MW01005944

BLINDSIDED

Hit from behind, Roshak's *Mad Dog* lurched forward under a barrage of fire so intense that warning lights flickered crimson on his cockpit console. His body strained as he twisted his 'Mech's torso to see what had hit him, then stopped. He knew already. He had been lured here. It was a deliberate trap.

The Clansman's choice was simple: fight or succumb. But he would not suffer an inglorious fate. Focusing on the *Stealth*, he fired everything he had left. The air filled with bursts of light as the charging *Stealth* sagged under the withering fire as armor seared and popped off.

The *Mad Dog* lurched again, becoming more ungainly and unmanageable. It staggered forward a step, then fell facedown against the muddy ground. Lying there, Roshak knew his 'Mech was finished. So was his life. He checked the tactical display one last time, wishing desperately for some chance, some hope.

There was neither. . . .

BATTLETECH®

OPERATION
AUDACITY

Blaine Lee Pardoe

A ROC BOOK

ROC
Published by New American Library, a division of
Penguin Putnam Inc., 375 Hudson Street,
New York, New York 10014, U.S.A.
Penguin Books Ltd, 80 Strand,
London WC2R 0RL, England
Penguin Books Australia Ltd, Ringwood,
Victoria, Australia
Penguin Books Canada Ltd, 10 Alcorn Avenue,
Toronto, Ontario, Canada M4V 3B2
Penguin Books (N.Z.) Ltd, 182–190 Wairau Road,
Auckland 10, New Zealand

Penguin Books Ltd, Registered Offices:
Harmondsworth, Middlesex, England

First published by Roc, an imprint of New American Library,
a division of Penguin Putnam Inc.

First Printing, June 2002
10 9 8 7 6 5 4 3 2 1

Copyright © FASA Corporation, 2002
All rights reserved

Series Editor: Donna Ippolito
Cover Design: Ray Lundgren
Cover Art: Doug Chaffee
Mechanical Drawings: Duane Loose and the FASA art department

 REGISTERED TRADEMARK—MARCA REGISTRADA

Printed in the United States of America

BATTLETECH, FASA, and the distinctive BATTLETECH and FASA
logos are trademarks of the FASA Corporation, 1100 W. Cermak,
Suite B305, Chicago, IL 60608.

Without limiting the rights under copyright reserved above, no part of
this publication may be reproduced, stored in or introduced into a
retrieval system, or transmitted, in any form, or by any means
(electronic, mechanical, photocopying, recording, or otherwise),
without the prior written permission of both the copyright owner and
the above publisher of this book.

PUBLISHER'S NOTE
This is a work of fiction. Names, characters, places, and incidents either
are the product of the author's imagination or are used fictitiously,
and any resemblance to actual persons, living or dead, business
establishments, events, or locales is entirely coincidental.

BOOKS ARE AVAILABLE AT QUANTITY DISCOUNTS WHEN USED TO PROMOTE
PRODUCTS OR SERVICES. FOR INFORMATION PLEASE WRITE TO PREMIUM
MARKETING DIVISION, PENGUIN PUTNAM INC., 375 HUDSON STREET, NEW YORK,
NEW YORK 10014.

If you purchased this book without a cover you should be aware that
this book is stolen property. It was reported as "unsold and
destroyed" to the publisher and neither the author nor the publisher
has received any payment for this "stripped book."

To my wife, Cyndi; my son, Alexander; and my daughter, Victoria Rose. This is also dedicated to Central Michigan University, my alma mater and keeper of many fond memories. To my parents; my incredibly stupid dog, Sandy; and everyone else out there who tolerates this weird hobby of mine.

To my friends Clan Rivenburg, Clan Huntt, and Clan Gramache. Thanks for coming along on this little hike as I got to tangle with the Jade Falcons.

Finally, to the fans out there who keep BattleTech® alive and thriving. BattleTech® is not just a novel series or a suite of software titles. It's a shared universe that perpetuates itself. It's a soap opera, war movie, sci-fi extravaganza.

ACKNOWLEDGMENTS

I'd like to acknowledge the other BattleTech® writers—Loren, Thom, and Randall. This book's story line tied into a massive, coordinated plotline, and everyone contributed a lot. Adam Steiner ended up here because of these guys, giving me someone to play the role of the antagonist.

Special thanks to John Kendrick for our Sunday mental therapy sessions during the writing of this book. Thanks as well go to Rob Martin for his forcing me to think first thing in the morning.

To my favorite author—Harry Turtledove—I thank you for setting the bar so high for the rest of us. Yes, this is beer-and-pretzel sci-fi, but that doesn't mean I can't enjoy the work of a true master.

And finally, to Matt Groening—thanks for my shiny metal ass!

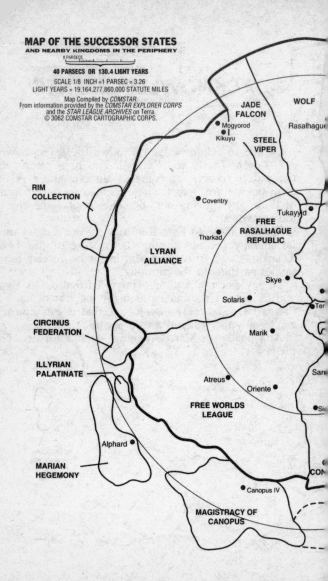

MAP OF THE SUCCESSOR STATES
AND NEARBY KINGDOMS IN THE PERIPHERY

8 PARSECS

40 PARSECS OR 130.4 LIGHT YEARS

SCALE 1/8 INCH =1 PARSEC = 3.26
LIGHT YEARS = 19,164,277,860,000 STATUTE MILES

Map Compiled by *COMSTAR.*
From information provided by the *COMSTAR EXPLORER CORPS*
and the *STAR LEAGUE ARCHIVES* on Terra.
© 3062 COMSTAR CARTOGRAPHIC CORPS.

WOLF

JADE
FALCON

Rasalhague

Mogyorod

Kikuyu

STEEL
VIPER

RIM
COLLECTION

Coventry

Tukayyid

FREE
RASALHAGUE
REPUBLIC

Tharkad

LYRAN
ALLIANCE

Skye

Solaris

Ter

CIRCINUS
FEDERATION

Marik

ILLYRIAN
PALATINATE

San

Atreus

Oriente

FREE WORLDS
LEAGUE

Si

Alphard

CON

MARIAN
HEGEMONY

Canopus IV

MAGISTRACY OF
CANOPUS

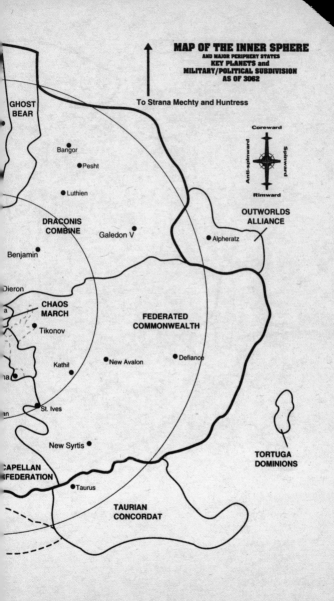

MAP OF THE INNER SPHERE
AND MAJOR PERIPHERY STATES
KEY PLANETS and
MILITARY/POLITICAL SUBDIVISION
AS OF 3062

To Strana Mechty and Huntress

Coreward

Spinward

Anti-spinward

Rimward

GHOST BEAR

Bangor

Pesht

Luthien

DRACONIS COMBINE

Galedon V

Benjamin

Dieron

CHAOS MARCH

Tikonov

Kathil

St. Ives

New Syrtis

CAPELLAN FEDERATION

Taurus

TAURIAN CONCORDAT

FEDERATED COMMONWEALTH

New Avalon

Defiance

OUTWORLDS ALLIANCE

Alpheratz

TORTUGA DOMINIONS

Prologue

Atholl, Halfway
Bolan Province
Lyran Alliance
23 May 3064

Leftenant General Archer Christifori could barely make out the building in the pre-dawn light, and the rain spattering against the windshield of the muddy hoverjeep didn't help matters any. As the driver, Demi-Precentor Rudolf Shakov of the Prince's Men, slowed and turned slightly, the vehicle's headlights further illuminated the old, weather-worn brick structure. At first, Archer took it for a quaint inn, then he spotted the red light, turned off, in the fixture near the front door.

"The Happy Harlot," said the name lettered on a small sign, which told the whole story. It wasn't the first time he'd encountered a place like this. There were countless of them on countless worlds, always located not far from a military base.

He looked over at Shakov and raised his eyebrows. "A bordello?"

"Yes, General," Shakov said, with only the hint of a grin.

Archer stared out the window. "Hell of a place for a meeting."

Shakov nodded. "We evacuated the entire village, saying there was a chemical spill on the nearby maglev line. Even the prostitutes didn't want to stick around, with the threat of toxic chemicals. Given some of the fighting for this world, it made a perfect cover story."

"Why not just tell them the Jade Falcons are on the way?" Archer asked, only half-joking. He didn't think it was funny, but the locals would be just as stunned as he was to hear that the Falcons had recently begun attacking the Lyran Alliance. Shakov had gotten the news just minutes ago, when he'd picked Archer up at the spaceport to bring him to a strategy meeting of Victor's commanders.

"I would have expected more optimism from you, General," Shakov said.

"Sorry." Archer waved one hand helplessly in the air. "I'm a little tired. I thought we'd be here discussing how to take the fight to Katherine, not dealing with a Clan invasion." Things had not been going well for the Prince in his civil war against his sister. The defeat at York had almost ended Victor's fight for good.

Shakov smiled ruefully. "Never forget that it is always darker somewhere else."

"Jerome Blake, I presume?"

Shakov laughed. "No, Rudolf Shakov."

Archer gave a half-hearted chuckle, then opened the side door of the jeep. Pulling the collar of his coat up around his neck, he half-hopped, half-ran to the door of the bordello. Shakov leaped out the other side of the vehicle and did the same. When they reached the entrance, four burly guards, in full Federated Suns attire, complete with assault rifles, checked Archer's ID and searched his briefcase.

The interior of the house was warm and cozy, which didn't surprise Archer. One of the guards took their dripping coats and disappeared down a dark, wood-

paneled hallway, while another one led Archer word-
lessly to a paneled door, where he knocked twice, then
opened it. All heads turned to look as he stepped in.

Some of the faces he didn't recognize, but their ex-
pressions showed that they knew him, or of him. All
but one were familiar more from the media and Archer's years in the military than from actual acquain-
tance. The face of the one man he did know personally
looked older and tireder than the last time Archer
had seen it, but his eyes had not lost their fire. Archer
walked over to the short, fair-haired man, then
stopped to snap a salute. He clicked his heels smartly,
his spurs jingling slightly as he did.

"Your Highness," he said.

Prince Victor Steiner-Davion extended his hand for
a firm shake and smiled with genuine pleasure. "Archer Christifori. Good to see you again. It's been a
long time."

"Yes, sir. The last time we met face to face, I was
a Major in the Revenants," Archer said, giving a
crooked smile. His gaze roamed the room. "Interest-
ing place for a strategy meeting."

"Jerry Cranston's idea," the Prince said. "Who would
think of looking for me and the rest of my generals in
a bordello?"

Still looking around, Archer chuckled slightly.
"Good point." The walls were covered with garish red
wallpaper, and the heavy maroon velvet curtains on
the windows were drawn shut. He relaxed slightly as
the others in the room turned back to whatever they'd
been doing before Archer came in. "I never got a
chance to express my condolences at the loss of your
brother," he told the Prince. "I was saddened to hear
of it."

Victor's face became serious at the mention of Arthur's death, the event that had triggered his declara-
tion of war against his sister Katherine. "As was I
when you lost your sister Andrea to all this madness."

Both men were quiet for a moment, then the Prince

motioned for Archer to follow him to the portable holographic display, set up near the communications relay work stations now lining the walls of the Happy Harlot dining room. "I believe Andrea and Arthur would be proud to see what we've done in their names. You've performed remarkably well in the last year and a half, Archer.

"Your campaign through the middle of the Lyran Alliance has tied up eight regiments all trying to track you down. In the process, you've crippled two of them and destroyed one, not to mention the job you did denying my sister the use of Snord's Irregulars and neutralizing Colonel Feehan's Highlanders at the start of your campaign. You're something of a contemporary Stonewall Jackson."

Archer flushed with embarrassment at the praise. "I appreciate the compliment, sir, but I think your media machine might have gone into overdrive." It was true that he'd been busy over the last year, however. He'd stayed on the move, liberating planets the Lyrans could ill afford to ignore. He had tied up a large portion of Katrina's forces in a never-ending snipe hunt to pin down his regiments. The press coverage of that, as well as the spin, had come from high command, but he'd never been comfortable with it.

The Prince grinned. "Archer, the Lyran people needed to see a military commander who was loyal to me and who they would find it hard to hate. My sister has proven herself such a master of the media, it only seemed fair to turn that against her. You were a war hero before all of this fighting began. You're not battling the Lyrans for any reason other than to remove Katherine from the throne. You've suffered the loss of your sister, and our polls show that that plays well with the women in the Alliance. All we did was build on your Robin Hood image, and in the process showed you as a force my aunt Nondi and my sister could not afford to ignore."

Another man, taller than Victor, came up and handed

the Prince a small box. "Thanks, Jerry," Victor said, then turned back to Archer. "There's a press release going out today from the decoy site of our meeting on Clinton, but I thought I'd give this to you now, before you saw it on the holonews."

The Prince opened the small box and took out the tiny three-bar insignia, then reached up to pin it in place. "For action above and beyond the call of duty and service to our cause, I hereby promote you to the rank of Major General."

"I don't know what to say, sir," Archer said, suddenly shy as some of the people in the room turned to nod and even wink in approval. It was more than he'd ever hoped for.

"You don't say anything. You've more than earned it. I need warriors like you on my side if I'm ever going to remove my sister from the throne. Besides, we've still got a long road ahead of us. The time has come to take the fight into the Federated Suns itself."

Archer could sense the mixture of relief and dread that passed through everyone at those words. The FedCom civil war was about to enter a new phase.

"I take it you brought your strategy outlines?" Victor said.

"I did. As we discussed sometime back, I've had my staff drafting for this contingency. Who'd have thought it would really happen?"

Victor's expression became hard as stone. "Yes, leave it to the Jade Falcons to spoil my best-laid plans." His reference to the Falcons drew some quick glances. None of them had gotten the news of the Falcon incursion until a little while ago. It was ironic that Archer and Victor had discussed this very possibility on one occasion, and Victor had asked him to come up with strategies for dealing with it.

Archer slid a small data disk into the table-top holographic display and took the tiny remote in his hands. His palms were sweating, and he couldn't remember the last time he was this nervous. He'd never been among such illustrious company all at one time. In addition to Prince Victor, he was awed by the presence of an older man who radiated authority and was instantly recognizable as Morgan Kell.

Victor rose, leaning forward with his hands on the converted dining room table. "As you all know, we recently received word that the Jade Falcons have suddenly decided it was time to take a stroll across the border. I've asked General Christifori months ago to come up with a strategy for dealing with them, in the event of such an attack, with the understanding that we cannot interrupt our offensive operations to remove Katherine from the throne." There was a murmur of agreement around the table.

Only one man neither showed or said anything. Phelan Kell, Khan of the Wolf-Clan-in-exile, sat with his arms crossed, staring down the table, as if meditating. From his various experiences with Clan commanders, Archer thought he understood the expression on Kell's face. It was a cross between extreme pride and an arrogant belief in his own superiority. If the Falcons were crossing the border, this was the face they would wear in battle.

General Caradoc Trevana scanned his noteputer as he spoke. "As you are all aware, the Jade Falcons have hit Blue Hole and taken out all but a few companies of the Third Alliance Guards RCT. They have also struck at Kikuyu, Kooken's Pleasure Pit, Ballynure, and Newtown Square. The Sixth Donegal Guards were badly mauled on Kikuyu, but the planet is still in the hands of the Lyran Alliance. On Newtown Square, the Fourteenth Donegal Guards were hurt, but managed an orderly withdrawal.

"This is not a driving assault like the Coventry campaign. Instead, they seem to be skipping some worlds entirely. At present, our intel shows that the deepest Falcon penetration is into the Melissia Theater. The planets they hit were well-defended, while the Falcons came in galaxy-size formations, in some cases multiple

Galaxies. This is not just a test of the border. They mean to keep coming, to drive deeper."

As he stopped speaking, everyone turned to Archer. He was nervous at first, but his thoughts seemed to flow anyway. "The Falcons' offensive extends all along the Lyran Alliance border, but they seem to be hitting worlds with proven defenders that allow them to test themselves in battle. Our regiments are grinding stones for them to sharpen their swords."

He activated the holographic display, which showed a rotating map of the border. Green smears showed where the Jade Falcons had come across.

"So you don't believe they're driving toward a specific target like Coventry or Tharkad?" Shakov asked.

Archer shook his head. "No. It looks more like they want to give their warriors a chance to sharpen their talons."

"So, General Christifori," Morgan Kell put in, "how do you suggest we deal with this violation of our sovereignty?"

Archer cleared his throat slightly. "Plainly put, we can't ignore the incursion and leave the border forces to fend for themselves. The Falcons are already pummeling the garrison troops on the border. I suggest that our ultimate strategy be aimed at forcing them to withdraw back into their occupation zone. We may lose a couple of worlds, but we have to make them realize that to stay and fight to hold planets will bloody them, and that to press forward will cost them elsewhere.

"As such, I propose a two-prong strategy. First, rather than toss forces in their path, we hit them on worlds they've already taken. This will force them to constantly reinforce their rear and to change their logistical routes. On its own, this will slow them down, but not stop them."

Archer thumbed to the next image with the controller, and the holographic display flickered, showing several different routes in red and blue plowing into the

Jade Falcon Occupation Zone. "To do that, we activate the second phase of the operation, which will require us to enter the Falcon OZ and take some of their own rear worlds. If we hit the right targets, we can wreck their support lifelines and force them to pull back to protect themselves rather than take our planets."

"General Sharon Bryan is in command of the Melissia Theater," Colonel Daniel Allard of the legendary Kell Hounds said from his seat near the Prince. "She's already sending out orders to concentrate her regiments on Melissia. It appears she's digging in, practically inviting the Falcons to hit her."

"Why in God's name is she doing that?" Morgan Kell demanded.

Victor shook his head. "It's Coventry all over again, where she wanted to dig in and take out the Falcons in one fight. She never understood my letting them go, that the cost was too high. She's letting her ego get the best of her. She always does."

"Then she will die there," Phelan said. "I know the Jade Falcons. They will see this as a chance to test their mettle. They will fight her until she is no more, then they will continue on. It is our way."

"Pray she doesn't," Doc Trevana said. "Her senior officer in the theater is Adam Steiner."

Victor didn't groan, but he looked as if would have liked to. Archer had read the reports, when they finally caught up with him, of what had happened on Newtown Square. Adam Steiner had taken out Victor's BattleMech, but his forces were ultimately defeated. Though Victor had released Adam, there was no love lost between the two men. Adam Steiner supported Katherine.

"Phelan," Victor asked, "what do you think of the strategy Christifori has outlined, from the Clan point of view?"

"It's sound," Phelan said. "Much better than what Bryan is attempting. He is right about one thing. You must bring the Falcons to bay, and the best way to do that is to hit them at home and hard."

Victor surveyed his command staff. "We need to continue our drive into the Federated Commonwealth. We can ill afford to give my sister the idea that the Jade Falcons would sap our strength. But I need someone to assume command of the Jade Falcon front, from Melissia down to the Pandora Theater. Whoever it is will coordinate with the ARDC forces as well as troops loyal to our cause to stop the Jade Falcons. That will mean also having to coordinate with the Lyran high command—which will not be easy. It must be someone who understands the Clans enough to beat them at their own game . . . before they devour the Lyran Alliance."

Silence followed, and the tension in the room was almost palpable. Some people looked to Morgan Kell, others to Doc Trevana. No one spoke for what seemed like an eternity. It was obvious that job would require a commanding officer man who could operate alone, without the burden of a tight command structure. Victor had to make his way toward New Avalon. He would not be in a position to coordinate the Falcon front at the same time.

Archer stood up and spoke, shattering the silence. "I can have my three regiments engaged with the Jade Falcons in the Pandora Theater in six weeks, and in the Melissia Theater in thirteen weeks, along with whatever regiments you can place under my command." He hoped his words wouldn't be misinterpreted as bragging or boasts.

Some in the room shook their heads in disb̲e̲l̲i̲e̲f̲. He thought, for a fleeting moment, that V̲i̲c̲t̲o̲r̲ ̲was going to dismiss the idea as outrageous. A ̲p̲a̲r̲t of him almost hoped he would.

Leftenant General Jerrard Cransto̲n̲ ̲spoke up first. "General Christifori, your forces a̲r̲e̲ on Odessa and Cumbres. You'd be pushing the̲m̲ pretty hard to hit that timetable."

"They'll do it," Archer said coolly, gaining confidence now. "They'll do it because the Alliance is still their home and they'll realize that if we don't stop the Jade Falcons, the outcome of the civil war will be meaningless. They'll do it because the reality of the situation is that we can still lose." He was most surprised by the expression on Phelan Kell's face. A slightly cocked eyebrow and a small nod of agreement.

Victor was studying him. "You'd be operating on your own command authority, General. I can't be on two fronts at the same time."

"No offense, Your Highness, but this is the first time we've met face to face since Huntress," Archer said. "I work best without someone second-guessing my moves."

Dan Allard said, "I would love to commit the Kell Hounds to this, Your Highness, but I believe they'll be needed to eventually deal with Tharkad."

Victor turned to Phelan Kell. "Phelan, what of your Wolves?"

Phelan uncrossed his arms. "If you are asking me to serve under General Christifori, the answer would be no. It is a position that diminishes the very nature of my people." He shot a quick glance at Archer. "Nothing personal, quiaff?"

Archer shook his head. He understood the Clan psyche and decided to leverage it rather than fight it. "And I would not think of asking a khan of the Clans to fight under me, Your Highness," he said, speaking to Victor, but looking at Phelan. "I have fought the Jade Falcons at your side on Twycross and other worlds, and nearly died on Huntress battling the battle Jaguars. I know the prowess of Clansmen in fighters of all, know that the Wolves are the fiercest spect for Phelan." His words were gauged to express respect for Phelan while establishing his experience, important in dealings with Clan leaders.

"We can't ask Khan Kell to operate under my command. However, perhaps the Wolf Khan would grant me the honor of coordinating my efforts with him instead. I can think of no other fighting force that I would want at my side than him and his skilled warriors."

Phelan looked at Archer with a hint of respect. "This is a man who understands our ways. I will fight beside him. May we both spill Jade Falcon blood on the same field of battle. Well-bargained and done, General Christifori."

Victor nodded. "I can think of no man better suited to this mission, Archer. I can give you twenty-four hours to advise me of your plan, including what troops you want freed up under your command."

Archer nodded once. "Yes, sir," he said, wondering for the first time what had possessed him to volunteer in the first place. "As I mentioned, there would be two phases. The first one—retaking planets the Falcons have already hit—I call Operation Bludgeon. The second phase of hitting them in their own occupation zone, well, I named that one Operation Audacity."

Phelan Kell chuckled. "From what you've told us already, I can think of no better name for such a thrust."

Archer had been working out of the library of the commandeered bordello, making his plans on the fly, drafting orders to his personal regiments, and meeting one-off with the other generals. It was intense work, but crucial. At some point, someone had lit the fireplace, which cast a yellow-orange light into the stately room. The Jade Falcons were on the move, and if not checked, would consume his precious Lyran Alliance.

At just before midnight, Archer glanced up and saw that Prince Victor had come into the room so silently that he didn't notice until the Prince was standing in front of him. He started to rise, but Victor waved him back into his seat.

"Relax, Archer," he said. "You haven't had to stand on formality for the last year and a half. Let's not get too hung up on it now."

"Yes, sir," Archer said as Victor pulled up a chair opposite the small writing desk Archer was using.

"You have a tough job ahead of you," the Prince said quietly.

"So do you, Highness," Archer replied, rubbing his temples as he squeezed his eyes shut for a moment.

"I know you want to be there, on New Avalon, when Katherine is brought to justice. Undertaking this mission might cost you that," the Prince said.

Archer sighed heavily. "I know, but what good is running off with you to confront Katherine only to find the Jade Falcon flag flying over more Lyran worlds? My troops will understand, sir. If anything, this invasion will harden their resolve."

"You've already sacrificed a great deal for this cause," Victor said. "And I'm going to ask you to do one thing more. Adam Steiner is a good general and a better fighter. He hates me because my sister has tainted his thinking. Despite the fact that he's head-strong and stubborn, he's pretty damn good in battle. You must do something for me when you eventually meet up with him."

"Yes, sir," Archer said, wondering what else he was going to have to undertake.

"You must convince him that I'm not the man my sister has made me out to be," Victor said. "You did a similar service with Snord's Irregulars. Now, I'm asking you to do the same thing with Adam. Make him see me for what I am. Do that, and this civil war will be over even sooner."

"I understand," Archer replied.

Victor handed him a holodisk. "Give him this for me. It's a personal message. It may help."

"Yes, sir," Archer said, taking the tiny diskette and placing it in his pocket.

"Good. Now, is there anything else you're going to need, Archer?"

"Someone to coordinate intel and communications," Archer said. "Running three regiments is one thing, but we're not likely to get much help from the Alliance command structure to coordinate movements. I need someone who's damn good at that stuff and can keep me up to speed."

"Done," Victor said. "I have someone in mind already. Anything else?"

"Sir, I've known you since I was just a green officer in the Lyran Guards. I've always considered fighting with you and for you an honor. I got pulled into this war because of my sister's death. You've let me handle my operations on my own so far, and I have appreciated that greatly. Now you continue to give me free rein to take the fight to the Jade Falcons in whatever way I see fit to end their incursion."

"You wanted trust, and you've got it, General," Victor said and offered his hand in a firm shake that went beyond commander to subordinate. "Now, then, finish up those orders and plans so that the Falcons can learn that we're serious about defending our homelands."

BOOK ONE

Where Angels Fear to Tread

1

Loveless Foothills, Melissia
Melissia Theater
Lyran Alliance
15 June 3064

Leftenant General Adam Steiner stood in the chill shadow of the DropShip, staring off across the tarmac to foothills in the distance. This region of Melissia was just entering its spring season, and the air was cool against his face, though the sun was already burning away the night frost. A light mist rose from the short grasses as the frost turned to thin fog under the sun's rays.

He wasn't admiring the view, however, but watching a hover jeep race toward him from across the valley. He didn't move. Behind him, from the DropShip, he heard the hissing and clanging of the bay doors opening, indicating that the first of his troops were about to deploy.

He and his force, the battered remains of the Fourteenth Donegal Guards, had just arrived on Melissia, obeying a summons from General Sharon Bryan to hightail it here at all possible speed. They had been deployed on Barcelona and Newtown Square, bracing to meet the Jade Falcons, when the order had come in via HPG. Adam assumed that the hover jeep racing toward him was bringing a member of Bryan's staff, who would explain why he'd been summoned here in the first place.

He glanced over his shoulder and saw his BattleMechs beginning to deploy. Even after a lifetime of living and working in and around them, they still inspired his awe. Three stories tall and bristling with lasers, missiles, and autocannon, 'Mechs had dominated the fields of combat for centuries. Adam saw them now as the thin, blood-red line between freedom for the Lyran Alliance and the caste-rule of the Jade Falcons.

The flat-green hover jeep swung in a wide arc to pull up sharply alongside of him. The plex-tarp top was in place, and the well-built infantryman at the wheel looked like someone not to be trifled with, even on his best day. The rear door on Adam's side opened, and he stooped to look inside.

"Good to see you, General Steiner," came a muffled voice from the depths of the jeep. Then he saw Sharon Bryan. "Climb in," she said. "We have a lot of work to do."

Adam got in, and the vehicle immediately shot off back in the direction from which it had come. Pushed back against his seat by the speed, he glanced over at the Melissia Theater's commanding officer. He was startled to see her grinning, and Adam couldn't help thinking that smiling was the last thing he'd do as theater commander, with the Jade Falcons coming across the border.

"Good to see you, sir," was all he said.

Her grin only widened. "And you, Adam. I'm glad you and your troops arrived on schedule. We have much to do."

Adam nodded. "We pulled some gees to get here, sir. Something big must be brewing for you to call me, the Ninth Lyran Regulars, and the remains of the Third Alliance Guards RCT here."

Her enthusiasm seemed oddly out of place to him. "Yes, it is here on Melissia that we'll end this Falcon incursion."

"What about Clermont and Barcelona? Aren't we abandoning those worlds by concentrating here?" he asked.

"Perhaps, but the Falcons might not even move against those planets. I think they're doing what they did on Coventry some years back—looking for a fight. Yes, we may lose a few planets, but in the end, the Falcons will be smashed against our anvil. We can easily retake those worlds once the Falcons are routed."

Adam shook his head twice, quickly. "I'm afraid I don't fully understand the strategy sir." *Routed? The Falcons?*

"The Jade Falcons seem to be striking at worlds where there are sufficient forces for them to test their mettle. The latest intel from last night, for example, shows them moving on the Com Guard 388th Division on Graceland—a real blood feud there.

"On Blue Hole, Storm's Metal Thunder and the Eighth Deneb Light Cavalry are falling back to re-group. I've ordered half of the Sixth Donegal Guards here, and the rest are en route to help on Blue Hole. We've got the cooperation of ComStar, which is giving us almost instant data feeds from all along the front. Leave it to the Clanners to take advantage of Victor's little uprising."

Adam winced slightly at her words. He knew the Jade Falcons, having fought against them many times. Sharon Bryan's assumption that they were taking advantage of the civil war to test the resolve of the Lyran Alliance made no sense to him. That wasn't the way the Falcons fought. To them, honor was everything. Hitting an enemy whose back was turned was not their style. It was much more likely that they were honing their skills, hardening their troops, against the Alliance's best forces.

He was also reacting to the mention of his cousin, Victor Steiner-Davion. Not only had Victor started a civil war in the former Federated Commonwealth, but he had fought and defeated Adam on Newtown Square at the start of the war. At first, Adam thought he had defeated Victor when he took down his 'Mech, but in the end, he'd suffered the humiliation of becoming his cousin's prisoner. He didn't know when he'd ever suffered a worse shame. Then, rubbing salt in the wound, Victor had tried to convince Adam that he was fighting his sister Katherine, the Archon-Princess, because she had killed their mother.

"Assuming you're right," he said coolly, "why concentrate our forces here on Melissia? We'd be better off hitting the Falcon staging worlds just across the border or else letting them come to us on the planets we're already defending."

Bryan shook her head. "Adam, you weren't on Coventry. I was. We blew our chance—or I should say Victor did—to cripple the Falcons there. He let them go even though we had enough concentrated force to demolish them. If we'd done it then, we wouldn't be facing them now. Well, I'm not going to make the same mistake again. I'm pulling all available forces here. The Falcons will come, and we'll bloody them. Their task force in this theater is much smaller than the one they sent to Coventry. We can pound them here and end this incursion."

"What about the other theaters?" Adam asked as the hover jeep started up a steep grade on the roadway. "Are you coordinating with the Arc Royal Defense Cordon and the Pandora Theater?"

Bryan chuckled. "No, I'm not. My orders are from General of the Armies Nondi Steiner herself. She told me to let Morgan Kell deal with his own problems. My responsibility ends with my borders."

Adam wasn't at all happy with her answer, and he

didn't try to hide his frown. "General, even if you stop the Falcon task force here, they could still be slicing up big pieces of the Alliance elsewhere."

Sharon Bryan's grin disappeared instantly. "General Steiner, rest assure that Nondi Steiner has these matters well in hand."

"What about the troops loyal to Victor?" Adam pressed. "Have you tried to mobilize them as well?"

"Funny you should mention that," she said, pulling some hardcopy from a side pocket of her gray dress uniform coat. "I received a message just two days ago from Victor Steiner-Davion on that very matter." She unfolded the sheet slowly and looked it over for a moment. "He sent this message to Nondi Steiner, with a copy to me, saying he has appointed a liaison to work with me and my staff to coordinate the troops that have sworn fealty to him."

Adam didn't let out a sigh, but he felt like it. The addition of Victor's supporters would be a big help in blunting the Jade Falcons' offensive, but he wondered how the hell they were going to be able to "coordinate" with allied troops who'd been their enemy for the last year and a half. "I'm not so sure I'm glad to hear that, sir."

She rolled her eyes slightly. "The man he appointed as liaison is General Archer Christifori."

Adam knew the name. Everyone in the Lyran Alliance had heard of Christifori by now. The stunning series of raids he'd accomplished over the last year and a half would surely become the stuff of study in military academies someday. Reports from over a dozen worlds at any point in time indicated that his three regiments were there, in force. When the Lyran high command had attempted to trap him, he'd turned the tables on them more than once.

Great, Adam thought, a celebrity-general. Why not send someone who could really help?

"Have you heard from him yet?" Adam asked, carefully neutral.

"Just a short message. He indicated that two of his regiments and three others were being mobilized and sent our way—whatever in the hell that means. He's coming with one regiment up the border, apparently with the intention of bolstering the Pandora Theater along the way. Here's what Victor says: 'I do this because nothing is to be gained by letting the Alliance forces loyal to my sister face this dire threat alone.'"

Bryan sneered as she read the words aloud. "He's not fooling anyone. This gives him a chance to steal some media coverage and, at the same time, shift his troops around within our borders under the guise of acting as our ally. Apparently, Victor takes me and his great-aunt for fools."

"General," Adam said, choosing his words carefully, "I'd rather not help Victor either, but we are talking about a Clan invasion. If we do dig in here to fight the Jade Falcons, we may need those additional troops."

Bryan shook her head. "I think not, Herr Steiner. You want to let Victor turn this into a media event where he's viewed as the savior of the Lyran Alliance? I don't think so, and neither does the Archon-Princess. If he wants to send in his troops to catch bullets that might hurt our forces, more the better. But don't forget this, Victor's people are still rebels and will be dealt with as such."

Adam could tell from her expression that others had probably presented the same argument to her previously, and that her patience was at an end on the subject.

Sharon Bryan's eyes narrowed to almost reptilian slits as she seemed to struggle to dominate her anger. "Let me make this clear to you as a subordinate officer, Adam. I'll deal with these rebel troops my way. If you can't handle that, you will be relieved of command."

A wave of anger surged through Adam, but he didn't give in to it. "I understand, General, and I don't necessarily disagree. I support the legitimate government of the Lyran Alliance—to the death if necessary.

I have no desire to provide Victor aid, either on or off the battlefield. We should be able to handle this on our own, if we act prudently." He gave the last words a degree of emphasis. Bryan's plan of force-concentration might work, but it was full of risks and tactics that had long proven ineffective against the Clans.

"You must trust me, Adam. And even if you don't, I can order it," she said, waving the finger of one hand in the air while pushing Victor's message back into her pocket with the other hand. Then, as if distracted, she twisted her head around to look out the window. "Ah, there it is!"

In the distance, Adam saw a hill whose green sod had been transformed into a bunker of concrete and firepower. It was ringed by several other hills, some of which showed signs of other fortifications. Two lances of BattleMechs, all assault-class, stood on the hillside of the main bunker. From the footprints in the sod, there were many more 'Mechs nearby.

"Is that your command post?" he asked.

"Yes. We've added to it significantly in the last few days. It's from there that I'll command our regiments and destroy the Jade Falcons."

Adam stared almost in shock. At no time had static defenses proven themselves against the Falcons or any other invading Clan. Mobile warfare and shrewd tactics, those were what governed the battle against this foe.

"Wouldn't it be wiser to arrange a mobile defense, General? Something less static perhaps?" He tried to water down the sound of his opposition, but his meaning couldn't have been clearer.

"Don't be ignorant, Adam," Bryan shot back. "I'll have multiple regiments using this as their focal point. It will draw in the Jade Falcons like a wave against a sea wall. And when they hit it, the results will be the same. They'll break here." She gestured toward the fortification as the hover jeep rose slightly toward it.

It had been a long time since Adam had seen such

a dangerous gamble, maybe not since the time of the Clan invasion. Deliberately drawing a concentration of the Jade Falcons to Melissia and then giving them a non-mobile target that could shatter the command and control was a scenario that seemed tailor-made for disaster.

Bryan continued on, ignoring his silence. "Between the 'Mechs we'll concentrate here and the defenses we've set up, the Falcons cannot ignore us, nor can they hope to defeat us. This is the rock that will break their spines."

"Be careful what you wish for . . ." Adam murmured, the words coming out almost before he realized it.

"What was that, General?"

"Nothing, sir," he said. He could tell by her enthusiasm for the plan that he had his work cut out for him if he wanted to stay alive long enough to mount any kind of a real defense of the Lyran Alliance.

Nadir Jump Point, Alocongo
Arc Royal Defense Cordon
Lyran Alliance

From the bridge of the JumpShip *Wayward Warrior*, Colonel Katya Chaffee watched in silent awe as another starship materialized several kilometers away at the nadir jump point of the Alocongo system in the Arc Royal Defense Cordon.

JumpShips traveled between stars, traveling nearly instantaneously from one star system to another at distances of up to thirty light years. The trips required tremendous amounts of energy, power a JumpShip obtained via a massive solar sail that collected the necessary energy—a task that often consumed days to gather enough power for the next leap through hyperspace. Some JumpShips carried powerful lithium batteries, allowing them to store a jump. The *Wayward*

Warrior was one of those. While JumpShips traveled between stars, the DropShips attached to their long spines were the means of traveling to and from a system's planets. Like her own, the new arrival was laden with DropShips, each one loaded with BattleMechs, troops, and the other tools of war.

Katya, second in command of Archer's Avengers, the three regiments that made up the forces directly under Archer Christifori's command, had been expecting the ship's arrival. Several other regiments, ones loyal to Prince Victor, had been placed under Archer's command. This was one of those regiments, joining her little task force.

Two of the Avenger regiments were with her—Second Regiment, known as the Muphrid Rangers, and Third Regiment, nicknamed the Minutemen. First Regiment had set off from Odessa to link up with Archer in the Adelaide system. Her orders were to take her task force to the Melissia Theater.

Katya stepped over to the communications station. The tech smiled, adjusted one of the controls, and pointed to her. "You're on, Colonel."

She stood straighter and pulled her uniform taut, not that it mattered. It was only her voice that was being broadcast. "This is Colonel Chaffee of Archer's Avengers aboard the JumpShip *Wayward Warrior*. Welcome to the Alocongo system."

There was a pause, followed by the sound of a deep male voice. "Colonel Chaffee, this is Lieutenant-General Anne Sung aboard the JumpShip *Saber Rattle*. I and the Second Crucis Lancers RCT send you and your Avengers our regards. The reputation of your unit has preceded you. Is General Christifori available?"

"I'm afraid not," Katya said. "He'll be hooking up with us at Adelaide."

"If you don't mind my asking, you seem to be a regiment short, if my count of JumpShips and DropShips is accurate."

"That's right," Katya said. "General Christifori thought we should send forces to link up with the Com Guard at Graceland to try and blunt the Falcons there. Though the push against the Melissia front is the greatest threat, he has command of the entire Falcon/Alliance border."

"Will he be able to link up with us in time?"

"Grand Duke Morgan Kell has issued some lucrative contracts with commercial JumpShip owners and is using them to shuffle troops. General Christifori will use the ships to travel quickly through the ARDC and link up with us."

"I look forward to meeting him, and with you . . . in person," Sung said.

"As do I, General Sung. I was impressed that you were able to coordinate a command circuit so quickly."

"Your intelligence man, this Captain Gramash, he was able to arrange it."

Katya nodded. She had worked hand in hand with Anton Gramash during the early phases of the war. Upon hearing that Prince Victor had assigned him to coordinate intel, logistics, and communications for Archer, she felt a whole lot better about this mission. So far, he'd been a ghost, a sender of messages and data-dumps tracking the progress of the Falcon incursion. "I've worked with him before. We're in good hands. *Very* good hands."

Sung cleared her throat slightly. "We're bone-dry on power over here. So we've got our work cut out for us."

"Agreed. We've just started charging the *Warrior*. I suggest that you commence with sail deployment and join us. We can make the jumps together to Adelaide. Do you need any replacement parts or gear?"

"We were mauled pretty severely," Sung said, "but I've been able to recruit some vets of the Clan wars and I also got my hands on some re-stocks. We should be good to go."

"That's good news," Katya said. She had little to

spare in the way or supplies. The three Avenger regiments had been operating by living off the land, capturing the supplies they needed. She knew that the Second Lancers had been pummeled earlier in the civil war, and had almost been wiped out.

"The Jade Falcons. . . ." Sung began, her disembodied voice sounding lost in thought as it came over the speakers. "Who would've thought they'd pull this stunt, now? We signed on to remove the Archon from the throne. After all of these years, I never expected to tangle with the Clans again."

"Same here," Katya said. "But if we don't stop them, the throne might just be painted Falcon green by the time the Archon does step aside."

Outskirts of Reston
Blue Hole
Lyran Alliance

The explosion went off nearly thirty-five meters in front of Jade Falcon Khan Marthe Pryde. She didn't flinch or show any reaction, even as the wet dirt splattered her face. Training from her youthful days in a warrior sibko and a lifetime of combat had hardened her to the explosions of mere artillery. Her only reaction was to casually wipe a speckle of mud from her high-boned cheeks.

She looked out over the hills near the city of Reston and watched as the company from the Third Alliance Guards RCT pulled back. The *JagerMech* III that had fired at her field camp was struggling with a Falcon *Vixen* from one of the newly formed freebirth units defending the border. The *JagerMech* III did not run from the fight like its comrades in the far distance, but instead slammed into the *Vixen* at a full charge, toppling the lighter 'Mech, then rushed for the forests in the distance.

She watched the attackers fade away as her forces

pursued. It was the fourth such attack by the remaining militia and Alliance Guards still on Blue Hole. She admired them. The planet had already fallen, yet they fought on, with bravado, attacking her base camp. Yes, these were enemies worthy of her Clan.

An older warrior, a Star Colonel, made her way to Marthe's side. She was a stern-faced woman, her right eye covered with a patch. The lacy pattern of the neural implants on her forehead were marred only by a deep scar that ran down her face. She was old by Jade Falcon standards, but Marthe respected her.

"Your new unit fights bravely, Star Colonel Redmond," she said, not even lifting her gaze from the last glimmer of battle in the distance.

"I thank you, my Khan," Kristen Redmond said, bowing her head slightly. "I would have thought that with their civil war, these troops would have been worn-down and weak. They have proven themselves able and innovative."

Marthe understood her sentiments. Too many of her subordinates thought that the Steiner-Davion civil war along her border meant that the Lyran forces there would be battered, unable to put up much of a fight. She knew better. Battles only made green troops veteran. "They have had much time to study these border worlds, learn every nook and cranny to defend them well."

"Yet we are victorious, aff?"

Marthe nodded. "Of course. We are Jade Falcons."

Redmond shifted slightly as she stood rigidly at her leader's side. "There are those who question the wisdom of such an attack, my Khan. Hitting much of the Lyran border at once is almost akin to a drive toward Terra."

Marthe turned to her aged comrade and shook her head slightly. "You, of all people, should understand Star Colonel. You were assigned to mere training duty, a solahma unit training freebirths. Now your young warriors gain a chance to sharpen their talons. And you get a chance to die honorably in battle rather than rot away like a useless piece of trash."

"For which I am grateful, my Khan," Kristen said, lowering her eyes. "I have borne my share of failures in life, and this offense gives me a chance to ensure my genes are carried into the future."

"There is more, though," Marthe said. "Only we and the Ghost Bears have worlds of the Inner Sphere that we can take. The Ghost Bears' private war with the Draconis Combine has made them lose sight of Terra as the ultimate goal. They will huddle in their caves, licking their wounds. We will take planets and resources that will make our Clan more powerful.

"The Wolves and Hells Horses must fight for whatever scraps we grant them. We have been idle far too long, allowing our enemies to become entrenched while preparing to fight us on their terms. We will take their border worlds until we are sated. This will force them to abandon years of planning, alter their defenses. Units they counted on will be bloodied and many destroyed. An offense of this type upsets their precious security."

"But what of the Wolf Clan, my Khan?"

"I learned from our last foray into the Lyran Alliance. This time our border is heavily defended. Khan Ward of the Wolves will try to take some token planets from us, but he will find that this time we are ready to hand him defeats that he cannot afford." She allowed herself a thin smile. She knew the Wolf Khan all too well, and if he decided to try any opportunistic moves, he would pay.

"What of the Star League?" Star Colonel Redmond asked.

"What of them?" Marthe asked, twisting her grin. "I do not fear them. They will see this as a matter for the Lyran people to deal with. My attack will show our fellow Clans that their unity is mere words."

"And when does this incursion end, my Khan?"

Marthe waved her hand in the air. "It ends when it is no longer to our advantage to continue it. While the Wolves and the Ghost Bears are bottle-necked by the Tukayyid truce line, I will expand our front, give us new avenues for reaching Terra. While they fight each other, I will show them what a true Clan can do when it chooses."

Kristen Redmond seemed to be putting it all together in her head. "So, by launching this assault, you manage to portray the other invading Clans as weak, while at the same time you force our enemies to react to our moves and shatter their years of defense planning."

"Aff, Star Colonel," Marthe said, smiling again. "And while some may believe that this is merely an attempt to give our new troops experience in battle, I will alter the face of the Lyran Alliance and lay the foundation for a dramatic drive for Terra when the time is ripe."

Redmond smiled, too. "Those who would criticize this assault within our ranks do not see the extent of your plans, my Khan."

"Aye," Marthe said. "But that is not what matters. What matters now is victories." She returned her gaze off into the distance as if she could see the battles of the future in the hills, rather than the dull red twilight falling over Reston on Blue Hole.

2

Ward Memorial Forest, Graceland
Pandora Theater
Lyran Alliance
6 July 3064

Don don?

As the Overlord-class DropShip *Colonel Crockett* touched down in a relatively small clearing of Ward Forest, Archer stared out over the tops of the trees that seemed to roll on forever into the distance. Graceland's brilliant sky and distant orange sun created an almost pastoral scene, at odds with the reality of the situation.

"Nervous, sir?" Colonel Alice Getts asked as she came up beside him, also surveying the endless sea of green.

Archer would have liked to make some humorous reply about the green of the leaves matching the emerald of the Falcons, but found it hard coming. "According to the splash-report I got from Com Guard Precentor Shillery, we're facing a reinforced galaxy of Falcons here. They've already bid and taken out the Eleventh Donegal Guards, and now they're working on the Com Guard 388th Division."

"You have issued a batchall," Getts said. "Under the circumstances, maybe we shou—"

A voice from the speaker cut her off. "This is Star Colonel Amado Roshak of the Lambda Galaxy, Seventy-fourth Battle Cluster of Clan Jade Falcon," the voice said. "Is this General Archer Christifori, who issued a batchall for control of this world?"

Archer leaned his hands on the communications console as the tech thumbed open the channel. "This is General Archer Christifori," he said. "With what forces do you defend this world?" He was repeating a formula he had heard before, from a time years ago when the invading Clans had attacked worlds where he was stationed. It was an echo of words he had spoken four days ago when he'd first arrived in the Graceland system.

"Our forces have crushed the Eleventh Donegal Guards in a Trial of Possession for this planet. We are currently engaged with the Com Guard defenders. Do you intend to supercede the batchall that was made with them, quiaff?"

Archer was a little caught off guard. The nuances of Clan batchalls, the challenges by which they prearranged the forces of combat, were somewhat lost on him. He wanted to ask for clarification, but a part of him knew that, as the challenger, the decision might be his. "Yes—affirmative."

"Very well," the Clan officer said. "We will break off our attack on the 388th Division and turn those forces against you. I will relay their current composition and force strengths to you, so that you can respond with what forces you will use against them."

"I believe I understand," Archer said. If nothing else, he might have saved the lives of a few of the Com Guardsmen who had been fighting the Falcons for the past several weeks.

"Well bargained and done," Star Colonel Roshak said, and the comm channel went dead.

The stocky Colonel Getts gave him a bemused look.

"Sir, with all due respect, you have no idea what you've gotten us into, do you?"

Archer returned the look with something of a cocky grin. "Neg, Colonel Getts," he said, mimicking Clanspeak. "Prepare your troops. I will go over the forces the Falcons are using here and let you know just how deep of a hole I've managed to dig."

Three hours later, Archer stepped into the field command tent and saw the Com Guard commander standing there. She was still dressed in the sweat-stained tee shirt, cooling vest, and combat shorts of her 'Mech cockpit. Her once lithe form showed both age and ruggedness like service stripes. She was obviously a veteran, scars from previous battles trailing down her arms like badges. There was the slight tang of sweat in the air, a scent familiar to Archer as that of someone who'd been spending days living in her cockpit

"General Christifori," Precentor Andrea Shillery said, giving a quick salute. "Welcome to Graceland, and thank you for taking the pressure off my men and women."

Archer shook her callused hand rather than salute. "I wish we'd met under better circumstances, Precentor. It wasn't my plan to take the heat off of you, but while we're here, we might as well do it. What can you tell me about who we're up against?"

"Tough bastards," Shillery said with a grunt. "The whole bloody Falcon Lambda Galaxy is here, all of them. Their Twenty-second Cluster waxed the Lyrans but good. Only a single company of them escaped, and they're in our ranks right now. This tough-nuts Star Colonel Roshak bid for a fight and tried to overwhelm us right off the bat. We're heavy with infantry and armor and fell back into the swamps about fifty kilometers from here. He's had a hard time prying us out of there. Though we whittled away at them pretty good, we sustained nearly thirty percent losses. I'd say they're doing a little better than that. I think they're toying with us, though, using us like some kind of target practice more than anything."

"How about this forest for defense?" Archer asked, sweeping his hand toward to door of the tent. "It's thick, heavily wooded, and hilly. It should serve to negate their extended-range weapons and allow us to use the terrain for some massed attacks."

Shillery nodded. "That might work. We thought the swamps would have done the same for us, but we got bloodied bad in there. This Roshak hits hard, then pulls back if he sees he's in too deep. He's a smart one, nothing like the Falcons were when they first showed up in the Inner Sphere. This one, he's learned to be wary of traps."

Archer walked over to the portable holographic display set up on a folding table and turned it on with a tap to the switch. A 3D map of the forest loomed into view.

"That's useful to know," he said. "That means we have to lure him very deep, very far and fast. Build up the Star Colonel's confidence until it's too late for him to simply fall back." He stared at the brilliant greens of the thick Ward Forest and saw that it offered kilometers of possible nooks and crannies that could be used to chip away at the Falcons.

He pointed to the display as Precentor Shillery came over to look at the map. "What's that clear area on that string of hills?" he asked.

"If my memory serves, it's a lumber concern. They've cleared that area out. It's about the only open terrain out there. But if you go there, you're playing right into Roshak's hands, sir. Open space and room to maneuver is what he wants—room to use his long-range fire advantage."

"So, he'll try to drive us there?"

"I would if I was him," Shillery said.

"Good. Then we'll put up enough of a fight to make him think things are going his way." Archer glanced over at Alice Getts, still standing near the door of the tent. "Alice, I've got some ideas, but I need your senior staff assembled before I respond to the bid."

"Yes, sir," she said smartly and left immediately to gather up the staff.

Shillery was obviously curious. "General, my people are worn out and in need of refit. The fighting stopped when you took over the batchall, but their blood is up, and some of them are going to want to keep slugging it out."

"Trust me, Precentor. There's plenty of Jade Falcon ass that's going to need whipping. Right now, let me finish up the fine job you started."

Star Colonel Amado Roshak brought his battered *Mad Dog* to a halt as he came to the roadway cutting across his path. His instinct was to be the first to rush forward and sweep the area with his weapons. But that was what the Inner Sphere commander would be expecting him to do. Those were the kind of rash mistakes that had gotten the Seventy-fourth Battle Cluster shuffled off to the Lambda Galaxy to begin with.

Not this time, he thought. The fighting with the Com Guard had already cost him a number of warriors, and all of their 'Mechs were damaged in some way. The good news was that the new foe, these Avengers, were tough but had been constantly falling back, driven by the furious pounding his forces unleashed every time they stopped to engage. If not for this dense forest, the whole thing would have been over hours ago.

He adjusted his sensors and picked up the faint signal of a lighter 'Mech, a *War Dog*, down the roadway to his right. It was joined by an older-model *Lancelot*, which opened up at another of the OmniMechs in Roshak's star. Both were using the natural grade of the road for some degree of cover. They probably thought he'd be foolish enough to rush into the road, but instead he made his way along the top of the tall embankment that loomed over the cut roadbed.

He spoke into his neurohelmet mic. "Command Trinary, this is Star Colonel Roshak, I have detected an enemy 'Mech on my right flank. Move to cut off his retreat."

Without hesitation, the enemy *War Dog* unleashed a silvery hypersonic slug from its gauss rifle. Finding its mark, the round plowed deep into Roshak's already damaged right leg, shearing off shards of armor plate and leaving other pieces looking as if they'd been torn by a jagged set of teeth. Roshak throttled his 'Mech forward, swinging the targeting reticle of his primary display onto the *War Dog*'s image just as it faded back behind a cluster of thick trees.

He bit his lip, then said, "All forces, download my coordinates and concentrate on the roadway of my current position."

"It shall be done, Star Colonel," came the voice of Bathol, commander of the Fire Star operating with him. "These new troops are tough, but they retreat like surats during a thunderstorm, aff?"

"This road leads to the lumber camp," Roshak said. "We'll use it as our axis. Sweep and Slasher Trinaries will assume flanking positions while the rest of us go up the middle. When they reach the open areas, we'll be able to concentrate ourselves and rout them off this planet."

He heard a flurry of "affs" in his earpiece. Yes, these Avengers were good, but they wouldn't live long enough to brag about their encounter with the Jade Falcons.

Archer angled his *Penetrator* toward the north end of the forest, turning to face the open, muddy fields where the lumber company had stripped the land barren. Fallen trees crisscrossed the muddy hillsides. To the south, near the almost wall-like expanse of trees, the Jade Falcons were pursuing Charlie Company. They were hitting his forces, driving them in what appeared to be a rout. Forcing them to flee across the open expanse.

He sidestepped the *Penetrator* toward a large tree, which provided him some degree of cover. Off in the distance, all along the edge of the forest, he saw the ground armor of Sledgehammer Company and the 'Mechs of the White Tigers spreading out, using the growth and trees for concealment. Almost two battalions of combat force were hunkered in, waiting for the Falcons to appear. Linked up, they formed an almost perfect horseshoe-shaped formation.

"This is Huntt on discreet for Avenger One," a voice crackled in his earpiece.

Archer toggled to the covert communications channel he was using. "Go ahead, Captain Huntt."

"We'll break through in about a minute," Huntt said.

Archer nodded to himself. "Roger that. We're in position." Then he switched channels. "Avenger One to the Sherwood Foresters." The Foresters operated as a kind of special forces unit within the Avengers. He had sent them and another company on a long trek through the forest. Making a large, sweeping arc, they would work their way into the rear of the Jade Falcon Seventy-fourth Battle Cluster. When the trap was sprung, the Foresters would provide additional "incentive" for the Falcons to keep moving out into the open field.

"Sherwood here," came back the voice of Thomas Sherwood, the Foresters' commanding officer.

"The show's about to begin. You ready, Tom?"

"Give the word and we're on top of them in three minutes' time," came back the rock-solid voice of the younger officer.

Archer checked his long-range sensors and saw Charlie Company reach the open stretch of land. "Foresters, do your duty," he said. Then he switched to the frequency being used by Alice Getts. "Alice, the show is yours. I've taken the liberty of ordering in the Foresters."

"Understood, General," she said, then immediately gave the order. "Attention, Avengers, just like we planned. Lock, load, and fire for effect."

*   *   *

Star Colonel Roshak was struck by a sudden burst of sunlight as he reached the clearing. Out in front of him, nearly three hundred meters distant, the company his force was pursuing had broken into a full run, fleeing from him. The rest of his cluster reached the edge of the clearing and kept right on going without the slightest pause. For the first time in many long hours, they had room to run as their opponents took flight. Roshak understood their emotions. For a warrior, there was nothing like seeing your enemy break and run before you.

Yet, he alone paused his 'Mech. The clearing would allow the use of his superior weaponry, but it could also be a trap. Surrounded on almost all sides, an enemy in the open could be exposed to fire from a concealed foe. One thing he'd learned about the warriors of the Inner Sphere was that—

A wave of short-range missiles ripped into his right-rear torso even before he heard the tone warning of their approach. His *Mad Dog* listed forward, quaking under the rattle-like wave of explosions.

"We have enemy BattleMechs to the rear!" he barked out. "Dagger Trinary, extend from the forest. Turn and deploy to meet the enemy from behind."

Roshak ran his *Mad Dog* forward, jutting slightly to the right to swing around and meet the enemy that had so dared to fire at him. His tactical display told him it was no small force coming from his rear. The threat was significant and would have to be met.

A *Stealth* 'Mech suddenly loomed in front of him, the one that had blasted his back side. "Very well, little one. Let us see your mettle," he muttered.

Then it happened. Hit from behind, his *Mad Dog* lurched again under a barrage so intense that warning lights flickered crimson on his cockpit console. He was engulfed in a rush of nausea and dizziness that he knew as a wave of neurofeedback into his helmet and brain. His body strained against the five-point restraint straps as he twisted his 'Mech's torso to get a view of what had hit him from behind, then stopped. He knew already. He had been lured here. It was a deliberate trap.

His choice was simple: fight or succumb. But he would not suffer an inglorious fate. Focusing on the *Stealth*, he let fly with his large and medium pulse lasers. The air filled with brilliant bursts of light, and the charging *Stealth* seemed to sag under the withering fire as armor plating seared and popped off under the barrage, hissing as the hot edges touched the moist ground.

Star Colonel Roshak's *Mad Dog* lurched forward again, and more red lights danced off his neurohelmet face plate. The *Mad Dog* became ungainly, unmanageable. It staggered forward a step, then fell face-down against the muddy ground. Lying there in his 'Mech, Roshak knew that it was dead, as was life as he knew it as a warrior. He checked the tactical display, wishing desperately for some chance, some hope.

There was neither.

Abhorring waste, he saw the futility of further struggle, but the knowledge ate at him like acid. He resisted what he had to say until training and logic won out over his emotions. "General Christifori, this is Star Colonel Roshak," he said on an open band. "I yield to you, sir." He struggled to keep his voice level. "All Falcons, stand down."

"You have fought honorably, Star Colonel," Christifori said in a formal tone that surprised Roshak.

"Graceland is yours," Roshak replied. "I will inform my superiors that we have lost this trial."

"I will take your equipment as isorla," Christifori said, using the Clan term for the spoils of war. "And those warriors we deem appropriate will become our bondsmen," he added.

Roshak was surprised. An Inner Spherer rarely honored Clan traditions in such a manner. "Thank you, General. You honor my command."

"Thank you, Star Colonel," Christifori said. "You have validated mine."

Five hours later, Archer and Precentor Shillery waited outside one of the cramped transmission booths inside the ComStar HPG in New Calverton. Archer needed to send out a number of messages, and was counting on an intelligence dump encoded and waiting for him there. Shillery had come along, and Archer appreciated the company. While they waited on the ComStar technician, they sat in one of the lounges, relaxing for the first time in two days.

"In case I hadn't mentioned it, I appreciate what you did, General," Shillery said, dusting off some specks of dirt from her light blue jumpsuit. "The Falcon Lambda Galaxy is leaving under a cloud of defeat."

"You wore them down for weeks," Archer said, rubbing his brow and wishing for sleep. "I just stumbled in at the last minute and happened to pick the right place to slug it out with them."

Shillery gave a hearty laugh. "You really believe that, don't you?"

Archer stared at her intently. "Precentor, may I confide in you? Off the record, of course?" She looked puzzled, but nodded silently.

Archer leaned forward, closing the distance between them and lowering his voice. "I'm feeling a bit like a fraud. I got sent here because some people think I'm some sort of strategic combat genius. The truth be told, I've been a front-line commander most of my life. I've never commanded this many troops before, not for real. I can't help but feel I'm in a little over my head right now."

Shillery listened, then had another good laugh. Archer felt as betrayed as a young schoolboy admitting a crush on his first true love, and his face got hot with embarrassment. But then Shillery reached out to touch his shoulder with one hand.

"If you think for one minute that I've bought all of that publicity about you being the incarnation of Stonewall Jackson, you're delusional," she said. "Truth be told, most of us on the front lines, even those of us who don't report to you, admire the way you came up through the ranks. The fact that you handed the Jade Falcons their asses in a bag proves to me you're not just some brass-ass general. You're the real McCoy. You beat them at their own game, fair and square."

Archer felt a little better, but he still felt some self-doubt. "I appreciate your candor."

"One question, sir, why did you choose me to share that little tidbit with?"

"Because you don't report to my chain of command. Because I wouldn't be risking my unit's morale."

Shillery smiled. "That's what you think. The Precentor Martial may hand me my rank on a plate, but until the Falcons fall back to the OZ, I'm going to follow your orders."

Archer cocked his head to the right. "Are you sure, Precentor?"

She nodded firmly.

"Very well," he said, sitting up in his seat. "Then, Precentor, I have another order to cut for you. In the meantime, get your division ready for immediate departure. If you're going to be in my command, you're going to earn your pay." And for the first time in a while, Archer allowed himself a smile.

3

Spitfire Island, Dustball
Arc Royal Defense Cordon
Lyran Alliance
30 July 3064

Phelan Kell stared out the cockpit of his *Wolfhound* toward the DropShips below him in the distance. A thin, dull brown haze filled the distant sky, shimmering like a live thing on the horizon. The bluff where he stood gave him a commanding view of most of Spitfire Island and its immediate neighbors.

It was really a string of islands, an atoll of five keys, with Spitfire the largest. Two major volcanic peaks dominated the terrain from the center of the island to its west coast. The rest consisted of rich, deep-black and brown soil and long beaches where the wind whipped the sands high into the air. Dustball was famous for its high-altitude sandstorms, even on this island where he had chosen to take up his defense.

Sitting between the mountains were rolling, rocky hills and dense jungles. Daily the rains came, brought on by the equatorial jet stream, flooding some areas and drenching everything for a few hours. Windstorms and mammoth waves constantly battered the desert-like shore of the Driscoll continent only twenty kilometers away, contributing to the shimmering, brownish haze on the horizon. Spitfire, however, was the key, isolated from the civilian community, yet strong for defense. Access to the other islands of the atoll was possible by BattleMech, if one knew the way.

And Phelan Kell made sure he knew those paths.

The Jade Falcons had arrived on planet, having issued their batchall en route. It was a challenge for possession of Dustball, but Phelan knew their real interest in the place was the presence of his Wolves in Exile. Based on the time delay in their response, the internal bidding for the right to battle his Wolves had taken the better part of two hours.

Phelan had bid the Fourth Wolf Guards Assault Cluster for the defense of Dustball and had chosen Spitfire Isle as the venue of the contest. The island provided excellent terrain for combat, wide and varied. The enemy's Seventh Falcon Regulars Cluster had landed and deployed on the wide beach to the east but had not rushed into battle.

"They are not acting as I would have expected," he heard Ranna Kerensky say from her *Warhawk* not too far below his position. "Star Colonel Icanza has not attacked with typical Falcon rapidity."

"They have also landed the Jade Hatchlings." Phelan adjusted his long-range sensors to confirm the additional DropShips he'd sighted.

"They must have lost the bidding for the right to bloody themselves," Ranna said.

"Two clusters on the ground and the rest of their Galaxy holding in orbit. Not a typical invasion."

"They have come to sharpen their talons against our armor," Ranna said. "I trust that you desire us to stick with your plan."

The plan that Phelan had created for the defense of Spitfire Island was not overly complicated and involved knowledge of the terrain and weather that only someone familiar with Dustball would know. The goal of his strategy was to grind away at the Falcons. He would push them until they were forced to recall their last bid, tying up even more troops, taking up more time. Each day here was a day that the rest of the Rho Galaxy was not marauding and hunting in the ARDC.

"Aff, Ranna," he replied. "Remind your warriors that we are in no particular hurry to clip the wings off of these Falcons."

The Jade Falcon OmniMechs had a difficult time pursuing through the jungles. The thick, sandy soil and the winding, often dead-end trails through the trees and growth made navigation difficult. The Wolves were plagued with the same obstacles, but had come to know the forests well, especially after four days of fighting. Phelan's Wolves had nipped at the Falcons, biting them, then fading back into the jungles between the two mountains. Each time, the Falcons fell further back, and each time it led to a new set of encounters on unfamiliar terrain. Today would be no different.

Phelan swung his *Wolfhound* out of the jungle facing a region known locally as The Flats, an open strip of sandy soil broken by the occasional volcanic rock outcropping. The sand-like soil was a powdery gray material that would suck down on a BattleMech's feet when dry. A band of nearly fifty acres of this sandy ground lay between two thick jungles; apparently, the soil was so acidic that none of the local plants even tried to live in it. On one side, Phelan and his Wolves. On the other side in the other jungle, the Jade Falcons. The heavy downpour had passed through less than an hour before, right on time.

Ranna's armor-clad Elementals burst out of the lush green of the jungle and rose into the air on their leg-mounted jump jets. As they landed, the armored warriors turned and fired back into the emerald depths. Bursts of green laser light lanced out at them, peppering the sand, leaving smoldering geysers of steam where they missed. The Elementals fired back, letting loose their shoulder-mounted short-range missiles, then dissolving back into the foliage. One Elemental was caught by a brilliant red lance of laserfire from an emerging *Fire Falcon*. The Wolf Elemental contorted as the beam seared off his right arm. The warrior fell motionless for a moment, then staggered to his feet.

Phelan knew it was time. "Wolves," he said over the open tactical channel to all his forces, "pick your targets well."

From all along the edge of the jungle, Ranna's Wolves stepped out and fired at the advancing Falcons. Long-range missiles swarmed toward the trinary pursuing her Elementals, who again lit their jump jets and moved across the flats.

The Jade Falcons suddenly saw the foes that had been eluding them for so long and wasted no time in rushing forward to engage. A full star of *Stormcrows* broke into a full run straight across the flats, bearing toward the Elementals that landed and fired back defiantly. A mixed star of Falcon 'Mechs, led by a lumbering *Behemoth*, broke into a sagging run toward his position. Down-range, at the other end of the flats, another star of mixed lighter 'Mechs attempted their run across the open space. Four days of sniping hit-and-run attacks had left the Falcons infuriated and hungry for a chance to take on the Wolves directly—which was what Phelan had been counting on.

The charge of the Seventh Falcon Regulars bogged down even as the first shots from the stationary Wolves found their mark. The flats were easy to navigate in Elemental armor or when the flats were dry. When soaking wet, however, the seemingly hard-packed sand became a quagmire that devoured Battle-Mechs. Running was impossible, and some of those that tried lost their footing and toppled, only to be swarmed by the Wolf Elementals that had turned and held their ground in the middle of the open expanse.

While most of the Falcon warriors concentrated on trying to wrestle for control of their 'Mechs in the muck, Phelan's warriors opened fire with everything they had. The air over the flats was alive with missiles, lasers, and the brilliant bursts of particle projection cannon fire. Explosions of red, orange, and sick black smoke seemed to consume the green 'Mechs of the Falcons.

The Falcons were too late in realizing their folly but still had enough firepower to be deadly. One *Stormcrow* let go at Phelan with a wave of twenty long-range missiles as it fought to maintain its footing. Phelan juked his *Wolfhound*, but not quite soon enough. Half of the salvo missed, but the remainder splattered up his legs and torso, pock-marking armor as they went.

He fired his pulse lasers back at the trapped enemy, pouring the stream of emerald laser light into the *Stormcrow*'s right torso, gouging and blackening the armor there. The heat in his cockpit spiked slightly, but it was nothing he couldn't handle. Next to his target, another Falcon *Stormcrow* turned around in an attempt to head back to the safety of the jungle, only to take a hit from a gauss rifle in its back. The slug caved in the thin rear armor and sent the *Stormcrow* face down next to Phelan's foe.

Phelan's enemy fired wild with his medium pulse lasers, two of them missing by a wide margin, and one hitting his cockpit just under the canopy glass. Phelan sidestepped for a moment, drew a long breath, and danced his targeting reticle back to the already damaged *Stormcrow*'s chest. He switched all of his weapons to the same target interlock circuit, and with the calmness of a priest, depressed the firing stud.

His cockpit temperature spiked momentarily, but the impact of the weapons was worth it. One laser hit the *Stormcrow*'s left arm, one created a nasty scar along its center torso. The rest all seemed to plow into the right torso. Whether it was the force of the impacts, internal damage, or loss of control in the muck, the Falcon *Stormcrow* staggered two steps, then dropped onto its side. The heat from its holed armor sent a wisp of steam into the air.

All down the line, Phelan saw the Jade Falcons attempting to turn or even fall back. All along the line, his Wolves kept firing. His Elementals swarmed a gigantic *Behemoth*, ripping away at armor plating as the Falcon warrior attempted to shake them free while still fighting the pull of the mud that seemed to only rise higher around his 'Mech's shins. A ninety-five-ton *Turkina* did not turn, but instead pushed across the wet mud, weathering the shots as it lumbered slowly forward, its gait uneven but determined. The Wolf warrior fighting it from his tiny *Phantom* dropped under the sheer firepower of the massive Falcon OmniMech, but the moment he fell, another Wolf stepped up to take on his role. Finally, almost unceremoniously, the *Turkina*'s knee joint gave way under a devastating PPC blast, and the 'Mech fell, plowing deep into the sandy-muck.

Its fall brought an odd silence across the flats. Smoke rose from damage where the Wolves stood and the Falcons had fallen. One trinary had been devoured, but the Falcons would not fall for the same ploy again. They would try to skirt the flats, but Phelan already had his troops deployed to receive them in the mountain pass where the mud flats ended.

"Excellent work, Star Colonel," he said to Ranna, who was down-range. It was not her well-loved voiced, but the unfamiliar one of another woman that answered over his neurohelmet earpiece. "Khan Phelan of the Wolves, this is Precentor Shillery of the Com Guard 388th Division. I am requesting permission to land my troops in support of your defense."

Phelan was stunned. "Precentor, I thought you were on Graceland."

The woman's rough voice came through even clearer after a few seconds of delay. "We were, Khan Phelan.

I was sent here at the behest of General Christifori. After he arrived on Graceland and dispatched the Falcons' Lambda Galaxy, he thought you might be able to use our assistance."

"Very well," Phelan said, unsure of what to make of this, but relieved to hear that Victor's trust in Christifori had been well placed. "Landing coordinates will be sent to you and your troops."

"Thank you, sir. I trust you left some Falcons for us?"

"Aff," Phelan said. He knew that the fighting for Dustball was far from over. The Falcons had ample forces in the system, and they intended to take the planet though it had no value to them strategically. If nothing else, he understood their nature.

He couldn't help a slight smile. "There are still plenty of targets everywhere, Precentor," he said.

4

Loveless Foothills, Melissia
Melissia Theater
Lyran Alliance
7 August 3064

Adam Steiner had come to loathe the dimly lit interior of the planetary command bunker where General Bryan had him reporting daily. It had nothing to do with the bunker itself, which was a fairly modern facility, clean and well ventilated. It was what it represented. Defense—stoic, boring, outdated, and outmoded defense in the face of an enemy he understood far better than his commanding officer.

For Adam, working with Sharon Bryan had become a painful and increasingly pointless exercise. She had herself convinced that concentrating her forces on Melissia was the way to beat the enemy and to protect the interests of the Archon Princess. She was so pleased with her own self-proclaimed brilliance that it took every ounce of self control he possessed to keep from saying what he thought of her so-called strategy.

She might think victory was assured, but Adam knew different. He'd fought the Clans before, and knew that the Jade Falcons were not likely to follow Bryan's desired path to their doom. To top it off, she continued to pat herself on the back what seemed like several times a day. Overconfidence was fuel for defeat just as much as battlefield information was the ammunition for victory. It was the mantra by which he'd been trained, and it had served him well as a warrior.

Adam paced around the command center, staring at the holographic map of the hills where they were attempting to plan the defense of Melissia. There wasn't much to work with. The spaceport at which he'd arrived was the only flat piece of ground for hundreds of kilometers. The surrounding slopes were grassy, but trees were virtually non-existent. Streams passed through the low valleys, but none were wide or fast enough to deter BattleMech crossings.

The center of the holographic display was the only real defensible point, the very command bunker in which he was standing. It possessed a maze of tunnels into the surrounding hillside, hidden repair bays for 'Mechs and gear. Gun positions provided cover to the area, with overlapping fields of fire outward from the bunker complex itself, which made it dangerous to anything but an all-out assault by the Falcons. Ringing the perimeter were pop-up mines, the mortal enemies of Elementals, as well as vibramines capable of hamstringing even the mightiest of assault BattleMechs. He knew that those were formidable defenses to everyone but the Jade Falcons. Somehow, someway, they would find and exploit the chink in the post's armor.

Bryan entered the room and quickly scanned the morning report on her hand-held noteputer, not hiding her impatience. Adam crossed his arms and tapped his toe on the concrete floor.

"So," she began, not even lifting her eyes from the report, "I see that Storm's Metal Thunder is slated to land shortly." The unit were staunch Steiner loyalists and well-equipped for mercenaries.

"Yes, though we still haven't gotten a unit-readiness report from them," Adam said. "I'm guessing they got pummeled pretty badly on Kikuyu." From what he'd seen of the scant reports transmitted, the fighting on that planet had been brutal.

In addition to Storm's Metal Thunder, the Sixth Donegal Guards and the Eighth Deneb Light Cavalry had also been posted on Kikuyu when the Jade Falcon Delta Galaxy had arrived. The Sixth Donegal Guards were hit first, mangled in only a few hours of fighting. Driven in a full rout, they had managed to scrape together just enough unit integrity to make it offworld.

The Deneb Light Cavalry had fared somewhat better, managing to combine operations with Storm's Metal Thunder, but the most recent word from Kikuyu was that both units were under attack. Their fate was unknown until a pair of DropShips had arrived in system from the Metal Thunder, requesting permission to land.

Bryan considered the defense of Kikuyu somewhat successful, despite the fact that the planet was now in Jade Falcon hands. She believed that the Falcons had been properly bloodied, but Adam wanted to see the real battle-damage assessments before he got his hopes up. "With their numbers added to our defense," she said proudly, "I'm sure we're going to prove a target that the Falcons cannot ignore."

Adam suppressed a wince. Bryan had placed him in command of several of the regiments operating around the perimeter of command post. The Ninth Lyran Regulars were well trained, but many of the recruits in the ranks had never previously fought the Clans. The remains of the Third Alliance Guards RCT had managed to flee Blue Hole to Melissia. Two battalions had been made field ready. He still had his reconstituted Fourteenth Donegal Guards—at regimental strength more on paper than reality—but loyal to him to the core. Victor had beaten them and him early in the civil war, and like many units, the Guards

were being rebuilt. The Sixth Donegal Guards were
at about the same strength, though Bryan had held
them under her direct control. Along with a handful
of local militia companies, this was what he had at
his disposal.

"General," he began, speaking slowly and choosing
his words with care. "Perhaps we should set up our
initial operations elsewhere. There's a forest about
two hundred kilometers from here. We can pull the
Falcons there initially, then fall back to this location
if we have to."

She closed one eye slightly more than the other in
thought. "No, General Steiner. The purpose of this
complex is to provide the kind of position the Jade
Falcons cannot take but that they will bloody themselves trying to. You and your mobile force are necessary to drive the Falcons against this position."

There was a hint of hurried frustration in her voice,
as if she had gone over the plans so many times with
him, had blunted his objections so often, that irritation
was taking over. "If the morning report is accurate,
Storm's Metal Thunder should be landing at the
spaceport now. Why don't we go out and meet them
personally, eh?" She was already on the way to the
door before he could answer.

"Any word yet on General Christifori?" Adam
asked as their hover jeep swerved away from the
guarded bunker and down the sloping roadway toward
the tarmac in the distance.

Bryan rolled her eyes at the mention of the man.
"Yes. Apparently, he was lucky, or else caught the
Falcons with their pants down on Graceland. He managed to hold onto the planet, though officially we're
crediting the Com Guard with the defense. Victor's
little toy general sent me a message advising against
concentrating my forces. Like he knows how to deal
with the Clans better than I do . . ."

"Where's he heading?" Adam asked, thinking that
at least Christifori had tangled with the Falcons, rather

than digging a hole in the ground and waiting for them to attack it. Still, Bryan was probably right; the Com Guard had probably done most of the fighting.

"Somewhere in the Theater, I presume. He probably thinks he's coming to save us. That's just like one of Victor's people, always looking for Indians so they can play the role of cavalry," she said with contempt, but her face lit up as she spotted the two Overlord-class DropShips on the spaceport tarmac.

"There they are," she said, pointing for the benefit of her driver. "Take us over to that pair of 'Mechs in the front. That's probably the command staff."

As they approached, Adam noticed that something about the two BattleMechs was amiss. One, a *Stalker*, was badly blackened from fire, and some of its armor plating had been ripped and twisted off, visible even from the hover jeep. As they got closer, he saw a streak of coolant pooling near its right leg.

The other 'Mech had been an eighty-ton *Salamander*. Its right long-range missile rack was more debris than actual weapon, obvious laser gouges having turned the armor on the torso to half-melted slag. The left leg bore a deep indentation as if it had been caved in by cannonball—most likely a long-range hit by a gauss rifle slug that had failed to penetrate. Adam glanced up at the cockpit and saw that the glass of the eye-like canopy was peppered with burn pockmarks from a pulse laser's vicious assault. This pair of 'Mechs had obviously been through one hell of a fight.

The hover jeep stopped, and he and Bryan dismounted. The two MechWarriors stood beside their 'Mechs and saluted. They looked weary, and their uniforms had obviously been drenched in sweat for days. Both had half-beards and sunken eyes that sent a chill down Adam's spine. Bryan ignored their worn appearance. She stood in front of them, and the two men snapped first to attention and then to parade rest.

"I take it you're the command staff of Storm's

Metal Thunder?" she asked. The two men gave each other slightly dazed glances, then one of them said, "Yes, sir. I'm Lieutenant Timothy Rivenberg. This is my brother, Sergeant Andrew Rivenberg. We're both attached to the command company."

"Good," Bryan said. "From the looks of it, your 'Mechs need some repairs. This is General Adam Steiner. He can assist you and your regimental command in getting repairs, refits, ammo, etc. As soon as Colonel Storm gets settled in, have him come to the command post."

"Sir," Lieutenant Rivenberg said, almost stuttering, "Colonel Storm was, well, killed sir."

"I sympathize with your loss, but we'll have time to mourn the dead once we beat the Falcons here," Bryan said crisply. "Get the rest of your command out and ready to deploy. General Steiner will coordinate integrating your unit with the rest of those we have assembled here."

Again, there was an uneasy look of confusion. "General, sir, I don't think you understand."

"Understand what?" she demanded, hands on her hips.

"We are all that's left of Storm's Metal Thunder. Our two 'Mechs are all that got off of Kikuyu."

Bryan's jaw hung down for a long and painful moment. "But you have two DropShips," she said, gesturing towards the vessels.

"It was all we could do to get out of there with the handful of survivors we did, sir," said the younger of the brothers. "The Falcons overran the drop zone. We were lucky to get off with our techs and the regimental families. Damn lucky—sir. We had to leave a lot of good people back there." He looked down at the ground as he finished speaking.

Adam was stunned. Storm's Metal Thunder was a top-of-the-line mercenary unit . . . *and the Jade Falcons had not just beaten them, they had devoured them.* The awkward silence was shattered when the driver came up, a portable comm unit in one hand. "Generals Bryan and Steiner, they need you back at the command bunker ASAP."

"Problem?" Bryan asked.

"A Jade Falcon task force just arrived at the nadir jump point. Their commander issued you one of their challenges."

"Who . . . who was it that contacted us?" she asked.

"Khan Marthe Pryde, sir," the driver said apprehensively. "They have issued a batchall, and are asking with what forces we will defend this planet. They're awaiting your response."

Adam Steiner felt his heart skip a beat. *It had begun . . .*

Marthe Pryde stood at the comm display on the bridge of her JumpShip, patiently staring over the commtech's shoulder. Though she usually traveled aboard her Clan's flagship, she planned to bid her command unit, the Turkina Keshik, for the right to lead the assault on Melissia.

At her side was saKhan Samantha Clees, commanding officer of Delta Galaxy and second only to Marthe in command of the Jade Falcons. "They are quiet," Samantha said, arms crossed defiantly.

Marthe nodded. "They are suffering a shock. Their general is somewhat dazed. First, we are striking at an important symbol for them—a Theater command world. This has not happened since our first invasion. Second, we came in at a pirate jump point. If I were General Bryan, I would probably be just as confused, at least for a moment." Her voice was deliberately cool and confident, as was expected of her.

"Our Watch did well in obtaining the coordinates of this pirate point," Samantha said.

Marthe caught her eye and grinned. "Aff. During our first invasion of the Inner Sphere, we had to strike out almost blind. Even during our strike against Coventry, I did not avail myself of our intelligence resources. If I had, Victor Steiner-Davion would never have been able to catch us off guard.

"This time, Samantha, the Jade Falcons will send a ripple of fear through Victor. We will maintain our honor, but we have also learned from the past."

5

"**A**re you sure about that?" General Bryan barked from her seat in the center of the command bunker's operations center.

"Confirmed, General," the commtech said. "Two JumpShips have arrived at Pirate Point Reho One. They are debarking DropShips on a fast burn toward our position."

Adam's eyes narrowed as he checked the sensor readings the comm tech was interpreting. "Corporal, those DropShips have ignored our signals to them?"

"So far, sir." The young officer couldn't hide his nervousness.

Adam stared at the screen, then turned to face his commanding officer. "Those are our DropShips. Their transponders correspond to the Lyran Alliance."

Bryan's brows furrowed with a hint of frustration. "And the Falcons are still on a burn in-system?"

Adam nodded. "They're coming in from a longer

distance." Pirate jump points were riskier to use, but closer to the planetary bodies than the standard system jump points. "They'll land a few hours before the Jade Falcons do."

Bryan rose from her seat and smoothed out her uniform. "I don't know who this commander is, but he's not here on orders from me, and now isn't the time for someone to be playing cowboy. I'm willing to bet it's one of Victor's people, maybe even the famous Christifori himself."

Adam said nothing. Help, *any* help, had to be appreciated and leveraged. At the same time, the part of him that had been raised and trained within the military command structure knew that a renegade force could spell problems.

Thanks to Bryan's disregard of the Clan bidding process, Khan Marthe Pride had not indicated what forces she would bring against the defenders on Melissia. From his own count of incoming DropShips and their capacity, he assumed she was bringing the better part of two galaxies of Clan warriors toward the planet. While he appreciated Bryan's bravado, he believed that the odds were heavy in the favor of the Falcons in this fight. Yes, they would only bid the number of forces they needed to defeat Bryan's and Steiner's defenders, but they had ample reserves. Bravado only counted on media footage.

General Bryan had been less boisterous about how she was going to destroy the Falcons. She had seen his and the intel people's estimate of the number of enemy troops. Her aide-de-camp, an aged, paper-pushing desk jockey named Kommandant-General Seamus Kinnell, kept pushing the idea that the fortifications, combined with the troops under Adam's command, would be more than enough to handle whatever the Jade Falcons tried to throw at them. Adam's protests seemed lost in the bustle of business in the command post, which frustrated him.

Bryan simply refused to deal with the issue of what to do if her plan didn't work. Adam had brought up the question twice, and both times had received a long and irritating lecture on how her strategy couldn't fail. He stood with his arms crossed, staring at the incoming DropShips, pretty sure of what would happen to her precious plan once the Falcons started fighting. He felt the blood rise to his face. "General Bryan, we've got to have a contingency plan for the Theater defense in case the Jade Falcons overrun this position."

He braced for her rebuttal but instead watched her shake her head in disbelief. "Talk of defeat can ruin morale, General. You, of all people, should know that."

"Sometimes things happen that we cannot plan for. What is your plan if we have to extract ourselves from Melissia?"

"We will not do that," Bryan said. "This is the place where we will bloody the Falcons so bad that they will stop and fall back."

"I understand, sir," Adam said, placating her. "But we still need a fall-back plan, sir. Even the best general with the best plan has one."

Sharon Bryan waved her hand in the air as though to dispel the thought. "You seem obsessed with this issue, General. Fine. Draw up a contingency plan if you want to waste your time doing so. I'll approve it, and we'll send it to the appropriate commands." Her tone was flippant as if to say she could care less.

Adam clicked his heels and bowed slightly. He felt that he had won the first real battle for the defense of the Melissia Theater.

The spaceport tarmac had a different look as Adam and Bryan climbed out of their hover jeep two days later. Buildings that had been bustling with activity were closed up. Sandbags covered entrances to structures, and windows were boarded over. Trenches had been dug on a nearby hillside. And for good reason. The Falcons would be landing shortly.

The five DropShips on the tarmac were still cooling

their fusion-powered engines as a lone figure made its way across the blacktop toward them. The ships had maintained communications silence on their trip in, but they had been identified as members of various units stationed in the Theater. Bryan was infuriated that a commander would come to her planet without her permission.

The man stepped forward. Wearing a Lyran Alliance dress uniform showing the rank of Colonel, his face showed a kind of stern determination that got Adam's attention. He saluted, and Adam alone returned the salute. Bryan stepped up to him and began her verbal barrage.

"Colonel, who are you? What are you doing on Melissia?"

"I am Felix Blucher of the Fifteenth Arcturan Guards," he said in crisp Germanic style. "When I heard of the Falcon invasion, I did not wait for formal orders but started out with those forces I had available. I managed to pick up additional companies of defenders along the way. We came as soon as possible."

"I remember you now. There was a reason I posted you to the hindquarters of the Periphery, too. It was because it was under your command that the Guards got plastered to begin with. Your command hasn't even been formally reconstituted yet," she bellowed. "You were on Bucklands recruiting and training. You have no authority to be here."

From his expression, Colonel Blucher did not seem to think he was in trouble. "Yes, sir. The request for transfer of posting of my unit was sent out, in triplicate, to you three months ago. You signed it, but apparently it was lost in the shuffle, with the civil war and all. The Gacrux FTM felt that this situation warranted their contribution as well, and we managed to link up. I took the liberty of contacting the Neerabup MTM, and they sent us a contingent of almost a battalion of strength. I come here to lead these troops in your defense of Melissia."

Bryan was unimpressed. "You came here with troops under my command, without my authority. All you're going to get, Colonel Blucher, is a trip to the brig."

Adam stepped forward into his commanding officer's field of vision. "General Bryan, we *can* use the troops he's assembled."

She turned, and he saw the fury in her eyes. "This man is a wash-out, General. The reason Archer Christifori has been running rampant through the Alliance for the last year and a half is because of him. If not for some political favors up his sleeve, he would have been sent packing to Outreach."

"With all due respects, General," Blucher said, his voice calm, almost soothing, "you are going to need every MechWarrior you can get to beat the Jade Falcons. Yes, I lost my command once, but I assure you that's not going to happen again. I've learned a great deal from the experience, enough to know that my place is here—now."

Adam wasn't sure why, but he found himself liking this Colonel Blucher, if only because General Bryan seemed to hate him. There was a dignity about the older officer as he stood calmly under her abuse. He seemed one cool character. Besides, anyone as dedicated to the defense of the Lyran Alliance had to be an asset. "General Bryan, let me take Blucher and his people under my command. I can make use of him, I think."

Bryan was still angry. "He had no authority to do what he did."

"Yes, sir," Adam said. "But the Jade Falcons are burning in as we speak. We don't have time to waste putting him in the brig, and we can't spare able troopers to guard him."

Sharon Bryan drew a breath and regained her composure. "All right," she said coolly. "He's yours to deal with." Then she turned and began walking toward the hover jeep.

Adam stepped up to Colonel Blucher and extended

his hand. "Welcome to Melissia, Colonel," he said as Blucher relaxed and took his hand.

"Thank you, General." Blucher nodded in acknowledgment of Adam's support.

"You'd better get your troops debarked, and I'll get you some coordinates so those DropShips can park somewhere other than the spaceport. The Jade Falcons are only a few hours behind you, and I think they're going to do what they can to take this planet away from us."

"Do you have a role or position for us to play?" Blucher asked.

"A beautiful one, Colonel," Adam said with a crooked smile. "You and your troops just became my only reserves for the defense of Melissia."

6

Nadir Jump Point, Adelaide
Melissia Theater
Lyran Alliance
15 August 3064

Arriving in the *Colonel Crockett*'s tactical operations room, Archer found his officers already gathered for the meeting he had called. With all his forces rendezvoused at the nadir jump point of the Adelaide system, the TOR had never been so packed. Some of the faces were familiar, and some were not.

Katya Chaffee, his best friend, closest confidant, and second in command of his own three regiments, sat at one end of the table. In large-scale operations, she handled command of the First Thorin Regiment. The hot-mouthed Leftenant Colonel John Kraff of the Muphrid Rangers, his second regimental commanding officer, looked red-faced and uncomfortable. Whether it was because of the heat or the presence of regular army officers, Archer wasn't sure. Also present was Colonel Harry "Hawkeye" Hogan, commander of the Minutemen, the Third Thorin Regiment. He looked both tired and stern.

Two other officers were strangers to him, both of them women. Colonel Anne Sung of the Second Crucis Lancers RCT looked sharp in her dress uniform, compared to the faded field fatigues that his own commanders wore. Given the fighting the Lancers had been through in the civil war, Archer was impressed that Sung still even *had* a dress uniform. The other officer, a woman with cropped jet-black hair and a dusky complexion, was Colonel Alden Gray of the Twentieth Arcturan Guards. Both officers and their troops had been attached to Archer's command by Prince Victor, joining up with his forces as they moved up to Adelaide.

"First off," Archer said in a controlled, firm tone to convey the seriousness of the meeting, "let me thank all of you for joining us. Right now, we're part of a much larger effort aimed at stopping the Jade Falcons, and I'm going to need everyone's input. Let's keep things informal, though. If you've got an idea, speak up. We don't have a lot of time to stand on formality."

He saw Colonel Sung's shoulders relax slightly with his words, but Colonel Gray looked like she might never be able to relax. John Kraff, with typical cavalier attitude, scraped his chair back and casually crossed his legs.

"What is the current situation along the border?" asked Anne Sung.

Archer pulled out the report he had received from an HPG data dump encoded and sent by Anton Gramash. He had no idea where Gramash was located physically, but the two had managed to stay in close personal contact, thanks to a series of codes and ComStar's cooperation. He had become Archer's eyes and ears along the Falcon occupation zone.

Archer put on his reading glasses, half-lenses that he had only recently begun to wear, and reviewed the long list of the data. Then he said, "The short version is as follows: On Kooken's Pleasure Pit, the Grave

Walkers lost sixty percent of their force and withdrew. The Falcons were defeated on Graceland, which is good news. The fighting on Dustball between the combined Wolf-Com Guard force and the Falcons has managed to tie up at least one of their galaxies. We've received word that Barber's Marauders II were totally destroyed on Koniz. Apparently, they dug in and fought to the last man—the Falcons didn't take a single one as bondsman. We've lost contact with the First Argyle Lancers on Crimond. So far, there's no indication that the Falcons have left, so we're assuming the Lancers are waging some sort of guerilla action." Archer though that last bit of news especially sad. Only two companies of the Lancers had survived the civil war, and now they faced extinction at the hands of the Jade Falcons.

When he glanced up, the faces looking back at him were glum. And they weren't likely to get any cheerier at the rest of the news. "Things aren't going well in the Melissia Theater. Blue Hole and Kikuyu have fallen, as has Newtown Square. For some reason, the Falcons are ignoring Barcelona for the time being, which seems to confirm that their reason for coming across the border is to increase their battle prowess. Fighting continues on Ballynure, but I don't know how long the Fighting Urukhai can hold out. The Falcons have arrived in the Clermont system, but have not landed troops. Apparently, they're using it as a staging point to jump into the Melissia system."

Without waiting for further comment, Archer activated a holographic map of the Melissia Theater, where the planet of the same name pulsed red. "Melissia is not the key to the defense of the region, but it has drawn two Jade Falcon Galaxies, thanks to the concentrating effort General Bryan has been kind enough to employ. According to our intel, the Falcons should be landing today."

"Is that where we're heading, to Melissia?" Colonel Gray asked, nodding toward the holographic map.

"I don't think we could get to Melissia in time to save them, but we can't afford to lose those troops and materiel if we're going to continue the fight." He caught a flash of anger in Colonel Gray's eyes as he spoke, but she still said nothing.

Archer let his gaze take in the whole group. "General Bryan's plan to dig in and let the Falcons hit her is not going to work at all. It's old thinking."

"It's damn stupid thinking if you ask me," John Kraff added.

Archer ignored the comment even though he agreed with it. They simply didn't have time to go down that road at the moment. "Bryan didn't respond to their batchall, so the Falcons are coming down in force. Even if there'd been bidding, I don't think our people have much chance on Melissia. I'm just hoping some of them will be able to retreat, so that we can hook up with them and pull them under our task force's umbrella. Then we start on Operation Bludgeon, as planned."

"Where do you think they'll fall back to?" Hawkeye Hogan asked.

Archer pressed the switch on the holodisplay's control, and another world lit up. "Nondi Steiner hasn't responded to our requests for information on their contingency plans in case Melissia falls, so I'm guessing . . . but it's an educated guess. Someone's ordered three reserve DropShips loaded with repair parts and expendables to Chapultepec, and we've got a report of a JumpShip fully recharged and ready to go. I could be wrong, but my money's on Chapultepec."

"That doesn't sound like Sharon Bryan at all," Sung said. "I've dealt with her a few times. She's not big on fall-back plans, from what I remember."

Archer nodded. "Adam Steiner is with her. I'm willing to bet he's the one who set this up but has simply not told her." From what Archer knew about Steiner, he didn't think such a move would be totally out of character.

"Well, if we're lucky," Sung said with a sly smile, "maybe the Falcons will have them both for dinner."

Archer couldn't let that go by. "Colonel, we've got to stop thinking like the civil war is the hottest fire burning right now. Yes, General Bryan seems to lack creativity in her thinking. Yes, Adam Steiner is a pain in Victor's backside. But we need them and everyone else in that Theater alive and focused on our strategy if we're to have any hope of success. Don't forget our operational objective. We've got to get the Jade Falcons to withdraw, fall back, or stop dead in their tracks. We don't achieve that by watching other people die."

"Chapultepec, eh?" Katya said, apparently hoping to take some of the edge off Archer's words. "Sounds good. Do you have a plan, sir?"

Archer smiled for the first time in a long time, despite the tension that had been stirred up. "Yes, I do, though it's more a rough guideline for an operation than a true plan. If we're lucky, some of our people will make it off Melissia alive enough to help us take the fight to the Falcons. We'll link up with them there and then pull back long enough to refit. Then, my good officers, Operation Bludgeon will earn its stripes."

Loveless Foothills, Melissia
Melissia Theater
Lyran Alliance

The roar of DropShips passing overhead seemed to shake the ground under Adam Steiner's *Thunder Hawk* as they headed toward the Loveless Hills. He didn't have to see them to know what was happening. Their hatches and ramps were opening, and they were disgorging their cargo of 'Mechs and Elementals onto the nearby hillsides. The Jade Falcons had come to Melissia, and they'd come with an attitude.

"All commands, stay in lance-size formations," he

barked into his neurohelmet microphone. "Concentrate your firepower on the larger 'Mechs first. Keep moving, and don't forget the overlapping fields of fire that we worked out."

"Guard One, this is Captain Mackey of the Third Alliance Guards. I have contacts on the outer marker at Sectors Two and Three. Make that Two, Three, Four, and Five. Multiple contacts on the seismic sensors and long-range sensors paint at least one, maybe two, clusters coming through." The voice was not terrified, but it should have been.

"Roger that," Adam said, calling up a tactical map of the region on his own secondary display. The Falcons had landed to the east of the command bunker, and they were coming toward it. All that stood between the bunker and the Falcons was the Third Alliance Guards and whatever else Adam could get into place in time.

"Fourteenth Guards, this is Guard One. Everyone to form up on my position, with my command lance as the center of the line. We can catch the Falcons' flank if we do it fast enough."

He broke his *Thunder Hawk* into a run. From his position on the south perimeter, he thought it just might work. By wheeling his forces to the south, he hoped to plow into the left flank of the advancing Falcons. From his cockpit, he saw the BattleMechs around him form up and break into a run as well.

"General Steiner, what are you doing?" came a shrill voice over his earpiece.

"Trying to save the Alliance Guards, General Bryan," Adam said as his long-range sensors picked up the first hints of signals from the Jade Falcons.

"Order them to fall to the south and let the Falcons hit our defense perimeter as we planned," she commanded.

As you planned, Adam corrected silently. "General, you've heard the odds. They can't possibly extract from two clusters assaulting them," he countered.

"General Steiner," she began, but Adam didn't wait for her order. He switched off his comm system from receiving from her, for now. Bringing his *Thunder Hawk* up over a small rise, he saw a wave of gray and green Jade Falcon 'Mechs rushing forward down. It was like a tidal wave rushing past him in the distance, heading straight toward the sagging line of the Third Alliance Guards.

"All right, Donegal Guards. Let's go save the Third," he said. Moving forward again, he managed to get twenty meters before a lance of red laser light slashed into his *Thunder Hawk*'s left leg. While the armor held, several plates beneath the knee joint bore a blackened slash that staggered his run. Adam juked slightly to the east, changing the angle of his run down the hillside, and found his first target, a *Black Lanner* that had turned to charge his line. He slowed almost to a walk, sweeping his targeting reticle over the charging OmniMech with a smooth motion. On his primary display, he saw its outline. Out through his canopy, he saw its faint green color grow brighter as it ran toward him.

He held his breath and slowly depressed the first two target interlock circuits on his joystick. All three of his gauss rifles whined for a moment, and his *Thunder Hawk* lurched back as they fired their metallic slugs down-range. One shot went high, just past the head of the Falcon. The other two both slammed into the *Black Lanner*'s torso. He didn't see the damage they did, only a blur in the distance as the Falcon 'Mech fell backward, then lay sprawled on the ground, knocked down by the kinetic impact of the hits.

"First blood," Adam murmured to himself, but a wave of long-range missiles riddled the armor on his *Thunder Hawk*'s arms and legs before he could indulge a smile of satisfaction. The 'Mech lurched and seemed to rumble under the impacts of the warheads, generating so much black smoke from hits all over his 'Mech's body that he could see very little through his cockpit viewscreen. Meanwhile, a *Grand Titan* at his side punched its huge fist into the cockpit of a *Goshawk* that had nearly breached his defensive line.

A quick glance at his sensors told Adam what was happening. He'd managed to get the attention of the Jade Falcons all right. Rather than rush the Third Alliance Guards, they had pivoted their drive and were headed right into his force of the Fourteenth Donegal Guards.

"We're in over our heads," he called. "Third Guards, see if you can draw their fire. Fourteenth Guards, fall back by companies to the southwest. If the Falcons don't want to take on the bunker, maybe some of that friendly artillery can at least hold them at bay."

Adam turned his *Thunder Hawk* around and ran back over the ridge, a flock of Jade Falcons hot in pursuit.

7

For Adam Steiner, the fighting seemed like an endless nightmare from more than ten years ago when the Jade Falcons had first invaded the Inner Sphere and had seized his homeworld of Somerset. The only difference from those youthful days of fighting the Clans was the mystique surrounding his then-unknown foe. Now they were a known quantity, though that did not blunt their ferocity in battle.

Khan Marthe Pryde had been personally leading her troops. He had even seen her once through the smoke of battle. Thus far, the Falcons had not shown much interest in the bunker complex, much to the irritation of General Bryan. They had ventured close on several occasions, only to be caught in a wave of long-range indirect missile fire or explosions from the vibramines hidden under the sod. Adam was impressed. He'd expected such threats to stop the Jade Falcons, but he was wrong. Dead wrong. Instead, Marthe Pryde had turned her troops loose against the defenders of the perimeters of the planetary-defense bunker complex under his command.

The battle had been a running slugfest so far, with Adam carrying out a series of fall-backs, using the hills as the best means of defense, but the cost was high. The Ninth Lyran Regulars, with twenty-five percent of their forces out of action, had suffered the least so far. His own Fourteenth Donegal Guards were down to just over a company of 'Mechs, all of them damaged in some manner. The Third Alliance Guards had been routed, but had managed to flee into the bunker perimeter, where they regrouped with the Sixth Donegal Guards still under Bryan's control.

That gave Adam at least some hope, thinking that the remnants of the Sixth Donegal Guards and the Third Alliance Guards could be leveraged to provide him some relief. He knew he could also pull Colonel Blucher in, but that would leave the only escape off-planet wide open. He wasn't ready to do that.

The mixed force that Colonel Blucher had brought was basically a reinforced regiment. Adam had managed to keep them concealed from the Falcons, hidden in a series of grass-covered ravines several kilometers away. Their mission was simple and twofold: to be the last line of defense in case he had to evacuate Melissia or to act as a reserve strike force to hit the Falcons when they were at their weakest.

He slowed the gait of his *Thunder Hawk* and checked his long-range sensors. The Falcons had slowed as well, but he knew it wasn't from weariness. They were preparing for yet another assault, one that would cost him more troops and from which he would have to fall back again.

"General Bryan, this is Guard One," he said into his neurohelmet mic.

"Bryan here, go." Her voice sounded tense and worn.

Adam took his *Thunder Hawk* to the top of the

highest hill and stopped. In the distance, only five kilometers north of his position, he could make out their
command post, which Bryan had insisted on calling
"The Rock". A rumble near him made him twist his
'Mech's huge torso to see a Vedette tank come to a
halt nearby, its turret sweeping to the northeast where
the Falcons were poised, still unmoving, out of line
of sight.

"General Bryan," he said, "I respectfully request
that you release the BattleMech forces currently under
your direct command to me. By sweeping through the
clear paths we have set among the minefields, they
should be able to hit the flank of the Falcons during
their next assault."

The answer didn't come right away, and Adam bit
his lip, wondering what her response would be. He
was counting on her professionalism to triumph over
her ego, but he knew that the contest would be close.
The wait was so long that he was about to repeat his
request when he finally heard her voice in his earpiece.

"The Donegal Guards are yours," Bryan said. "The
Third Alliance Guards only have a lance of 'Mechs,
but we have them repaired. Take them, too."

"Thank you, sir," Adam said, suppressing his sigh
of relief.

"Why aren't they coming at the bunker?" she
asked, more to herself than him.

"They have their reasons, sir," he said wearily. Over
eighteen hours in the cockpit had nearly drained the
last of his strength. "They keep throwing units at us,
then they pull back only to send in another unit . . .
a fresh one."

Suddenly his long-range sensors blared out a warning. The Jade Falcons were moving, en masse, toward
his line. The Vedette tank next to him adjusted its
aim and fired.

"General, we're under attack," he managed, swinging his *Thunder Hawk* to meet the threat. His eyes
darted down to his tactical display, and he saw the

lights, appropriately tagged in emerald, moving all along his front. At the far end of the line to the southeast, the Ninth Lyran Regulars advanced slightly into the Falcon line and seemed to be preventing them from enveloping the Alliance forces.

A wave of five long-range missiles peppered his *Thunder Hawk*'s arm and chest, slicing off armor near the site of previous damage. Two of the missiles missed and flew past him, into the unknown.

Adam held his stand on the hill and locked onto a rushing *Hellhound*. The Falcon 'Mech moved into the valley below and began to sweep to his left as Adam locked onto it. He fired two of his gauss rifle slugs, and the Thunder Hawk almost lifted in the air from the force of their launch. Both hypersonic slugs found their marks on the running Falcon 'Mech. One hit in the *Hellhound*'s right torso, cratering the armor plating like a massive bullet wound on man. The other slug tore into the hip joint.

The enemy 'Mech staggered in its run, seeming to trip, but catching itself at the last moment. It saw Adam and fired its large pulse laser. A brilliant rippleburst of green death dotted the *Thunder Hawk*'s upper torso. The armor plating seemed to moan under the assault, then pop off with an echo that made Adam's joints hurt.

He swept his four medium lasers over the *Hellhound* just as its pilot regained his sense of balance, and fired. Two of the shots stabbed downward and into the already-damaged legs of the Falcon 'Mech, and two missed entirely. The crimson lances literally sliced the armor off the legs, and the already-damaged left leg lost not only its remaining armor but was burned through to the myomer bundles underneath. A puff of white smoke rose from the gash near the hip, and the leg of the *Hellhound* dropped off, hanging in place by a few myomer-muscle strands that refused to give way. Still upright, it was a deadly foe, but it wouldn't be running anytime soon.

Adam glanced over to his left and saw the forces
that Bryan had released to him racing up and then
down the grassy green hillsides, mindful of the paths
through the minefields.

"Hauptmann-Kommandant Calvin," he called on
the tactical frequency to the commanding officer of
the Sixth Guards. "This is General Steiner on discreet."

"*Jawol*, General," Calvin said, his tone almost Prus-
sian. "We understand you need some help, *ja*?"

"That's an understatement. I need you to take your
forces into the flank and, if possible, the rear of the
Falcon line." As he spoke, Adam sidestepped his
Thunder Hawk just in time to avoid a brilliant burst
of charged particles rising from the valley below him.

"Understood, General," Calvin responded, and
Adam saw the outline of the other warrior's massive
Grand Titan appear at the top of a hill on the edge
of the bunker's defensive perimeter.

He didn't have time to see more because his attention was suddenly drawn to the Vedette next to him.
The tank attempted to move backward, then stopped
abruptly. A shadow fell over Adam's cockpit as a
Night Gyr dropped on its jump jets next to the tank.
They were separated by a scant fifteen meters and, as
Adam swung to meet the threat, the Jade Falcon warrior opened up with his Ultra autocannon. A stream
of shells hit the tank's turret, ripping it up. The Vedette quaked and seemed to jump as internal explosions gutted its interior.

Adam cursed his hesitation and fired his medium
lasers at point-blank range into the side of the Clan
machine. The ruby-red spears of light energy seared
into the right arm and torso of the *Night Gyr* before
its pilot could focus his attention to him. A wave of
heat rose in Adam's cockpit. It lasted only a few seconds, but it was enough to remind Adam to check
that he wasn't building up too much heat. He took a
step backward, then began moving along the hillside

to get enough room to employ his gauss rifles. The *Night Gyr* fired a dozen Streak short-range missiles at him, most of which hit, twisting armor and shaking his *Thunder Hawk* violently.

The shaking got to him. He stopped for a millisecond, then charged his one-hundred-ton BattleMech forward, straight at the *Night Gyr*. The Clan 'Mech seemed to lean forward, toward him, as if to brace for the impact. Adam didn't disappoint him. He hit him at a full run with incredible grinding force. The *Thunder Hawk* seemed to sway for a moment, and Adam's head felt like it was in the middle of a church bell on a Sunday morning as his biofeedback attempted to compensate for the change in balance. Just barely holding on, all he was aware of was the ringing in his ears and the sharp, grinding sensation of armor mangling on impact.

The Jade Falcon OmniMech fell on its side, sliding nearly twenty meters down the hill, digging deep furrows in the sod. It rolled slightly as the warrior attempted to turn and right himself. Adam checked his tactical display for his own damage, and saw that he had lost much of his frontal armor. He was not long for this fight. But he was still in it. Adam took a step forward, then drew back his right leg for a pulverizing kick into the top of the *Night Gyr*.

This time, he heard the thudding-crunch of the impact much clearer as he stepped back to keep his balance. Glancing down, he ignored the damage readout and looked instead at his victim. His 'Mech's foot had caved in the cockpit of the *Night Gyr*. There was no sign of the warrior inside, but Adam wasn't surprised. Whatever was left wasn't much more than a DNA sample, hardly identifiable as human anymore.

He spun slightly just in time to see an explosion on the hilltop where he had last seen Hauptmann-Kommandant Calvin. It was a blast from at least three PPCs, a mix of blue-white light that devoured the hundred-ton *Grand Titan*. The 'Mech's arms reached upward to the sky, not in a gesture of surrender, but as a sign of its total destruction. As his eyes adjusted to the flash, Adam saw the blackened and charred remains of the *Grand Titan* twist, drop to its knees, then fall face-first down the hillside. The other BattleMechs of the Sixth Guards seemed to be in disarray, some falling back toward the bunker, some making their way toward his position. None seemed to have punched through the Jade Falcon flank or rear as he had hoped.

His tactical display again blared out a warning. This time it was a triple pulse tone—an air-threat warning. His eyes darted to the sky, and he saw a lone *Broadsword*-class DropShip swing through the air over the battlefield, then toward The Rock. It dipped slightly in its flight, then dove in lower, bearing directly for the command bunker. Adam watched in dismay as dozens of little figures emerged from the ship, the tiny lights of jumps jets flashing around their ankles.

Elementals.

A chill seemed to sweep his body. "General Bryan!" he screamed as the first troops hit the ground. Even at this distance, he could see that they had landed perfectly. The Falcons had bypassed the minefields and the defenses, coming down directly on top of the command post. From there, not even the defending artillery could fire on them without risk of hitting the bunker complex. Signs of battle—small laser bursts, explosions, and the flash of machine-gun fire—appeared on top of the bunker. It was a miniature battle compared to what he was fighting, yet it seemed all-consuming.

A hiss of static came over his earpiece, followed by a desperate, fear-filled voice. "Oh god, they've killed her. General Bryan is dead. Oh my—" The voice screamed, and there was the sound of a machine-gun burping out death, then utter silence.

Adam looked at his long-range sensors and surveyed their interpretation of the battlefield. The planetary command post was lost. General Bryan was dead. The Jade Falcon assault had lost enough momentum for him get some distance between the two sides, if he wanted. To fall back, again.

This was never the planet where he'd wanted to fight, nor was it the ground he would have chosen or the way he would have chosen to fight. The only reason he was there at all was because he'd been ordered—by a dead woman.

"Colonel Blucher, this is General Steiner," he said, his voice hoarse with exhaustion.

"Yes, General."

"Roll out your troops. We're on our way to you."

"We're leaving, sir?"

"Yes, Colonel. The Falcons have played a trump card and dropped Elementals smack dab on top of General Bryan. All the defensive perimeter work proved pointless. The fight for Melissia is over . . ."

Now all they had to do was try and get out of there alive.

8

Hazi Highlands, Blue Hole
Melissia Theater
Lyran Alliance
25 August 3064

Phelan Kell stood on the small plateau in the Hazi Highlands of Blue Hole where the DropShips of the First Wolf Legion had touched down, then deployed. Five trinaries of force moved away from the ships as the late fall sunrise burned off the morning frost from the grass. He watched as Star Colonel Daphne Vickers' massive *Turkina* lumbered to a stop near him. The OmniMech was honor-won isorla, captured in the Refusal War against the Jade Falcons, and she had more than proven her prowess in the machine. Long gone was any trace of the Falcon green that had originally been the 'Mech's paint scheme. Now, the symbol of the First Wolf Legion—a pack of wolves cresting on a peak against a half-moon—showed on the left torso. The unit was known as the Stalking Death.

"Khan Kell, they have not responded to our batchall yet, quineg?" Daphne asked impatiently. This was the second time she asked since landing two hours ago. Any other time, Phelan would have rebuked her impatience, but he felt the same way.

The Falcons had attempted to find a pass over one of the high mountains, and became trapped in a narrow defile with barely enough room for them to twist their torsos. A patrol from ComStar's 388thDivision had stumbled onto them and had engaged them before the Falcons had a chance to fully deploy. Two trinaries of Jade Falcons had been defeated there, turning the tide of the battle once and for all. While Ranna and the Com Guard repaired and refitted, Phelan had decided to employ the Bludgeon strategy that Archer Christifori had drawn up. Blue Hole seemed a good target, already captured by the Falcons in their initial thrust into the Lyran Alliance.

"I understand your frustration, Daphne," Phelan said, not bothering to repress a sigh. "If they do not respond soon, I shall give them reason to do so." If the Jade Falcon commander did not tell him with what forces they intended to defend Blue Hole, Phelan would deploy his forces around their base of operations to apply the appropriate pressure.

He was moving his *Wolfhound* forward slightly when his comm system crackled to life. "Phelan Kell, this is Star Colonel Daniel Kyle of the Seventh Talon Cluster of the Gyrfalcon Galaxy of Clan Jade Falcon. I acknowledge your batchall, but you are not of the Clans, and I am not obligated to tell you with what forces I am defending this planet. Instead, I order you to depart this Jade Falcon planet immediately or I will be forced to destroy you."

Phelan responded the best way he knew how, by laughing long and hard. "Star Colonel Kyle, we are the Wolf Clan. Your fledglings have had their wings clipped by us several times. I was a Khan of Clan Wolf while you were still in a sibko. How can you deny we exist or say we are not entitled to the honors of battle?"

"What other Falcon warriors fail to do is not of my

concern, Phelan Kell," Kyle said, deliberately avoiding the use of Phelan's title of Khan. "We defeated the defenders of this planet, and it is now part of the domain of the Jade Falcons. I do not recognize you as Clan. Come at me if you wish, but know that I will order my forces to treat you as they would any Inner Sphere trash-warriors. In our eyes, your so-called Wolves are nothing more than bandit caste, a blight that must be removed and all memory of your lives erased. I will not obligate them to fight you with any degree of honor."

Phelan considered for a moment. Kyle was a hard-liner, that much was obvious. The implications for battle were equally clear. In an honorable fight, warriors would not gang up and concentrate their fire on enemies, but Kyle intended to turn his warriors loose. Phelan guessed that the fighting would indeed be vicious if the Falcons would throw honor to the winds for the sake of victory.

"Then I will be forced to use all of my forces," Phelan said.

"What you do," Kyle said airily, "means nothing to me."

"My forces will fight honorably," Phelan continued. "Any violation of Clan traditions will be on your head. The honor on our field of battle can be won or lost by your actions."

"My honor does not concern you. What you think or do is of no interest to me."

"So be it. Poorly bargained and done, Star Colonel Daniel Kyle," Phelan said.

He switched to a channel that would let him address all of the Wolves with him. "Golden Keshik and the Wolves of the Stalking Death, prepare to move out. It is time we teach these Jade Falcons a little humility and the meaning of respect."

Warrens of Dean, Chapultepec
Melissia Theater
Lyran Alliance

Adam stepped off the ramp leading down from the
DropShip and looked around him at Chapultepec's
Warren of Deans. They were here because it was
where Adam had set up a makeshift repair facility
with a supply of spare parts and ammunition, just in
case the defense of Melissia should fail.

And it had failed, miserably.

Events were still a blur to him, even after the pas-
sage of the days. He had managed to flee to the south
of the command post with the remnants of his force,
fighting each step to the DropShips. The arrival of
Colonel Blucher's forces, now informally know as the
Hodge Podges, had been just enough to break the
wave of the Jade Falcons. Blucher had bought enough
time, through the sweat and blood of his command,
to let Adam's forces withdraw.

There were eight DropShips present in the small
valley where he'd established his makeshift landing
zone. Their engines still glowed red-orange from the
flight in, and there was a bustle of activity around
them as the crews and techs debarked and began their
work. The ships were all opening up, and what was
left of the forces Adam had managed to evacuate from
Melissia was now descending the downloading ramps.

He saw a few vehicles and BattleMechs from the
Ninth Lyran Regulars, their gray and brown camou-
flage caved in, burned, and battered from battle.
Adam watched as what was left of the Third Guards—
less than a company of 'Mechs—deployed and attempted to make some sort of formation. Most were
far from battle-worthy at this point. The 'Mechs of the
Sixth Donegal Guards seemed almost apprehensive as
they shuffled forward, pummeled, weary, and more
like shambling scrap-heaps than viable weapons of de-

struction. The only sight that gave Adam any hope was the pair of 'Mechs from Storm's Metal Thunder in the distance. Somehow, the Rivenberg brothers had managed to survive the hellish onslaught that had devoured and mauled his command.

Adam lowered his head and rubbed his brow. Repairs would begin immediately, but he knew that the Jade Falcons had sent a force after him. They were behind him by some thirty hours, and his DropShips had detected their arrival in-system. He knew they were coming. Not so much to take Chapultepec from the Lyran Alliance, though that would be a bonus to them. No, they were coming to find his force and defeat it. They were coming to fight.

An older man strode up to him, and Adam tried to ignore him, but the man just stood there waiting. "Yes," he said slowly, finally looking over at Kommandant-General Seamus Kinnell. As the late General Bryan's aide-de-camp, Kinnell had been hovering like this for several days, obviously intending to assume the same role with Adam.

"General Steiner, I took the liberty of forwarding your after-action report on to the General of the Armies," Kinnell said in his crisp, almost high-pitched voice. "It was sent priority to Tharkad while we traveled in."

"Thank you, Seamus," Adam said, hoping that the man would leave—which he didn't. "Is there more?"

"ComStar apparently has bumped up the priority of our messages. We've already got a response back from General Nondi Steiner."

Kinnell seemed happy, which Adam found irritating at this time. "Go on," he said.

Kinnell pulled out the small printed transcript. "By order of the Archon-Princess's Designate, General of the Armies Nondi Steiner, I hereby appoint General Adam Steiner Commanding General of the Melissia Theater, effective immediately."

"Wonderful," Adam said sarcastically.

"A great honor, General, for one of your age."

Adam shook his head, totally frustrated with this man and his attitude. "Honor? Are you insane, Seamus? Honor? Did you bother to tell the damn General of the Armies or the Archon-Princess that they'll have to change the name of the Theater because Melissia is in the hands of the Jade Falcons? Did you tell them about the men and women we lost in a pointless defense?"

"Nondi Steiner sent her deepest regrets at the loss of General Bryan in battle," Kinnell said in a softer tone, his enthusiasm vanished under the verbal barrage from the much younger man who was now his commanding officer.

Adam shook his head. "General Bryan was an idiot," he said, almost under his breath.

"I worked for her for many years and I beg to differ in my opinion of her, Herr General."

Adam stared at Kinnell, disregarding the man's indignant tone. "Your differing opinion doesn't concern me at all. She's dead. Oh, I'm sure she'll be given a big formal state funeral on Tharkad, but I don't care about that. We have to deal with the living. Right now, the Falcons are burning in after us. I want you to supervise getting our forces refit and repaired. When the Clanners land, they're going to come right for us."

"Yes, sir," Kinnell said, snapping to attention. "And where will you be, sir?"

Adam checked his chronometer, then glanced back at the older man. "I'm going to be looking for some suitable terrain for us to slug it out on when they do land."

Archer felt like the pit of his stomach slopped to one side of his gut as the jump through hyperspace was completed. The *Little Sorrel*, to which the *Colonel Crockett* and several of other DropShips were attached, materialized in the Chapultepec system at the same instant he did, though it felt like his stomach had lingered in hyperspace a few milliseconds longer from the way it pitched. His face got hot, and beads of cool sweat formed instantly as he held back his breakfast.

Licking his lips slightly to fight back the bile, Archer glanced over at the captain. "What's the situation here, Captain?"

Captain Talbert Renfrew, a burly man with thick black hair and one long dark eyebrow, leaned forward and checked the sensors, then glanced out the view port. "Damnation," he muttered.

That was not the word Archer wanted to hear. "What is it?"

Renfrew waved his hand to the screen. "It's like a parking lot up here. I count a total of eight military JumpShips."

Archer pushed off and came to a stop at the control station near the captain's command seat. He glanced at the sensor readings, then looked out the bridge window of the JumpShip as well. He could see the larger dots of light in the distance—JumpShips, some with large circles of light indicating deployed jump sails— recharging their batteries and drives. "Great. Who do they belong to?"

Captain Renfrew checked the monitor and adjusted some of the controls. "I'm getting IFF transponders indicating that half are vessels belonging to the Lyran Alliance Armed Forces. The rest"—he paused as if to double-check his readings—"the rest appear to be non-Inner Sphere in origin."

Archer said nothing. He didn't have to. Non-Inner Sphere. That meant the Jade Falcons were already in the Chapultepec system. Damn, he thought. They beat us. Things on Melissia must have gone worse than he'd anticipated.

Katya Chaffee went over to the communications console and began to scan through the report. "We're getting a data-dump from a relay satellite in orbit.

Apparently, our friend Gramash was able to transmit the latest and greatest for us, General."

"Go ahead, Katya," Archer said. "Tell me a story."

"Melissia has fallen. General Bryan's dead," she said, scanning through the reports and giving only the highlights. "Phelan Kell should be landing on Blue Hole by the time this got here."

"What happened to the forces defending Melissia?"

She studied the screen, oblivious to the fact that every eye on the bridge was glued to her, awaiting her answer. Her eyes seemed to flicker as she devoured the report on the monitor, then rose and turned to face her commanding officer and best friend. "General Adam Steiner is now in command. He's here on Chapultepec."

"Good," Archer said.

Katya didn't blink. "So are the Jade Falcons. They're two days ahead of us on a fast trajectory to the planet."

Not what Archer had hoped to hear, but this war was far from over. "Then we'd better get our butts in gear. Captain Renfrew, start the recharge cycle. We'll be back in a few days, if we're lucky. Katya, let's transfer command to the *Colonel Crockett*. We'd better arrange for a transmission to General Steiner. I want to get down to Chapultepec before the party's over."

9

The fast-moving *Battle Cobra*, most likely a relic of some battle between the Falcons and the Steel Vipers, raced around the rock formation at almost point-blank range in front of Adam Steiner's *Thunder Hawk*. The pair of Galleon tanks behind him fired at the same time he let go with his own lasers. The heat in the cockpit rose slightly as he heard the whine of the capacitors release their deadly lances of crimson death.

Two shots went wide; the others hit it on the right side. The Galleons missed with half of their shots, while the rest poured into the arm and torso of the Jade Falcon 'Mech. The *Battle Cobra* reeled as the barrage sheared off its right arm at the shoulder actuator, and thick gray smoke rose from the severed limb. The *Battle Cobra* contorted slightly under the assault, stopped, then fired its remaining medium and small pulse lasers.

The Galleon closest to Adam bore the brunt of the

barrage, and Adam jerked his head over to see the results. The frontal glacial plate melted away under the green pulses of laser light. The green and brown tank quaked under the burst. The small laser pulses penetrated even deeper. In an instant, the Galleon stopped moving. Its hatches burst open, and twisting black smoke bellowed from within.

Adam turned to face the *Battle Cobra*, but it was gone, leaving behind the severed arm, blackened and smoldering. It had been that way for the past day or so. The Falcons would hit, do their damage, then fade away before he could make a kill. The Warrens of Dean, a twisting maze of rock formations and hills, were tailor-made for the kind of quick, all-out assault that was the Falcons' favored modus operandi.

He checked the sensor-feed on his secondary display and saw that they had indeed pulled back out of range. If true to form, they'd stay back for at least an hour or so. Maybe he could get some repairs done in that time. "Kinnell, give me a sit rep," he barked into the command channel.

"Sir, we've confirmed the arrival of multiple clusters of Jade Falcons in-system a few hours ago, and they have discharged their DropShips. They read like the ships that hit us on Melissia. Galaxy-strength."

"I assumed they hadn't turned around and run. At least they're several days out," Adam responded curtly. "What about those other ships?"

"General Christifori has maintained communications silence since first arriving insystem and sending you that greeting."

The greeting was a short message that Christifori was in-system with multiple regiments coming to relieve and, if possible, rescue Adam's beleaguered force. That had infuriated Adam. Who was this man to come in and think he needed rescuing? Yet, Adam knew his force could not hold out much longer, especially with Falcon reinforcements burning in-system.

Since Christifori's initial message, silence. He was on the ground somewhere on the planet, that much was known, but so far, no one had heard another word from Christifori or his people. If the man waited much longer, there wouldn't be anyone left to rescue. Damn desk general, Adam thought, he's probably waiting for a camera crew to arrive.

Archer Christifori took one more look at the long-range sensor feed showing his force's disposition. A part of him wanted to smile in satisfaction, but he didn't allow himself the luxury. He'd seen enough battles in his time to know that things could change instantly or that unknown factors were in play that could turn the tide of battle in a heartbeat. He was proud of what he had pulled together, but not cocky.

He had brought with him three regiments, two of his own command and one of those that Prince Victor had attached to him. It had been tempting to bring them all in, but he didn't think that was necessary to fight a single cluster of Jade Falcons. He had other reasons as well. For the last year and a half, he had been operating with his three regiments in a relatively independent manner, without needing to coordinate with the regular army. Now, he had a mixed command of full-time military and his quasi-militia forces. This was the first time he'd ever attempted to coordinate a joint command, and he wanted to start with something manageable.

The temptation to rush his forces into battle—to drop right on top of the Jade Falcons and to hit them hard and fast—was seductive. But that would be giving the Clanners exactly the kind of fast and furious clash they favored—and at which they excelled.

So, Archer had deployed his forces outside of their sensors in a sweeping arc around the Falcons. While they encircled the Warrens of Dean, he encircled them. It took time, painful time, but in the end, he would have the Jade Falcons wedged between him and whatever was left of Adam Steiner's force. The *key* was the deployment, and the timing.

Katya Chaffee's voice came over the tactical line.

"General, I'm getting a priority message for you on a scrambled Lyran frequency."

Archer slumped somewhat. "Patch it in." Katya was somewhere nearby, in her converted Badger tracked transport, overseeing the communications intercepts and satellite data. Her job was rough in combat; his was about to get worse. He had a feeling he knew who it was. A person he had been ignoring for the last few hours. This was the fifth priority message he'd received. The time had come for him to deal with this man once and for all.

"Christifori, this is General Adam Steiner. Please respond," came the terse voice in his earpiece.

"General Steiner," Archer said as professionally as possible, "I bring you greetings from Prince Victor."

"To hell with my cousin," Steiner replied angrily. "You've been on planet for hours. You've ignored me up until this point. If this is any indication of Victor's commitment to the Lyran Alliance, why bother to show up at all?"

Archer felt his face get hot at the contempt in Steiner's tone. "General Steiner, I am getting my forces in place to come in and relieve you. Additional Jade Falcons are in-system, so I am aware that time is precious, but so are the lives of those in my command. We'll be ready to launch our relief effort in a few minutes."

"If you're afraid to get into the game, Christifori," Steiner said venomously, "just put your troops under my command and I'll get them into the fight."

Afraid? Archer had been called many things by the Lyran high command in the last few years, but coward was not one of them. For an instant, he wanted to blast the man verbally, but he held back. If it weren't so laughable, maybe he wouldn't have. Besides, he hadn't been sent to the Melissia Theater to take over command, but to coordinate with the Lyran Alliance. That meant that his personal feelings had to be set aside so he could make this joint effort work.

"We'll be there in a few minutes, General. Hold onto your brass," he said, allowing himself one tiny verbal barb. He switched to the tactical channel with the rest of his command. "This is General Christifori to all commands. I'd prefer to have a few more minutes, but it appears that our Lyran hosts have a burr up their butts. On my signal, all units advance by lance. Clan rules of engagement be damned. Take them out. Hit them with everything you have. Concentrate your firepower on the larger BattleMechs first. Mass your attacks. Watch your IFF transponders because somewhere out there are the Lyrans we've come to save."

"The Muphrid Rangers are ready, sir," came back John Kraff's voice.

"The Twentieth Arcturan Guards are in the center of our line and are locked and loaded, General," said Alden Gray.

"The Minutemen are ready," said Hawkeye Hogan, commanding the Third Thorin Regiment.

"Good," Archer said, angling his own *Penetrator* slightly as his command company formed up on his sides. "Tonight, dinner's on the Lyran Alliance. All units . . . charge!"

His seventy-five-ton *Penetrator* hop-stepped forward like a bird, rushing nearly two hundred fifty meters before his sensors began to scream about targets. They had caught the Jade Falcons all right, apparently concentrating for an assault on the surrounded Alliance force. He was sure that the Clan sensors were painting his units as targets as well, but the Falcon commander was faced with a deadly and suddenly desperate situation.

A trinary of Falcon 'Mechs turned from the Alliance units, and charged right back at the center of his own line, straight at the 'Mechs of the Twentieth Guards. The fifteen 'Mechs were all medium-to-assault-class and did not seem impressed or daunted by the sudden appearance of three regiments half-

surrounding them. They charged at a full run, breaking out of the Warrens and into the sparse open fields
to his left. They looked almost like a blur to Archer.

"Command Company, wheel to the left flank. Engage at maximum range. Let's give the Arcturan
Guards an assist if we can," he said, suddenly angling
his running *Penetrator* toward the running Falcons.

The attacking trinary did not seem to care that it
was being flanked. If anything, the first shots seemed
only to prod it into racing faster at the Arcturan
Guards. Archer slowed only to assist in bringing his
own extended-range large lasers to bear. His weapons
were captured Clan equipment, courtesy of the Smoke
Jaguar demise at the hands of the Star League.

He brought his lasers in line with the lead 'Mech,
a mighty *Gladiator*. Its pulse lasers were spewing emerald destruction before it like a hailstorm as it headed
toward the center of the Guard line. Two of his shots,
the pulse lasers, missed totally. Two of the large lasers,
however, found their mark, the scarlet beams slicing
off armor plating from its left leg. The *Gladiator*
slowed briefly, turning to look at Archer as if seeing
some kind of nuisance. Then the giant machine turned
again toward the ranks of the Twentieth Arcturan
Guards, which had halted.

The Guards let go with a barrage of fire, and a
wave of Arrow missiles smashed into the chest of the
Gladiator, shaking it violently. A pair of *Vulture*s
moved up beside the Falcon 'Mech and added their
firepower to the first impressive burst. A stream of
autocannon slugs stitched up across the *Gladiator*
while more than forty long-range missiles lanced
downward at the *Vulture* closest to Archer.

He opened the tactical channel. "John, this is Archer. Detach some of your 'Mechs to cover the center.
Let's not let Gray's Guards bear the brunt of this."

"I'm not blind, sir. Already on it." Archer ignored
the comment. Kraff was a damn good fighter with a
hot temper and hotter vocabulary. At least he wasn't
cursing—yet.

An orange blossom of explosions seemed to engulf the 'Mechs, but Archer managed to keep his target lock on the *Gladiator* as it swayed under the beating. One of the Arcturan Guards, a squat *Bushwacker,* poised itself almost directly in front of the *Gladiator,* firing with everything it had. Archer slowed to a walking pace, letting his lasers recycle their power charge and cool enough to fire again. He carefully centered his targeting reticle on the humanoid head of the *Gladiator* as it belched its fire down at the *Bushwacker* in front of it, nearly toppling the smaller Guard 'Mech in a single burst of laser fire.

Archer knew he was risking heat buildup, but he had to draw their attention. At a full stop, he waited for the targeting tone in his ear, then fired. First, the large lasers, then all six of his medium pulse lasers. In a heartbeat, the cockpit of his *Penetrator* went from mildly warm to the heat of a steaming, humid summer day. His heat indicator spiked as his weapons fire tore away at the *Gladiator*. The left arm, torso, and head bore the brunt of the damage. It was hard to see through the smoke down-range, but as the *Gladiator* sidestepped, Archer saw a number of pockmarked armor plates along the side of its head. Its huge arm was blackened from damage, but was still serviceable, still firing.

The rest of the Jade Falcons seemed to rush straight into the line of the Guards, as if they intended to punch through. Archer was angling himself at a slow gait to get closer to the *Gladiator* and the *Vulture*s, when one of the *Vulture*s erupted, its ammo going off from within. The CASE storage system compartmentalized the blast, sending the pop-off doors flying into the air as the yellow burst of fire and explosion toppled the Jade Falcon. A Falcon *Goshawk* landed in its spot and added its firepower to that of the *Gladiator*. The Arcturan Guard *Bushwacker* toppled, bathed in fire and smoke.

Archer drew his breath and took a moment for thought. What were they doing? Trying to punch through to escape? No. That didn't make sense. Their DropShips were not in the direction the Guards had just come from. There had to be a reason. He adjusted his long-range sensors to get a better picture and saw some of what was unfolding. The trinary that was charging the Guards was doing a perfect job of slowing the assault, drawing fire, slowing the advance.

They were buying time for the others.

Crudstunk! He switched to tactical just as the *Gladiator* staggered back a step, then dropped onto the ground, withering and twitching under impacts from short-range missiles that Kraff and Gray's Guards were pouring into the area.

"Colonel Gray, you'll have to hold the rest of those Falcons alone. Finish them off, then join up with us. Minutemen, form up on me double time. We're heading to the northeast. Kraff, get your people out of that fight and move to the Warrens as quickly as possible."

"Problem, General?" came back the voice of Colonel Gray.

"Yes and no. That trinary was sent to hold us off to allow the others to escape. It *was* working. Now, let's see if we can give the rest of the Falcons a run for their money." He broke his *Penetrator* into a full run again, turning to link up with Kraff. The race was on.

Twenty minutes later, Archer came over the ridge at the same time the Jade Falcons reached the bottom below him. John Kraff and the Rangers poured down the hill like water dumped from a bucket, rushing in a wave of metal and destruction off to his left. To his right, Archer watched as the rest of Third Regiment formed on top of the ridge, awaiting his command.

In the distance, on a flattened hilltop, he could see the oblong and rounded shapes of the Jade Falcon DropShips. Some of the Jade Falcon 'Mechs were already boarding.

"Take them," Archer said on the broadband channel. "Take them all. Head straight for the DropShips."

A star of five *Kraken*s, halfway to the ship, reeled

around and began to make a last stand, to buy time
for the other Jade Falcons. Archer watched as the
Ranger 'Mechs sagged under fire from the enemy's
long-range autocannons. Several BattleMechs toppled,
and chunks of ferro-fibrous armor flew into the air
from the impact of the shells. As powerful as the Clan
'Mechs were, they were no match for their opponents'
sheer number. Kraff's forces ran right up to them,
some firing as they passed, some even slowing enough
to punch or kick the *Kraken*s. The lone star of Jade
Falcons was virtually swallowed up in the assault.
Soon, Archer didn't see their fire.

The Minutemen joined in the pursuit, rushing down
the hillside as well, charging toward the DropShips.
Overhead, two lances of heavy fighters peeled off,
strafing and bombing the DropShips. Smoke rose in
the distance as the ground forces pounded the re-
treating Jade Falcons. All but one DropShip rose from
the ground on a plume of fusion-heated hydrogen.

Archer was about to start down, to survey the damage himself, when he noticed another force forming
up on the ridge around him. On both sides of him
were battered BattleMechs, all Inner Sphere designs.
All showed signs of heavy fighting, some worse than
others. They were not moving fast, but looked almost
groggy as they surveyed the last bit of the fighting
taking place off in the distance. Smoke plumed up into
the air from the landing zone, from either a downed
'Mech or some other collateral damage.

Archer looked to the right and left and saw what
he realized had to be the beleaguered remnants of
Adam Steiner's command. He watched them as they
stared off into the distance. Finally, his comm system
came on from a direct laser-signal feed:

"You there," a voice said, "can you tell me which
one of these people is Archer Christifori?"

He looked off to see the sender, a bruised and burned
Thunder Hawk. "Today seems to be your lucky day,
soldier," Archer called back. "I am General Christifori."

"Well, this is General Adam Steiner in command

of the forces on this planet. You let the Falcons get away, General. Why?"

Archer resented the insinuation that he had messed up. "I didn't let them get away, General Steiner. I drove them away. And I did it to save your butt."

"There are other Jade Falcons in the system," Steiner said impatiently.

"I know."

"We need to establish a defense against them. I have some ideas as to where your troops would be of use."

Archer gritted his teeth for a moment. "I believe the words you're looking for are 'thank you,' General Steiner."

"Thanks for what? You let them get away." It was clear that Steiner didn't understand the gravity of the situation he had been facing, or maybe he was posturing. Either way, Archer didn't care.

"Okay. Let's try this a different way. Is there someplace we can meet face to face?" he asked.

"I'll send you the coordinates of my command post," Steiner said abruptly.

"I'm looking forward to it," Archer replied, lying more than he had in a long time.

10

Archer stood near the campfire, and for a fleeting moment, was transported to the days of his youth, when he and his family had camped out in the forests of Thorin. Bathed in the fire's warmth, the surrounding darkness at bay, he was not fighting a civil war or any other war. Gone were the losses, the deaths, the destruction. All was well with his universe. Such moments seemed more rare these days. He closed his eyes and held his coffee cup with both hands, savoring a rare sense of peace

"You Christifori?" a voice asked from behind him. Archer opened his eyes slowly and turned around. Behind him stood a shorter, younger man dressed in a jumpsuit similar to his own field green fatigues. The newcomer had brown hair, a tight, even rigid expression, and a hint of the Steiner nose. Behind him, outlined by the light of the bonfire, a pair of BattleMechs stood mute as statues.

"Yes," Archer said. "And I take it you're Adam Steiner?" He extended his hand in greeting.

Steiner seemed to regard Archer's hand cautiously, then reached out to give it only a single, hard shake. "Yes, I am."

"Pleased to meet you face to face," Archer said, trying to shake off some of his weariness.

Steiner seemed irritated, but as if he didn't want it to show. "I appreciate the assistance your troops gave us," he said slowly.

"I came because we share a common enemy."

Steiner averted his eyes momentarily. "Don't take this the wrong way, Christifori, but I wish to hell you hadn't let that cluster of Jade Falcons get away."

A few years ago, Archer might have taken offense, but the civil war seemed to be teaching him patience. "There's a full galaxy of Jade Falcons now in the system. That one cluster was already badly beaten. There was little to be gained by trying to wipe them out, other than the senseless destruction of life."

"They fled to the Guffin Continent. They'll be refitting and repairing. Their kin are coming in-system. Because you let them go, we'll probably have to fight them again."

Archer took a long drink of coffee, using the time to stay on top of his emotions in dealing with the prickly younger general. He savored one last gulp, then turned and tossed the rest into the roaring flames. "I didn't come to Chapultepec to defend it from the Jade Falcons," he said. "I came to save you so we could combine our forces to take the fight to them."

"We have to save Chapultepec," Steiner said.

Archer set down his coffee cup on a nearby tree stump and ran his hand through his sweaty hair. "No, we don't."

"So much for the help Victor's willing to commit to the Lyran people," Steiner said, walking off a few steps as though talking to himself. "I should have expected as much from him."

Archer pulled himself up sharply. "Wait a minute there. Before you say something you regret, let me remind you that I am Lyran."

Steiner's eyes narrowed. "You're one of Victor's people."

Archer felt his skin tingle with anger, but he kept his voice slow and calm. "You don't have to like Victor. You don't have to like me. But we both love the Lyran people and know that the Jade Falcons are a threat. The question I have for you, as a general, is what do you want to accomplish in facing off with the Falcons?"

"That's easy," Steiner spat back. "I want them destroyed."

Archer shook his head. "No, I don't think you do."

"Are you insane?"

"Maybe, but I'm willing to bet that what you really mean is that you want them off the worlds they've taken. Destroying them is a moot point. Unless the Star League commits the kind of resources they did to obliterate the Smoke Jaguars, we can't hope to wipe out the Jade Falcons. So, my question, again, is what do you want as a result of our engaging the Falcons?"

"I stand corrected," Steiner said curtly. "I want them off the Lyran worlds they've taken."

Archer smiled broadly. "Then we've found some common ground, General. Because that's what I want, too."

"We should be fighting them wherever they are and beating them. And they're here, on Chapultepec. Fight them here, fall back if we lose, then do it again on the next planet. Pound them until they get sick and tired of fighting." There was a fury and passion in Steiner that Archer really appreciated.

"I understand your feelings. But I'm afraid that won't achieve your goal. We tried that strategy during the initial Clan invasion of the Inner Sphere. It didn't stop them and it didn't force them off of our worlds. No, we have to do something more, something bolder."

For the first time in several minutes, Adam Steiner looked curious instead of furious. "What have you got in mind?"

Archer crossed his arms and stared intently at the other man. "If we want the Falcons to stop or even turn around, we have to make it costly for them to advance. First, we need to hit some worlds they've already taken. Something close to the former border. That will pinch their logistics. It takes a lot of hardware, parts, and ammo to keep those galaxies operational."

"Those worlds are likely to be defended with frontline units," Steiner countered.

"Yes, but we know from the original Clan invasion that the worlds they've taken are where they usually put their units in need of repair, refit, and replacements—units not at peak fighting form. In some cases, we may also run into provisional garrison clusters as well. Besides, that's only one part of the plan. First, we take back a world or two from them, like what Phelan Kell is doing right now. Then, we punch into their occupation zone. We hit a target they can't ignore, something that strikes a chord with them. Eventually, no matter what, the Jade Falcons will have to turn their offensive operations around and come back to their roost."

Steiner shook his head. "What about their vanguard in the meantime, their advance forces? There would be nothing to stand in their way. If we set off for the occupation zone and let them walk off with Chapultepec, the rest of the Melissia Theater is nothing more than a hollow balloon."

Archer smiled slyly. "They didn't come just to conquer. You've noticed it, haven't you? They're pitting their best units against our best. Sometimes they roll in a green unit, too. They're honing their fighting skills against our troops. We're a training ground for them."

"You didn't answer my question."

"They'll eventually turn around and come after us. Deep down, you know I'm right. They can't occupy all of the worlds they've taken. Digging in didn't help General Bryan at all, and it won't help us. If we want them to stop advancing, we've got to give them a good reason. And the reason will be that they risk losing their holdings if they stay."

"So, do you have some targets in mind?"

"Some," Archer said. "But, frankly, I'd like your help. Whatever we pick, it's got to be big enough to shake up the entire Jade Falcon clan."

Adam Steiner stared into the fire, and Archer let his gaze drift to the flames as well.

"It's a gutsy strategy. I'll give you that much," Steiner said thoughtfully.

"I'll take that as a compliment," Archer said.

"Don't." Steiner turned away from the fire, his eyes flaring slightly. "From where I sit, you're still a holovid actor playing the role of a general. Victor's touted you as some kind of living legend, but you took a hell of a lot of time getting deployed while the Falcons ate my troops for dinner. So far, you haven't proven yourself to me."

"Fair enough. I guess if I was in your boots, I'd feel the same way. But remember this, General," Archer said, stressing the title, "I came halfway across the Inner Sphere and brought top-of-the-line regiments to save you and your force. You might not like the way I do things . . . but I've spent the last two years humiliating the Lyran Alliance Armed Forces, and now I'm ready to do it to the Falcons."

Archer reached into his jumpsuit and pulled out a silvery data disk. He tossed the disk to Adam. "This seems as good a time as any."

"What is this?"

"A message from Victor, for you. It's private," Archer said coolly. "I'm going to turn in. Tomorrow we should pool our staff and start laying out targets."

Adam sat in his tent, staring at the tiny image on his personal holoprojector. It was the only source of light in the field tent and cast odd, long shadows about him. His distant cousin, Victor Steiner-Davion, stood facing him as he had in real life only a year earlier. He was dressed in the crisp uniform of the Federated Suns, complete down to the spurs. The projected image stood casually, its arms sweeping out with almost passionate gestures.

"Adam, I know that you don't fully trust me. I know that a part of you believes that I might have actually killed my mother, despite the evidence. None of that matters. I sent Archer Christifori and the forces under his command to the border region for one purpose—to stop the Jade Falcons.

"Regardless of your personal feelings about me, I can't stand by and let the Lyran people suffer at the hands of the Clans. By the time you get this, I will have taken other regiments loyal to me and pressed into the Federated Commonwealth to remove my sister from the throne. I could have taken Phelan Kell and Archer as well, but I didn't. It would have made more military sense to keep them with me, but I made a choice—a choice to save the Lyran people from the Jade Falcons. No press releases, no play up for their support. This is the reality of the situation, and I thought you should hear it from me personally.

"The reason I'm sending you this disk is simple. I know you well enough to guess that you and Archer aren't going to see eye to eye about everything, but it's important for you two to work together to beat the Falcons. United, I think you can bloody their noses enough to force them back across the border or at least stop their progress. If you get caught up in petty arguments or don't work as a united force, then the Jade Falcons have already won and you might as well pull back to Tharkad and wait for them to come for you there.

"I know that this does not set everything straight between us, nor would I be so presumptuous. When this is all over, all I ask is that you consider my actions for what they are, not what my sister might paint them to be." The tiny holographic figure of Victor Steiner-Davion flickered out, and darkness again filled the tent.

Adam glanced up and saw a shadowed figure standing at the door of the tent. Setting the holoprojector on the ground, he rose and went over to the flap to find Colonel Felix Blucher standing at parade rest. "Is there a problem, Colonel?" he asked.

"I wanted to see you for a moment, sir. I heard you listening to something so I stayed outside."

"I appreciate that." Adam waved Blucher inside the tent, and turned on the small field light. "Is there a problem?" he asked again.

"No problem, General. I just wanted you to know that I have my regiment rearmed, and we've salvaged a lot of the Clan equipment. Refitting will take time, and I've given orders to spread the gear out among our forces as evenly as possible."

"Good work," Adam said. "An old colleague of yours is here—Archer Christifori." He spoke the name as if it should get some kind of big reaction, but all he got was a narrow grin.

"I heard. I trust you've met with him."

"Oh yes," Adam said. "He's not quite what I expected."

Blucher nodded slowly. "There's more to that man than what shows on the surface, General."

Adam didn't speak for a moment, wondering about that. "You know Archer Christifori better than I do," he said finally. "Just between you and me, I'm having a hard time accepting him. What I mean to say is that he's been fighting Lyrans for a long time, and beating us. Now he shows up and I'm supposed to work with him? I still think there's something phony about him, what with the way the press tried to turn him into god's gift to war. I think he's more a creation of the media than some big hero."

Felix Blucher chuckled, a response Adam thought totally inappropriate. "Did I say something funny?"

"In a way," Blucher replied. "I would agree that Archer Christifori isn't what the propaganda machines of either side have created. He's no devil, nor is he some romantic Robin Hood figure. He's a man and a leader of men—a man who lost his sister because of the actions of the Archon. I think you and others are looking for some devious motive that simply isn't there. He doesn't have some complex political agenda or plot. He's been fighting the war because of a sense of moral outrage, pure and simple."

"That's an odd statement coming from you. Christifori cost you your career."

"No, he didn't," Blucher said without missing a beat. "My career was ruined by the politics the Archon has been playing. I was beat by Christifori in battle, there's no doubt about that. Pundits and critics chose to paint me as too incompetent to lead troops in battle, but too talented to let go. They were the ones who failed, though, not me.

"No one could have stopped a man like Archer Christifori because he's driven by ideals, and military force can't be used to suppress an ideal. The pressure only makes the ideal stronger. He's spent the last two years standing on a hill of moral high ground and has beaten off all comers. No, General Steiner, my career was ruined because I blindly followed orders in the way I had been trained to do. If I'd been smarter, I would have broken the rules and gone with my heart. I was bitter for a while, but then I realized just how misplaced my emotions were. Truth be told, a part of me is jealous of Archer—he did what he felt was right and hasn't stopped doing that since. I denied myself that right once, but I won't again."

Adam allowed himself a crooked, sarcastic smile. "You speak as if you were one of Victor's rebels."

Blucher looked away for a moment, then back at Adam. "Knowing what I do now, I might very well have chosen to fight alongside Archer Christifori." Then he turned to leave, but stopped and turned back. "Then again, we *are* fighting alongside him, aren't we?"

With that, Blucher stepped out into the darkness, leaving Adam alone to wrestle with his demons.

11

It was more a drizzle than a full-blown rain that marked the weather the next day. Dark purple clouds obscured the sunrise, and there was a chill in the wind as Archer hustled to the tent where he and Adam Steiner had agreed to meet in the Warrens. The weather on Chapultepec had proven to be as temperamental as the enemy.

Entering the tent, he saw that his officers had beaten him to the meeting. As he came in, Alden Gray began to rise to her feet, a reflex upon seeing a senior officer. Archer waved one hand for her to stay seated, then smiled at John Kraff and Katya Chaffee. They knew him so well that they hadn't even tried to rise.

General Adam Steiner sat at the portable table, arms crossed defiantly. Next to him was another officer, a woman who looked almost as defiant as Steiner, her icy gaze virtually screaming contempt. She wore a dress uniform, in contrast to Archer who wore his faded field jumpsuit. From the Alliance Star on her chest, he made an educated guess that this was Leftenant General Jeanette Scarlett of the Ninth Lyran Regulars. Standing behind Steiner was the man Archer assumed to be Kommandant-General Seamus Kinnell, Steiner's aide-de-camp. Archer had seen him before, at a distance, when he'd first relieved Steiner's force.

Seated to Steiner's other side was an older officer in a dress uniform whose presence surprised Archer. Catching his eye, Archer walked over to Colonel Felix Blucher, who had once been his commanding officer. One of the hardest moments in his career had been fighting Blucher, who he respected as an officer. Blucher rose slowly to his feet, holding Archer's gaze.

Archer could feel the eyes of everyone in the room on him, especially the penetrating stare of Adam Steiner. In a move that caught everyone off guard, he gave Felix Blucher a sharp salute. Blucher returned the salute.

"It is customary, General Christifori, for the lower-ranking officer to salute the superior grade," Blucher said with a wry smile.

Archer nodded and moved to a seat opposite Steiner at the table. "I've got far too much respect for you, Colonel, not to break a few rules." Across the table, Steiner's face flushed an angry red as he listened to the exchange.

"The purpose of this meeting," Steiner interrupted, "is to determine how we will work together and what our objectives should be. General Christifori and I met last evening, and we have agreed that the ultimate goal of our operations should be to drive the Jade Falcons out of Lyran space, either by force, or by giving them a good reason or incentive to leave."

Archer reached out to turn on the holographic map so that both sides of the table could see it. A dark green slash showing the Falcon incursion ran along the top of the Melissia Theater, near the Periphery.

Smaller cuts of Falcon green showed where the invasion had been blunted or at least slowed in the Arc Royal Defense Cordon and the Pandora Theater, which comprised the rest of the border. "As you all know, Barcelona, Kikuyu, Clermont, Newtown Square, Melissia, Koniz, Ballynure, and Kooken's Pleasure Pit are still in Jade Falcon hands."

"We beat the initial push on Newtown Square," Steiner put in.

"They came back after you withdrew," Archer said.

"What about Blue Hole, Graceland, and Dustball?"

"I was present on Graceland when the Falcons were driven off," Archer said. "On Dustball, the Com Guard 388th Division and Phelan Kell's Wolves beat the Falcons off-planet. As for Blue Hole, I have received word from my intelligence person on-planet that the Jade Falcons were defeated several days ago by Kell's Wolves."

"We know that one galaxy of troops is headed here, and one is headed for Machida," Steiner said. "The Jade Falcons have cut quite a swath."

Archer nodded. "Yes, but there are limits to what they can do. I proposed a strategy to you yesterday, General Steiner. The first phase is the one Phelan Kell and his people are carrying out right now, Operation Bludgeon. They're hitting planets after they've fallen to the Falcons, forcing the Clanners to tie up resources and shift their logistics lines. The second phase of the strategy is called Operation Audacity, and involves hitting targets deep in the Falcon Occupation Zone to force them to pull out of Lyran space. You've had some time to think about it, General. What do you think?"

Adam Steiner looked to the people seated on either side of him. No words were spoken, but Archer could tell there had been some disagreement, or at least some debate, between Steiner and Scarlett.

"I went over your idea with my staff earlier this morning. There are some reservations." Steiner

glanced again at the stone-faced Jeanette Scarle.
"But for the most part, my commanders agree—it's
best if we take the fight to the Falcons rather than try
and tangle with them here."

Archer allowed himself a smile. "I'm glad we're in
agreement. What do you propose for the next step?"

"Let's pick some targets and determine who's going
to go where, and when," Steiner suggested. "We still
have some time before the Falcons arrive on-planet.
Let's make the best use of it."

Hazi Highlands, Blue Hole
Melissia Theater
Lyran Alliance

A Wolf Elemental marched the man in before Phelan
Kell, bowing slightly in the presence of his Khan. The
fighting against the Jade Falcons on Blue Hole had
ended three days ago, and Phelan had been using the
time to repair and refit his troops. This man had been
demanding to see him for a full day, but Phelan had
ignored him until he provided the password Archer
Christifori had been using in his communications. Phelan's people had long since verigraphed and verified
his identity.

"Khan Kell," the shorter man began, "I would like
to congratulate you on your operations here. You
soundly beat Star Colonel Kyle."

The fighting had been vicious. Phelan had allowed
Kyle to begin an encirclement maneuver but had sent
two stars far around to his rear area. In the middle of
his attempted envelopment, Kyle suddenly thought *he*
was the one surrounded. He'd lost his nerve, if only
for a few minutes, and attempted to pull out, but Phelan did not allow it.

A running battle broke out, one that destroyed any
threat the Seventh Talon Cluster had operational. For
all of his posturing, Star Colonel Kyle had been cap-

tured and made a bondsman by the Wolves in Exile, and the last time Phelan saw him he was scrubbing down armor plating on a row of Wolf OmniMechs.

"Your assessment is accurate, but I am not sure it is welcome. You are, after all, a total stranger."

The small man smiled, combing a lock of black hair off of his brow with his fingers. "Actually, we do know each other already, just not personally. I am Captain Gramash. I'm the person who has been coordinating your intelligence efforts along the front." He extended his hand and Phelan took it, suspiciously.

"You are our spy, quiaff?"

Gramash raised one eyebrow almost playfully. "Yes, though I prefer to think of myself as your intelligence coordinator."

"You must forgive me, Captain, but I have a natural distrust of military intelligence organizations."

Gramash chuckled. "Based on experience, no doubt."

"Indeed."

"Very well. I can't stay long. I came here in person because I need ready access to the border."

"How is Christifori doing?" Phelan asked.

The small man pulled out a noteputer and stabbed at the tiny button controls, reviewing the material on the screen. "He has linked up with General Steiner on Chapultepec."

Phelan couldn't resist a smile. "Good, though I wonder how that meeting is going, considering Adam's rather stormy past with Victor. I'm prepared for the next phase of this operation."

"As am I. It's always best if we hold the initiative in these kinds of situations. However, there is an intelligence matter on this planet that needs addressing. Thanks to some work with ComStar's ROM, I was able to learn that a member of The Watch is here on Blue Hole." The Watch was the Clan version of an intelligence network. Each Clan maintained its own arm, and though they were new to the idea of spying, they had learned from their experiences in the Inner Sphere.

"Which Clan?"

"Vlad Ward's Wolves."

Phelan drew a long breath and paced across the room slowly, wrapped in his thoughts. "You know where this person is, quiaff?"

"Yes," Gramash said. "He is being held by several agents loyal to Prince Victor."

"And you came here to tell me . . . why?" Phelan found himself doubting the man claiming to be his intelligence coordinator.

Gramash swept his hands in front of him. "The last time the Jade Falcons came across the border to Coventry, they were stopped for two reasons. First, they knew they'd be severely bloodied if they stayed, perhaps even crippled. Second, Khan Ward's Wolves struck at their rear, and they were at risk of losing their occupation zone. I wanted you to know that this person exists in case you want to pass any information to Clan Wolf, perhaps something that might prompt them to apply pressure to the Falcons."

"Khan Marthe Pryde is no fool, Captain. She learned from what Vlad did last time. She left behind at least four galaxies of troops to defend her occupation zone. Your own intelligence has told you that, quiaff?"

"Yes. My intelligence has told me that. But do we know what Khan Ward knows?"

Phelan grinned. Gramash was right. He had learned the Falcon disposition, but who knew what the Wolf Clan Watch had yet uncovered? "You understand a great deal about the Clans, Captain Gramash, if that is your real name."

The spy smiled in response. "It's not, nor is the rank real. Such is the nature of the life I live."

"You have the Wolf spy's name?"

"I do."

"Give it to me. I have a meeting to attend with this man."

"Good luck, Khan Kell."

"We both need luck in our chosen lines of work,"

Phelan said. He strode over to shake Gramash's hand and to get the Wolf spy's name from the noteputer.

The trip there took less than a half an hour. The Wolf Clan spy was being held in a small, dingy cinderblock structure in the country. Two men stood guard, though from a distance they looked more like farmers than heavily armed sentries. They stepped aside silently as Phelan and Gramash entered the small one-room structure.

The interior was dimly lit by thin shafts of sun poking through the mud-spattered windows. A thin layer of dirt covered the wooden floor, and in the center of the room, lit by a single bulb, was a man strapped to a chair. He was aged by Clan standards, with gray-white hair and a face weathered like someone who had worked outdoors his whole life. Phelan studied him, and the man stared boldly back.

"I know you," Phelan said.

"I am nothing more than a trader here," the man said.

"Neg," Phelan said with a single light laugh. "You are of the Carns bloodline. I can see it in your nose and eyes. I believe we once met, though it was long ago."

The man said nothing, nor did he flinch when Phelan pulled out his knife. He stabbed the knife forward, cutting first the bonds on the man's left hand and then those on the right. The "trader" silently rubbed his wrists.

Phelan sheathed the knife rapidly and stepped forward. "You are of The Watch," he said slowly.

"I have no idea what you are speaking of."

Phelan smiled like a hungry wolf. "Of course not. That is of no matter to me. What matters is that you can get word to Khan Ward."

The trader shrugged.

"By now, you know that that the Jade Falcons have crossed the border into the Lyran Alliance. What you do not know is that I am part of a task force that plans to take the fight into the heart of the Jade Falcon occupation zone."

The captured spy still did not speak, but his silence betrayed his interest.

"The Jade Falcons in the occupation zone have been weakened," Phelan continued, "and their frontline galaxies are in the Inner Sphere. We have stopped them here, but they will move on to new targets."

"Why is this of interest to me?"

"Because if you are who I think you are, the blood of Kerensky runs in your veins. You know that if the Falcons push much harder, they will be poised to seize worlds that would make a thrust to Terra much easier. You also know that they are waging this fight to sharpen their green troops in battle, perhaps against the Wolves."

The man shrugged again.

"Perhaps I have the wrong man. If so, this is a waste of breath. But let me tell you this. I am going into the occupation zone to stop the Falcons. If you are who I believe you are, tell Khan Ward that I will be on Sudeten in a few months. Perhaps we can then 'reconcile' our old differences."

With that, Phelan turned and walked out, Captain Gramash at his heels. When they had gotten a short distance from the building, they stopped.

"Sudeten is the Jade Falcon capital," Gramash said, showing surprise. "To go there would be madness. I know that Operation Audacity calls for crossing the border, but that . . . that is too much."

"I have no intention of going to Sudeten, Captain," Phelan said flatly. "I am going to cross the border, and it might look like I'm going that way, but I'm not."

Gramash smiled broadly. "Ah, so you lied, because no matter what, it works to your advantage."

"Aff. Your assessment is correct. This man is a former Wolf warrior. He is of The Watch. He will pass this word onto Vlad. As a Wolf Khan, Vlad will do one of two things. One, he may attack the Jade Falcons and drive toward Sudeten, an effort that will help us. Two, if he plays the political angle, he may pass that information onto Marthe Pryde of the Falcons. She, in turn, will re-deploy her forces to blunt such a strategy. But since we are not going there to begin with, either outcome is acceptable."

"Brilliant," Gramash said.

"Neg. It was well bargained. Now let us see that it is done."

The air inside the command tent hung heavy with moisture as the pelting rain continued to pour down on the Warrens of Dean. The debate had been lively for the last two hours, and Archer could still sense some distrust on both sides of the table. The civil war that Victor had been waging had left its mark on them all. He had remained quietly in the background, letting Adam Steiner and his subordinates do most of the talking. Finally, he rose from his folding chair and stood staring at the holographic map.

"Problem, Christifori?" Adam Steiner asked.

Archer crossed his arms, one hand cradling his chin in thought. "All of this talk isn't getting us anywhere. We're all in agreement that we need to take the fight to the Jade Falcons, preferably in the occupation zone. The truth of the matter is that we need a target, one that will shake them up so much that they are forced to respond. Maybe such a target doesn't exist, but I think it does. We've got to find it."

"Sudeten," Leutnant-General Scarlett said. "As I said before, if we strike at their capital, they will be forced to respond."

"It's too damn heavily defended," Kraff argued. "We might be able to take it if we go in together, but they've got enough force within one or two jumps to pulverize us."

"I'm just trying to point out an option," Scarlett retorted, glaring across the table. Throughout the discussions, Adam Steiner had all but encouraged his staff's belligerent attitude toward Christifori's staff. After almost two years at each other's throats, the two sides were not going to have an easy time putting the civil war behind them, even for a few months.

Archer raised his hand, and Kraff, whose mouth was just opening to argue the point, slowly sat back into his seat. "Maybe there's another option," Archer said thoughtfully. "Katya, according to our esteemed intelligence officer, where are the Falcon Guard?"

Katya checked her noteputer. "They did not successfully bid to participate in the Falcon incursion. Right now, they're split up over a couple of planets, Seiduts, Evciler, and Twycross . . . just in case Clan Wolf gets adventurous."

"The Falcon Guards are considered the best of the Jade Falcon Clan," Archer said as his mind played over several ideas at once. "Twycross?"

"Yes, sir," Katya replied. "Twycross. I don't have much data on it, but apparently the Falcon Guards always keep a trinary there as some sort of honor guard."

"Twycross," Archer repeated, fixing his gaze on Adam Steiner.

"You want to attack Twycross? That's suicide. It's close to the Falcon border with the Wolf Clan zone."

Archer felt his blood surge and renewed energy pulse through his extremities, as if he had just consumed a liter or so of coffee. "We don't have to hold it. We just have to beat the Falcon Guards there."

"What's so important about that?" Sean Kinnell asked as if he were annoyed with the concept.

"To us it's not a big deal, but these are the Jade Falcons. When I was with the Tenth Lyran Guards, we wiped out the Falcon Guards there. They rebuilt that unit, and that was the reason the Falcons won anything at all in the Trial on Tukayyid. Later, the sole Falcon Guard warrior who survived our attack defeated Natasha Kerensky, the Wolf Khan, on Tukayyid."

"It's an honor issue with them," Adam Steiner said, nodding.

"Right," Archer replied. "To us, Twycross is a dust-ball with no strategic value. To the Falcons, it's a crucible of honor. If we go there and beat the Falcon Guard on that world, it will force every unit in the region to respond. They'll *have* to halt their drive into the Inner Sphere."

Adam Steiner pointed to the map. "No offense, Christifori, but you're talking the same sort of suicide as hitting Sudeten. Any troops with you will be wiped out."

Archer grinned. "I'll be gone by the time they arrive. I know you don't want to hear this, but that's been the hallmark of my unit's operations against the Lyran Alliance so far. I don't plan on sticking around long enough for them to kill us."

Adam got to his feet. "It's possible to get there, but I think the real key is to have a place you can fall back to. One that has supplies and reinforcements. Otherwise, you're going to be on the run and will get whittled down along the way."

"What have you got in mind?" Archer asked.

"We go in two prongs. You hit Roadside and I take Black Earth. Both worlds are inside the occupation zone, just across the border. Taking both planets will force the Falcons' logistical chain into a frenzy because it will cut them off from the border. I stay on the border while you drive to Twycross. You hit the Falcon Guards, stir up the hornet's nest, then get out. We meet on"—Steiner squinted at the map—"Black-jack." He pointed at a tiny dot of light.

Archer leaned toward the map as well, pulling out his glasses to better see the planets. "I could ask Phelan Kell if he and his force could be leveraged best against the Falcons here in the Inner Sphere. It's a modification of our original intent, but may prove useful."

"It's a plan," Steiner said.

"You don't sound too sure."

"Christifori, if you want to take your regiments in there, I'll support it as best I can. I'll do it for the Alliance, plain and simple. But you need to know what's going through my mind if we're going to try and work together. From the standpoint of the Lyran Alliance, if you go in and die there, and we still push the Falcons out of the Alliance, we win. If you come out alive, that's merely a bonus."

"This plan," Archer replied sternly, "requires us to work in unison. If you abandon us, General Steiner, the whole thing will collapse."

"You have my word as an officer and a gentleman, Christifori. I'll support you in every way reasonable."

Archer took note of the word. "Reasonable" was not the same as "possible." He nodded, but a part of him wondered if he was being set up for a last stand that would rival General Custer's at the Little Big Horn. It was a chilling thought. He had tried to put the civil war out of his mind, but apparently it was still very much a part of Adam Steiner's thoughts.

"Very well. Let's get prepped, orders out, and break camp. There's still a Jade Falcon galaxy bearing in on this system, and we need to be out of here by the time they land."

12

Khan Marthe Pryde watched as her laborers and technicians worked to clean up the burned interior of the bunker the enemy had been using as a command post. The air still stung slightly with a hint of burned plastic and an almost electrical smell that left a coppery taste in her mouth. The walls were scarred black from laserfire, and the floor was covered with shattered pieces of equipment that the workers were sweeping up and otherwise removing from the bare concrete.

A blast-proof window provided some view of the exterior of the command post, and what Marthe Pryde saw everywhere were signs of her Clan. Jade Falcon technicians were working on field repairs to their BattleMechs, while old but still dignified solahma infantry labored to dig up the mines that had been laid to kill her troops. Though she couldn't see it, she knew that somewhere overhead, fluttering in the afternoon breeze, was the flag bearing the image of the emerald green Jade Falcon.

She turned at the sound of the door, then saw sa-Khan Samantha Clees come in, a thin sheet of hard-copy in one hand. Crossing the room, Samantha stepped over a kneeling technician as if he were a mere scrap of trash to be avoided. "Greetings, my Khan. I bring new word from the Omega Galaxy on Chapultepec."

Marthe nodded permission to continue, and Samantha glanced quickly at the hardcopy report, then spoke in a crisp tone. "According to confirmed reports, the Inner Sphere forces on Chapultepec are departing for the jump points."

"All of them?"

"Aff, my Khan."

Marthe said nothing for a moment. "How many regiments were present?"

"There were at least two at the jump points that never deployed. There were two Lyran Alliance regiments on-planet, and they were joined by three more regiments."

"And two of those regiments we have never heard of, quiaff?"

"Aff. They are apparently newly formed units, a result of this civil war being fought. Combined, three of these regiments call themselves Archer's Avengers."

"Chapultepec is ours then. I assume that Galaxy Commander Von Jankmon will want some time to rebuild."

"He has made the request."

"Allow it. After all, the foe that we desire is leaving."

"But where are they going, my Khan?"

"It has been a long time since we have faced the Inner Sphere in battle. For that reason, they will likely assume we are heading for Coventry or even Tharkad. I would estimate that they are moving to Medellin to be in a position to block us."

Clees nodded. "That is logical."

"We shall take some time to catch our breath, then sweep in there to meet them. Besides, pushing further across the Melissia Theater gains us nothing but Periphery worlds. If we must take planets, let us take those with an industrial base to support us when we finally begin the push to Terra."

"What of the rest of the front, my Khan?"

Marthe frowned. "Phelan Kell is proving troublesome. We will have to give him something to think about. Strike at the Com Guard on Crimond and at Rasalgethi. Phelan will feel obligated to respond, given the mantle of protectorship that Phelan Kell wears. That will tie him up and keep him from meddling."

"An excellent plan," Samantha said. "Rasalgethi widens our front facing the Terran Corridor. I would be remiss, however, if I did not point out that such a move may stir the wrath of this farcical Star League. They may feel obligated to respond with military force."

Marthe couldn't help an almost wicked smile. "The Lyran Alliance is embroiled in a civil war. The Star League will not step in for fear of tipping the balance of power in favor of one side or the other. Furthermore, Rasalgethi does not cross the Tukayyid line, so our truce is held. Finally, it will infuriate the Wolves. The Com Guard position in Rasalhague has blocked the way to the Terran Corridor for all of us. Taking Rasalgethi gives us a potential path to Terra with only the Lyran Alliance to defend against us." Rasalgethi had played a key role in Marthe Pryde's mind in the planning for the incursion into the Alliance. "For that matter, I would not mind losing all the territory we have gained except that it would seem a loss of honor in the eyes of the other Clans. But, know this, Samantha. That alone is a planet I desire."

"Perhaps we should pull another galaxy from the occupation zone to the border, quiaff?"

"Neg, Samantha. When I drove for Coventry, Khan Ward of the Wolves took advantage of the situation to take worlds from us. I have learned. We must leave galaxies in place to blunt any Wolf aggressiveness. This time, we will fight on only one front against a foe that will crumble before us."

"And where does it end?" Samantha asked.

Marthe smiled, feeling that everything was going very much her way. "We stop when what we have captured is too difficult to hold and when I see that our troops have honed their skills enough. And not before."

Samantha bowed her head slightly, properly respectful. "As you desire, my Khan."

BOOK TWO

The Stuff of Memories and Legends

13

Star System Woodbine 211
One Jump From Roadside
Jade Falcon Occupation Zone
3 October 3064

Archer had decided to hold the staff meeting in the cavernous 'Mech bay of the *Colonel Crockett* rather than the more traditional tactical operations room for a couple of reasons. The first was that even after almost two years' ownership, his technical crew could still not get the temperature in the ship's TOR to stay comfortable for more than fifteen minutes. The second was that he was feeling cramped and needed room to pace. He'd been spending so much time on DropShips and JumpShips lately that he just needed space around him, enough to let him stretch his legs more than just his daily exercise regime.

With the unit's BattleMechs mounted in their transport positions, two teams of technicians simply worked around his command staff. Some of what they did was routine maintenance, and some of it involved adding captured Clan technology to the Avenger machines. A few of the 'Mech pods contained OmniMechs newly captured in the recent fighting on Chapultepec, and they had already received priority repair jobs.

Arms crossed, the usual scowl on her face, Colonel Alden Gray of the Twentieth Arcturan Guards stood in the middle of the bay. Archer wondered if she ever really relaxed or smiled. His three regimental commanders were also present. The only one missing was Anne Sung, commander of the Second Crucis Lancers RCT. After some serious closed-door negotiations, Archer had persuaded Sung to go with Adam Steiner to help balance their forces.

She had a hard time accepting orders from Steiner, but Archer had convinced her that it was what Prince Victor would have wanted her to do. His parting words to Sung were blunt: "For what it's worth, Colonel, the man hasn't once addressed me by my·title. I understand your apprehension, but I need someone to know there's someone with him who I can trust and who knows what she's doing. You're one of the best. If it doesn't work out, I'll send over the Twentieth Arcturan Guards in your place. And as hard as it is, please avoid punching out General Steiner." Archer kept a certain lightness to his tone, but he was half-serious.

He stopped pacing and turned to his commanders. "Okay, people, listen up. Our target is Roadside. Rho Galaxy usually maintains a unit there, and they may still be doing so, but our latest intel has them facing off against Khan Kell and his Wolves."

"So we don't know what's there?" Katya asked.

"Captain Gramash thinks the world's location on the old border means there's a good chance it would be garrisoned by either a unit up for refit or else a solahma unit."

"Pray for solahma troops," Kraff said under his breath.

"I wouldn't if I were you," Archer said. "Don't be fooled by the Clanners' own propaganda. Those solahma units are pretty tough. Their members may be old by Clan standards, but most of them are our age, and they're determined to go out in a blaze of glory to preserve their honor. Many of them fought suicide assaults during the initial invasion." He deliberately spoke slowly to let his words sink in.

"Point taken, General," Kraff said.

"We also know that the Jade Falcons have an ammunition production plant there. It's not big, but chances are that's where any garrison force would be concentrated."

"You want us to blow it up?" Colonel Hogan asked.

Archer shook his head. "No. We're going to need those supplies for ourselves. We're making a long hop into enemy-held territory, but we'll follow the same routine that's gotten us through the civil war so far. The Avengers didn't need logistics to survive. We made it using supplies we picked up along the way. Same rules here, people."

Gray had a question. "Sir, if we take Roadside, how are we going to hold it and still have a force that can push into the Falcon occupation zone?"

Archer grinned. "I've sent a request to Khan Kell to see if he can release the Blue Star Irregulars to both Roadside and Black Earth, where General Steiner's jumping. I'm hoping he can spare them enough to garrison those systems."

"The Blue Star Irregulars are outstanding troops," Gray said appreciatively. "But aren't they under your control? Why ask Kell?"

"On paper, they're under my command, but the defense of the ARDC is falling into Phelan's lap, and the last thing I want to do is to step on his toes. After all, he's had the most success at blunting the Falcons up to this point."

Archer looked around at his commanders. "The Blue Star Irregulars are some of the best. I say 'some' because, from what I can see, I've got the best there is with me, too. No matter what happens, we have to stop the Jade Falcon drive.

"Now then, let's make our plans to take Roadside and do it quickly. We jump in five hours to a pirate point in the system, then begin burning for the planet as soon as we emerge. Let me tell you some ideas I've come up with . . ."

Outskirts of New Houston, Black Earth
Jade Falcon Occupation Zone

General Adam Steiner swung his *Thunder Hawk* onto the top of a hill just outside the city of New Houston on Black Earth, then paused to survey the area. By arriving at a pirate jump point, his force had been able to travel to the planet's surface much quicker than from a standard jump point. He had been challenged twice on the way in by a Star Colonel named Cewen Newclay, who Adam remembered from the fighting on Barcelona. He'd tangled with Newclay at the start of the incursion, bloodying his Third Talon Cluster until being ordered to withdraw by General Bryan. Apparently, the Third had been ordered by Gamma Galaxy command to Black Earth for repair and refit. Well, now Adam would get the chance to set matters straight.

New Houston, a refinery and production city, had been the site of the original fighting for the planet during the Clan invasion. In the distance, he could see the maze of pipes, storage tanks, and buildings stretching out to Newport News Bay. The city was in a low pocket, surrounded by hills. Hanging over it, the dull brown and gray air cast cloud-like shadows below. From pre-Clan maps of the planet and the city, Adam could tell that the Jade Falcons had expanded operations there. All of it was meant to feed their war machine, but he was going to see about changing that.

"Any sign of the locals?" he asked on the command frequency. Adam commanded a mix of forces, including the remains of his own unit and the Ninth Lyran Regulars, which added up to a reinforced regiment.

"Nothing here," Colonel Blucher called from his left flank.

"Too quiet, if you ask me," Colonel Sung said from his right flank.

"Keep your eyes peeled," Adam ordered. As if on cue, his comm system flashed a yellow warning light, indicating an incoming message from the Jade Falcons. He tied it in with his command channel.

"This is Star Colonel Cewen Newclay of Clan Jade Falcon. Who is it that dares land on this holding of the greatest of Kerensky's Clans?"

Adam leaned back into his seat. "General Adam Steiner of the Lyran Alliance."

Newclay chuckled once. "The same General Steiner who fled Barcelona, quiaff?"

Adam's jaw tightened, but he forced himself to speak calmly. "The same. I'm sorry I was ordered off Barcelona before we could finish our little contest."

"It was over from the time we landed, General."

"That remains to be seen. I suppose I should ask you with what forces you plan to defend this planet, but I'm willing to bet it's everything you've got."

"My entire cluster stands ready to repulse you," came back Newclay's deep voice.

"Where are you located?" Adam asked. "So we can come and finish what we started on Barcelona."

"You shall see soon enough," Newclay said, and the channel went silent.

Suddenly, an incoming air-threat warning lit up red on Adam's console. Aerospace fighters. Two stars of them, ten in all, were bearing down from the north on the center of his line. Adam turned his *Thunder Hawk* just as they began to dive in.

Some of the fighters let go with bombs. Others sprayed downward with salvos of long-range missiles and autocannon fire. Massive explosions in what had been his rear area seemed to roll forward toward him.

BattleMechs and vehicles began to move as Leutnant-General Scarlett ordered her forces to disperse.

Adam did not break. None of the shots were aimed at him. As the aerospace fighters began to bank for another pass, a trio of captured *Kraken* BattleMechs, now repainted in the gray-green of the Ninth Lyran Regulars, turned and began to fire. The long-range Clan-built autocannon carried by the *Kraken*s were welcome additions to his force. The stream of shells were invisible to the naked eye, but he watched as two of the *Jagatai* fighters seemed to quake in mid-turn, one visibly losing an armor plate as it banked.

"Where did those fighters come from?" he demanded.

"Unknown," came back the responses from several of his command.

Adam gritted his teeth. On Barcelona, Newclay hadn't deployed any fighters. This time, he wasn't going to make it easy.

The two stars of fighters didn't complete their banking. Instead, they swung out over the waters of Newport News, and continued on out of sensor range. They were deliberately keeping the location of their base a secret.

And as long as Newclay was using fighters, Adam knew he would have his work cut out for him. "We've fighters, too," he said. "Let's get them and some satellites in the air. I want that airstrip found so we can take it out, or else our friendly Star Colonel is going to whittle us down with bombs and strafing runs."

"I'll order our fighters up immediately, sir," Scarlett said.

"Same here," Sung put in.

"Make it snappy. The last thing I want is for this to drag out for days. We've got a timetable to keep."

≡ 14 ≡

Tyler Munitions Works, Roadside
Jade Falcon Occupation Zone
4 October 3064

Outlined against the purple morning sky, the Tyler Munitions Works on Roadside sat on an open plain, isolated from the nearby city of Dehl. Its nearly twenty acres of interior structure were ringed with heavy fencing. No trees, no real cover, just the occasional low hill. From the vantage point of his *Penetrator*, Archer studied it as the orange sun of Roadside slid behind the clouds. The Jade Falcons were supposed to be here. This was the place. According to the challenge he received upon landing his troops last night, a Star Captain named Michael and his trinary would defend this planet from outside of the Tyler Munitions Works.

It wasn't like the Jade Falcons to be late.

Kraff's wish seemed to have been fulfilled. The trinary defending Roadside was a solahma unit, composed of screw-ups and "aged" Falcon warriors from the Jade Dark Wing Cluster. That didn't mean they were pushovers. After the age of thirty, a Clan warrior's career was considered to be on the downslide, which tended to make solahma warriors more ferocious because they were more desperate. They lived for one thing—a chance to earn the honor of having their genes preserved for use in the genetic breeding program. The only way to do that, as a warrior, was to die gloriously in a great battle. This attitude combined Jade Falcon cunning and training with a recklessness that often proved to be a deadly combination.

"Anything?" he asked on the tactical channel.

"Looks deserted," Katya Chaffee said. "I'm bouncing scans off a satellite, and I think those 'Mechs are in the complex."

"Bingo!" called out John Kraff. "At oh-niner-three, I have multiple targets emerging."

Archer turned his gaze and long-range sensors in the direction of Kraff's sighting. Sure enough, a star of five BattleMechs stepped out.

"Star Captain Michael," Archer said into his helmet mic. "Our forces outgun and outnumber you. You don't have to do this."

"Honor demands it," the Jade Falcon warrior said, halting his aptly named *Behemoth* 'Mech.

Only the Jade Falcon commander and his star were visible. The trinary's two other stars were unaccounted for. Archer stared for three seconds at the five BattleMechs, and spotted the structures behind them at about the same time that Katya Chaffee did.

Her voice rang like a warning bell. "All troops, hold your fire. Those buildings behind them are munitions-storage bunkers."

Archer was pleased that Katya had caught on so quickly. A stray shot in the wrong direction would set off the perimeter building behind the 'Mechs. Yes, the building would likely be destroyed in such a blast, but so would a good portion of the facility. Despite the bunkers and reinforcement partitioning between the buildings, a lot of damage would be wreaked on his forces even at this distance if the buildings were full.

Staring intently at the row of Jade Falcons, Archer guessed that others were hiding in the complex, their signatures masked by the metal infrastructure and production equipment.

"Star Captain Michael," he said firmly, inflecting his voice with as much respect as possible, "move away from those buildings, and we will give you a fight that will earn you the honor you seek."

"You know nothing about the honor I or my people seek. Come and get us. Fight us here, on our terms, if you dare, you freebirth tick on the hide of a surat!"

With those words, Michael's star moved just slightly forward and began to fire at the First Thorin Regiment. True to their orders, none of Archer's troops returned fire, but began to fall back. A pair of silvery streaks from the *Behemoth*'s gauss rifle tore outward at Katya's command company. A lightweight *Scarabus* toppled backward, spewing a thin cloud of grayish smoke from the gaping holes in its torso.

"General," Katya said, sounding nervous but still in control.

Archer stared at the image in front of him. "We don't have time for games. We can't be sure they've already evacuated the civilians from the plant, but we'll have to operate on that assumption. All units, this is General Christifori. Fall back to maximum range and open fire. Fall back and then fire at will!"

The star of second-line Falcon BattleMechs stopped dead in their tracks. One of them, a *Galahad*, bent at the knees and braced itself as it spat round after round of gauss slugs. Another, a *Hellhound*, tried to sidestep into a better firing position. Archer could only see them for a moment as the First Thorin Regiment—some two battalions of BattleMechs, tanks, and infantry—poured their fire down on the lone star of Jade Falcons. There was the bright flash of eight or nine particle projection cannons, waves of missiles so thick the air filled with smoke from their contrails, and lasers and pulse lasers stabbing downward. The ground seemed to quake, then moan audibly as the star of Falcons all but disappeared, enveloped in a cloud of death and chaos.

Archer saw another Falcon star break from the factory complex and charge his line, firing wildly now that the Clan rules of engagement were off. He only saw them for a second or two before something set off the building behind them. A rumble followed by a thunderclap of explosive force knocked him back two meters and toppled almost half of the 'Mechs in his line of sight. A brilliant cloud of sparkling orange and billowing black rose hundreds of meters in the sky. All firing stopped along the line of his regiment.

"My God . . ." Katya said.

"I assure you that God had nothing to do with that," Archer said. "They assumed we wouldn't attack them there. They were wrong, but in the end, they died a glorious death, which is what they wanted anyway. Colonel, get your infantry in there on fire control ASAP and make sure no green birds somehow survived."

The wind shifted direction, and the cloud cover cast a long dark shadow over Archer's *Penetrator*. One thing was certain. The rest of the Jade Falcons would know he was in their back yard pretty damn soon.

Manocchio, Suburb of New Houston
Black Earth
Jade Falcon Occupation Zone

The force of the blast knocked Adam Steiner out of bed, leaving him momentarily disoriented. He grabbed his wrist communicator, which was still on the nightstand somehow, and fumbled with it in the dark, attempting to activate it. Through the partially closed blinds of the apartment building he had confiscated as an HQ in the suburbs of New Houston, he saw a flicker of red and orange light. Outside, a fire was burning.

"Striker One here. What was that?" he bellowed.

"Bombing run by the Jade Falcons, sir," came back the comm tech's voice. "They must have come in too low for sensors to pick up until the last moment."

"Are our fighters in the air?"

"Launch orders went out automatically, sir, but the Falcons aren't sticking around."

Adam pulled himself up off the floor and tossed the communicator down on the bed while he searched for his pants. For two days now, it had been the same thing. The Jade Falcons sent in fighter/bombers that hit his units, then peeled away to an unknown fighter base. He had ordered out three battalions, a regiment's worth of troops, to try and find the base, but they'd struck out so far.

Twice, his own fighters had managed to maintain a close enough pursuit to force the Falcons to turn and deal with them. Twice, his fighters had been driven back by the Clan aerospace pilots, and Adam had lost five fighters in the process. Star Colonel Newclay was not fighting the same kind of battle as he had on Newtown Square. Instead of the usual Jade Falcon rush into a fast and furious fight, he was frustrating Adam with these harassing attacks. Thus far, the Falcon 'Mechs hadn't even surfaced . . . just the fighter craft.

Adam made his way to the ad hoc command post in the basement of the building, where his portable sensor gear and communications equipment was set up. A handful of techs and officers were studying maps and attempting to plot the Clan fighters, but thus far, every attempt to pin them down had failed. Adam ran his hand through his hair as he, too, stared at one of the maps. "Let me guess. We have no idea where they're coming from."

The leutnant on duty shook his head. "This time they came in from Newport News Bay, sir, flying in just above the surf. By the time we picked them up, there wasn't time to send up a warning."

Adam shook his head as he picked up the headset

microphone and pulled it on. "Colonel Sung, this is General Steiner."

"I read you five by five, sir."

"Good," Adam said, looking at the map showing the latest digital track of the fighters. "We just got bombed again. They flew out over your search sectors. Do you have a reading on where that damn base is?"

"We had multiple sightings here, sir, but they seemed to split up when they spotted us and went off in different directions to confuse us."

"Their base should be right where you are. It's the only place on the continent that we haven't fully mapped. They should be landing right inside your sectors."

"I understand that, General," Sung said, "but your wanting isn't going to make it so. The fact of the matter is that they aren't here. I've deployed troops on the mountaintops in the Upperville region, and we still haven't spotted a secret base or a hidden landing strip."

Colonel Blucher came in on the same channel. "My command company picked up a *Scytha*-class fighter here. It tangled with us for three passes before departing."

"Colonel Blucher, you're covering the southwest. Did you pick up any indications of where that base is?" Adam was just slightly more civil than he had been with Sung.

"Negative, General. They seem content to hide from us."

"Damn! There are no carriers in orbit," Adam said. "I have one of our DropShips up running surface scans, but they seem to fly right up into the ionsphere where sensors get reflective bounce-back. We launch a satellite, and they shoot them down within a few orbits. They have to be somewhere on this continent."

Adam didn't hide the fact that he was tired, frustrated, and angry. "Colonel Sung, I've had you, the

Ninth Regulars, and half of Blucher's people all over this continent. We haven't been able to find those bloody-damn fighters or the Falcon BattleMech forces. Every time they make a sortie, we get weaker."

There was a slight pause before Sung spoke up again, this time more calmly. "If we apply logic to this, we can make the assumption that the fighters are not based on the continent."

"That's not helping, Colonel," Adam returned through gritted teeth.

"It may, sir. Have we sent out patrols over the oceans or the ice caps?" Sung asked.

Adam paused. "What?"

"Logic, General. If they're not using the continents, maybe they're based where we aren't looking. That leaves the oceans. Maybe they've got some sort of floating flight deck out there. Or else maybe they're out on the polar ice caps."

Adam frowned in thought. He didn't like Colonel Sung, mostly because she was such a strong supporter of Prince Victor that Adam had considered her blinded by Victor's light. Christifori had sent her, but Adam was convinced it was more to keep an eye on Adam Steiner than to really help in a stand-up fight. He had to admit that Sung's idea was sound, which made it all the more frustrating.

"Very well, Colonel Sung. I'll order up flights from the Ninth Lyran Regulars in a few hours as soon as we have daylight. We'll test your theory."

Archer stood on a small pile of bricks that had been a wall, still wearing his lightweight jumpsuit and cooling vest as his infantry poured water onto the smoldering pile of debris. Soot stuck to his boots, and he looked gray where the material stuck to his sweaty skin.

The fighting for the Tyler Munitions Works had proven to be both fast and brutal. The Jade Falcons recovered from the shock of the blast much faster than his troops did. Both stars came out of the narrow alleys between the buildings, weapons blazing, firing everything they had before they could be downed. A *Baboon* 'Mech had somehow made its way to the roof of one building and rained down long-range missile fire at the Avengers. Then a pair of *Goshawk*s lit into the air through the billowing smoke of the blast, weapons razing a lightweight *Hollander*.

His forces rallied quickly and finished the job they had begun. In the end, five Jade Falcons were captured, two of them knocked unconscious in their cockpits in the heat of the battle. Four of the buildings in the munitions works had been blown, burned, and blasted apart. Katya Chaffee's people had scoured the factory and found stockpiles of short- and long-range missile ammunition, but not as much as expected. Apparently, the Falcons had already been actively shipping the materials off-world, into the Inner Sphere.

That supply chain ended now. Archer was relieved but at the same time worried. They'd taken a planet back from the Falcons, a thrill he hadn't enjoyed since the Smoke Jaguars were defeated by the Star League Defense Force. At the same time, he was now behind enemy lines. He was working with Adam Steiner, a man who openly defied and disliked him. From this point forward, he knew he was risking waking a sleeping giant.

He only hoped Prince Victor had picked the right man for this job . . .

15

The Lytle Glacier Field on Black Earth was a kilometer-thick slab of solid ice that had taken thousands of years to form. While many glaciers were created by compressed snow, Lytle Field was formed more from seasonal freezing of the floating ice cap. It was mostly white with a marbling of green, almost beautiful. It extended for thousands of square kilometers, stretching out as far as the eye could see. Adam Steiner might have enjoyed its scenic value if not for the fact that the Jade Falcons had converted the area into their base of operations.

It had taken more than a week of searching the ice fields, both from space and from the ground, before his men had found the converted base. The location bordered on genius. The ice served as a landing strip, while the Falcons hid their fightercraft in caves they had carved and tunneled deep into the glacier itself. From above, the location was almost invisible. Adam had found it more by luck than anything else.

It happened when elements of the Ninth Lyran Regulars had tangled with a patrol of Elementals and Omni-Mechs at the south end of the glacier, where Adam had shuttled over his force. The fight had not gone well for the Lyran Regulars. They had been soundly defeated and forced to withdraw, but the outcome confirmed what Adam had suspected—the Jade Falcons were close by. Now, it was simply a matter of finding them. And for that, he had a plan. It had taken time, though, precious time he didn't have.

"The surface of the glacier is slippery," came the voice of Leutnant-General Jeanette Scarlett over the comm channel. "One of my recon lances lost their footing and are stuck in a crevasse."

"Injuries?"

"Mostly equipment damage."

"Keep sharp," Adam said, advancing his *Thunder Hawk*. He made it only a few meters more when it happened, a roar overhead as the aerospace fighters of the Jade Falcons took off on another sortie.

"Bingo!" Adam said, his sensors picking up the five fighters roaring just above his weapons range. "All right, fighter lances, you know what to do." His own fighters were now scrambling, not to provide air cover, but to attack the airstrip. With the Falcon fighters in the air, part of his plan was to deny them their landing strip. In just a few minutes, his bombs would destroy the airstrip, stranding the Falcon fighters. His ground forces were the bait.

The Jade Falcon pilots didn't seem to care. They dove in on the Ninth Lyran Regulars even as Adam heard warnings of 'Mech sightings. Star Colonel Cewen Newclay's Third Talon Cluster had finally emerged from hiding.

"Do we have confirmation of Newclay's force? Is this the full cluster?" he asked, hoping for a reply from one of his senior officers, preferably Leutnant-General Scarlett. He didn't get it.

Instead, a crimson beam from an extended-range

large laser struck his center torso. Hearing a hissing sound followed by a crackle as some of his chest armor melted and popped off, Adam instinctively swung to his right, side-stepping. As he did, he spotted a Jade Falcon *Mad Cat* in the distance, lumbering across the glacier toward him.

He swung his gauss rifles to bear on the threat. With the ease and skill of long experience, he guided the joystick to bring the targeting reticle onto the form of the approaching *Mad Cat* as it loosed a salvo of long-range missiles at him, oblivious of the death he could bring down on it. The reticle dropped onto the image of the 'Mech on his display and changed color from dull gray to yellow and then red. He heard the tone through every fiber of his being as he hit two of the target-interlock triggers on the joystick.

A trio of gauss rifle slugs cleared their barrels at the same moment the wave of missiles enveloped his *Thunder Hawk*. The long-range warheads went off everywhere at once as they hit. This time, Adam Steiner's BattleMech rocked and buckled under the blast. Some of the shots must have missed, plowing into the ground in front of his 'Mech, spraying the cockpit canopy ferro-glass with shards of ice that melted almost instantly. He fought the controls of the huge *Thunder Hawk*, keeping it upright. Yellow and red damage-warning lights flickered on the faceplate of his neurohelmet.

Another laser sliced into his chest as Adam regained his balance. To one side, he saw the image of a Manticore tank pull up and add its firepower to his own. Glancing quickly at the Jade Falcon, he could see deep gouges in the armor plating of the Omni-Mech's torso, where at least two of his shots had found their mark. The Manticore fired almost everything it had, long- and short-range missiles and its large pulse laser. Some of the missiles missed wide. The green fire from the laser danced up the left arm of the *Mad Cat*, doing little to slow its determined pace.

General Steiner brought his Defiance medium lasers to bear, again adjusting his sighting of the *Mad Cat*, then squeezed the thumb trigger of his joystick. The heat in his cockpit didn't worry him much on the glacier, where it would bleed off faster. One of his beams missed, just barely. The other three dug into the *Mad Cat*'s chest, brilliant red stabs of light that cut away at the thick armor plating there.

The *Mad Cat* slowed, then twisted slightly at the torso. Adam saw what was happening, and realized there was nothing he could do to stop it. The Falcon 'Mech was targeting the Manticore tank. It fired, not just its lasers, but everything in its arsenal. Only twenty meters away, Adam watched as the tank was bathed in fire. Explosions rose up with dark black plumes from the missile hits. His own 'Mech quaked from the nearby savaging. The tank's turret blew at the ring, flying five meters into the air and landing nearby. There was no hope for the crew.

Adam's jaw clenched as he turned and fired everything he had at the approaching *Mad Cat*. At the same time, another 'Mech had joined in from off to his left. He didn't look to see who it was. He didn't care. All that mattered in that moment was the destruction of the *Mad Cat* before it could kill again. The Jade Falcon contorted under the salvos smashing into it, but tried to keep upright. A wave of short-range missiles ripped off one of its boxy missile racks, leaving ragged shards of metal reaching upward where it had been. A barrage of lasers slammed into its torso, and from the billowing smoke, Adam could tell that some of the shots had penetrated beyond the armor, into the literal guts of the OmniMech.

The *Mad Cat* sagged slightly, as if its warrior was fighting to control it. It turned off to Adam's left and fired off a few laser shots, then fell over. A cloud of hot steam rose from the glacier as it fell. The surface of the 'Mech sizzled as it slid and sank slightly into the surface of the ice.

Adam threw a glance at his sensors, which showed that the Jade Falcons had struck with fury all along his line and that of the Ninth Lyran Regulars. Their trinaries had punched through in some locations. In the air, he saw a flicker of silver in the sky, a Falcon *Sabutai* banking off in the distance. He knew that many kilometers away his own fighters were carrying out their bombing mission. He and his ground forces would have to contend with these foes.

A flash of green lights around the *Sabutai* surprised him. They weren't rising from the ground but coming from another distant flicker of light. He checked his long-range sensors and could see that another Clan fighter was tangling with the Jade Falcon *Sabutai*. It was a large *Jengiz* fighter, cutting loose with its pulse lasers and the occasional blue flash of its particle projection cannons.

Where in the hell did that come from? Adam wondered. For a moment, he was worried almost to the point of panic. Was another Clan in the Black Earth system? He had already taken more time on Black Earth than he and Christifori had planned for. Now the thought of fighting another Clan seemed to be the death knell for Operation Audacity.

"Incoming message for you, General Steiner," came the high-pitched voice of Seamus Kinnell.

"Go," Adam said, watching the *Sabutai* contort in the air under a hit of PPC fire from the newcomer.

"This is Star Colonel Hampton Schroeder of the First Wolf Strike Grenadiers," the voice said firmly. "I bring you greetings and solicitations from Khan Phelan Kell. He regrets that he cannot be here in person, but thought you might need our help."

Adam let go a long sigh of relief. "It's good to see you, Star Colonel. I take it that Khan Kell received my call for garrison forces from the Blue Star Irregulars."

"Aff. Your *orders* and General Christifori's *request* reached him. A battalion of the Blue Stars will be here in a week or so. We were sent in case you needed help."

"What does this mean?" Kinnell asked with some degree of urgency.

Adam shook his head inside his neurohelmet. "It means I may have been wrong about my cousin Victor's commitment to this operation."

Jade Falcon Heavy Cruiser **Black Talon**
Orbital Dry Dock **Star of Ironhold**
Butler
Jade Falcon Occupation Zone

"Slow day, quiaff?" Star Admiral Martin Thastus said as he glanced around the bridge of the Aegis-class heavy cruiser *Black Talon*. The temporary dry-dock scaffolding obscured some of his view out the main viewport, but he wasn't really looking. His attention was on the only other officer with him on the bridge, his XO, Star Captain Stanley. Only a skeleton crew was still aboard, just enough for emergency operations, should they be needed. The other crewmen present were repair technicians from the *Star of Ironhold* dry dock facility. It was not a full-blown repair port, but one used for maintenance operations exactly like those the *Black Talon* needed most right now.

"We should be with the primary task force or at least on patrol against the Wolves," said Stanley.

Martin Thastus nodded. "I regret that we lost the bidding to participate in the assault, but we needed the time to rotate the crew planetside for recuperation and to get maintenance work on the weapons and engines."

"I wish to be fighting in the Inner Sphere. There's no glory to be won here," Stanley said, gesturing around the bridge with one hand. "We deserve better than to sit out this fight."

Thastus rubbed his jaw. "Have patience, Stanley. We'll get our chance. In the meantime, let us go and tour the engine room. Scaring some of the technical crew with our presence will cheer you up."

DropShip Colonel Crockett
Inbound Trajectory, Butler
Jade Falcon Occupation Zone

Archer stared at the tactical readout the *Colonel Crockett*'s sensor officer had just handed him. "You're sure about this?"

The man looked pale with fear. "Yes, sir, General, sir. The WarShip is in a floating, pressurized dry-dock facility, but according to our scans, their engines have yet to even power up." Everyone on the bridge of the DropShip was listening intently. For the last few minutes, they had all been on edge since the first sensor readings confirmed that a Jade Falcon WarShip was in the system.

"Seems like they haven't spotted us yet," Katya said.

Archer nodded. "They're in dry dock. They could be down for repairs."

"Or they could be suckering us in for the kill."

Archer looked over at his old friend, the slightly portly Captain Lee Fullerton, in the command seat of the DropShip. Nervously twisting one end of his mustache, he wore his perpetual air of gloom.

"Lee, we came out at a pirate point. How far out are we?"

Fullerton checked the arm of his command seat to read the data streaming into the small console there. "At present burn rate, we'll be on top of them in five hours."

"And if we want to abort the burn in-system?"

Fullerton shook his head. "You can order it, but Isaac Newton is more in control of this than I am. We're at full speed for our turnaround. I can slow us down, but we'll be in range of that ship by the time we start heading back to our JumpShips. Besides, the JumpShips won't have had enough time to fully recharge. We drained our batteries making the pair of jumps to get to this system. If that WarShip follows us, it can take out the entire task force."

"What's the tactical data on the ship?" Archer asked.

"The Aegis-class is a heavy cruiser. Forty-two naval autocannon. Sixteen naval lasers. Twelve anti-ship missiles launchers. The good news is that she can only carry about twenty fighters, if she's loaded with them."

"Leave it to you to find a ray of sunshine in all of this," Archer said.

"Just the facts, sir," Fullerton replied.

Katya came over. "How do you want to handle this?" she asked in a low tone.

Archer could see the glowing, white-blue orb of Butler slowly closing in through the DropShip viewport. "We don't have much choice. We have to take out that WarShip."

"Fighters?" she asked.

He nodded. "Every one of them. The Twentieth Arcturan Guards have ample fighter support as well. I wish I hadn't left behind a battalion of them on Roadside, but our garrison forces hadn't arrived yet."

"General," Katya said, lowering her voice even further, "many of our pilots are green. None of them have experience in this kind of fighting."

Archer threw up his hands slightly. He knew the odds were stacked against them and that once more he was going to have to send people off to fight and perhaps die. Even with the heavy cruiser in dry dock, she could power up at any time to intercept them. Worse than possibly sending a lot of young people to their deaths, he might be sending them to the slaughter. He rubbed his brow, struggling with the thought.

"We're going to get one shot at this, Katya, and we're going to have to act soon. Assemble the fighter crews on-deck. Tie in the other ships via lasers—I don't want the Jade Falcons listening in. I want our people to know what they're up against and what they've got to do."

An hour later, Archer stood on the flight deck of the *Colonel Crockett* facing the lance of four fighters assigned to the ship. A tripod-mounted holocamera picked up his image and broadcast it to the rest of the DropShips of the task force. Without pulling any punches, he had laid out the situation for his regiments.

"So, there you have it," he said, looking into the camera. "I don't need to tell you how important this is or that I think you can do it. Hell, I *know* you can do this. How do I know? Plainly put, if we don't take out this ship, the Jade Falcons are going to keep plowing through the Lyran Alliance, and none of us want that. So far, that WarShip has been blind to our presence. We have to make this first pass good, and make it count. You've got to take her out. If you don't, we're all as good as dead. So, I know you'll succeed because we don't have any other choice. We either beat the Jade Falcons now or your families will become their bondsmen.

"I know none of you signed up for this kind of a fight. Until recently, the only war we had on our hands was the one between Katherine Steiner and Prince Victor. Well, today, we're all Lyrans at heart, no matter where we were born, no matter what prior political allegiance we have. Today, we strike a blow for the Inner Sphere. Today, we kick the Jade Falcons squarely in the balls, so high, so hard, that we'll wake Nicholas Kerensky himself from the dead."

He couldn't see or hear the reaction on the other ships, but from the lance of fighter pilots on the *Colonel Crockett*, he got a roar of support.

16

***DropShip* Colonel Crockett**
Inbound Trajectory to Butler
Jade Falcon Occupation Zone
17 October 3064

"I should be out there," Archer mumbled to himself as he paced the bridge of the *Colonel Crockett*, the magnetic shoes used for null-gravity squeaking slightly with each step.

"You're not a pilot," Katya said, catching up to him.

"So what? I can always sit in a jump seat," he snapped, then caught himself. "Sorry, Katya. This is just the hardest part of this job, sending good people into battle. And every time they promote me, I get to send more to their possible deaths."

"I know what you mean," she said, keeping her voice low enough that no one else could overhear. "Things sure were a lot easier when we were just a tiny militia unit."

Archer nodded. "Seems like a lifetime ago," he said, then broke off when he saw Captain Fullerton jump up from his command seat and go toward the primary sensor station. He was staring at it intently, with a look of such concern that Archer hurried over to him, with Katya close behind.

"What is it, Lee?" Archer asked.

"What's what?" Fullerton didn't lift his eyes from the sensor screen.

"Come on, Lee," Archer said. "I know that look. You're on to something."

Fullerton continued to stare at the sensor output for a few moments more, then finally lifted his gaze. "General, I'm no hotshot admiral. I'm just a simple ship's captain."

"Out with it, Lee," Archer said.

The portly captain pointed at the sensor display. "It's been quite a while since we launched our fighters. Though they're in sensor range of that WarShip, there's been no movement from the vessel. She's just sitting there in dry dock. Our fighters are screening each other on approach, so they won't initially show up as a flotilla, but those Jade Falcons should be cutting moorings, maneuvering that ship for battle. Hell, they should've started firing already."

Fullerton stroked his chin in thought. "Maybe," he said slowly, "just maybe they can't move."

"What do you mean?" Katya asked.

"WarShips need routine maintenance, just like DropShips. Yet, our active sensors haven't picked up even a trickle of fusion-reactor power from the *Talon*. Without them, there's no power to the main engines, the primary weapons, and so on. That ship's sitting in dry dock, which limits what she can do anyway. I'm just guessing, but maybe her engines are in the middle of a maintenance cycle."

"Our fighters are slated to target the fore and aft of the ship, where her armor is thinnest," Archer said.

"The only reason you'd go aft is to take out those engines," Fullerton said. "I can't say for sure, but maybe we should pour all of our resources into an attack on the prow of the vessel. If her engines are down, why waste fighters trying to take them out?"

Archer looked over at Katya, but these waters were as uncharted for her as for him. He closed his eyes and took a long breath, knowing the high stakes riding on this decision. He suddenly remembered one of his professors at the NAIS, years ago when he was still in officer training. She was an older woman whose name he could no longer remember, but he'd never forgotten the lesson she'd tried to drill into her students time and again.

"When all else fails," she'd said so many times, "trust the instincts of others. If you trust those in your command, in the end, your force cannot be broken."

Archer opened his eyes and let out the deep breath he'd taken. "Captain Fullerton, send a message to the flight leaders. Have all lances concentrate on the bow of that ship."

Fullerton looked worried. "Sir, I might be wrong."

"I might have been wrong to send them in to start with, Lee. The truth of the matter is that your hunch is based on more practical knowledge than anything I've got to offer right now."

"But those pilots . . ."

"Those pilots will do their duty," Archer said in a tone of total resolve. "At this point, that's all any of us can do. Now, send the message to them. And if you're right, I'll see to it you're made a vice admiral."

Star Admiral Martin Thastus reached out and stabbed at the audio-warning control blaring on the bridge of the *Black Talon*, muting it instantly. "If we're still alive when this is over, I will meet you in a Circle of Equals and make you regret this failure to your Clan, Barry," he said to the red-faced technician standing nearby.

"We are in the middle of our occupation zone in dry dock," the young officer stammered. "I thought it was safe to use the head, sir."

"Always prepared for battle, that is our standard," Star Captain Stanley barked, backhanding the warrior

across the face. Then he turned back to Thastus.
"Our primary drive is in pieces, Admiral. The Inner
Sphere fighters will be on top of us in just a few
minutes."

Star Admiral Thastus was a man who believed in
tests of destiny. This was one just like the kind faced
by the great Falcon hero Aidan Pryde in earlier times.
He relished the opportunity. "I'm aware of our condition. Time to get the fusion reactor back up?"

"Hours."

"Very well," Thastus said calmly. "Get whatever
crew we have at the dry dock aboard immediately and
seal the ports."

Stanley responded instantly, rapping out a long
string of commands into the comm system. Thastus
moved rapidly as well, walking over to the helmsman's
seat and dropping into it. The *Black Talon*'s pilot was
not currently aboard and might not get there in time.
Today, Thastus would prove his honor. Though he
cursed himself for being the one who'd signed off on
shore leave for his pilots, he would show himself a
true warrior no matter where or how he fought.

"Clear all moorings," he barked to Stanley and the
two other bridge crewmembers present. He switched
comm channels quickly.

"We have a star's worth of fighter pilots on board.
I will scramble them, with your permission," Stanley
said.

"Aye," Thastus affirmed. "Engine room," he called
over the comm.

"Senior Repair Technician Jorgass on line, sir. Your
engineering chief did not make it aboard in time."

"You are in command of engineering then, quiaff?"
Thastus asked quickly.

"Aff," came back a nervous voice.

"Our reactor is down. You've got to tap our jump
batteries and channel that energy to maneuver and
fire-control, now."

"I am not sure if that can be done," Jorgass said, a

quaver still in his voice. As a tech based on a dry dock, he lacked the combat experience of seasoned Jade Falcon naval warriors.

"It can, and you will. I have done it before. You have five minutes. That should be ample."

"It will not be a great deal of power, Star Admiral. And what we have will not last long."

"It will be enough for this battle," Thastus replied, grinning broadly. He glanced over at Captain Stanley, who was furiously attempting to bring whatever power he could to the weapons bays.

Stanley noticed the big smile. "If I did not know better, Star Admiral, I would say that you are enjoying this."

"Know better, Captain. I am not enjoying this—I am *savoring* this. We'll transfer command to the CIC and coordinate the battle from there. Locate the enemy commander's DropShip. I have a message to send him."

Archer could not see the battle itself save for the occasional flash of light far off in the distance. Though concentrated on the long-range sensor display, he couldn't help looking out through the bridge viewport from time to time. The *Black Talon* had disengaged itself from the dry dock and had slowly maneuvered a short distance away. From information provided by the *Colonel Crockett*'s sensors, he knew the ship was not moving under the power of its reactors. It had also begun to fire its weapons, though with nowhere near the full, raw firepower that the Aegis class possessed.

With great bravado, the Jade Falcon commander, Star Admiral Martin Thastus, had issued a Trial of Possession for Butler and demanded to know what forces were in the system. That was a strange move coming from a defender, but it told Archer several things about his enemy. First, that Thastus was bloodnamed, which meant he was one of the Jade

Falcon best. Second, by issuing a challenge, he was fully prepared to go down in battle, a fight to the end.

The fighters of Archer's task force came in on the heavy cruiser. Diving at the slanted flat front of the Clan WarShip, they came straight into the maw of the naval autocannon located there. The weapon was useless against the sheer number of craft coming at it, wave after wave of fighters sweeping in on the vessel's fore end. The ship tried to turn, but was no match for the fighters. A number of aircraft were hit and some destroyed, but Archer was surprised at how one-sided the battle was thus far.

He winced as a salvo of Barracuda and Shark-class missiles tore out from the port side of the other ship, the dots of light slamming into the tiny specks representing his fighters. The star of five Jade Falcon aerofighters had dived into the middle of his formations, inflicting damage but too outnumbered to hope to protect their vessel. When he glanced up briefly to see out the *Crockett*'s viewport, Archer noticed that his hands were aching from his tight grip on the support rail.

"We're going to be in range of their anti-ship missiles in a few minutes," Captain Fullerton said cautiously.

"This will be all over in a few minutes, if we're lucky," Archer returned, still looking through the bridge window. Fullerton leaned forward and stared at the tactical display, squinting slightly. When he stood up and craned his neck to get an even better look, Archer quickly walked over.

"What is it?" he asked.

"Oxygen. She's venting a lot of it from the bow region," Fullerton said.

"What does that mean?"

"I'm not entirely sure, sir. I've never tangled with a real WarShip before. But I'd say we've punched through the armor and are causing a little damage."

Lee Fullerton pulled himself up to standing. "And if I'm right, I just made Star Admiral."

Martin Thastus leaned back against the pressure-hatch he'd just managed to crawl through and heard the hissing near its buckled seal. It was an imperfect seal, but it would be enough for a while. He glanced over at the limp form of Star Captain Stanley and one of the technicians still gasping for breath.

The hits had torn into the Combat Information Center, forcing them out. The emergency sealant had filled the hole, but not before Thastus had almost passed out from the sudden loss of pressure. His ears were still popped, and he was sure that one, if not both of them, was bleeding. A high-pitched tone filled his head, and he tasted a salty-metallic flavor in the back of his mouth . . . blood.

The main bridge had been evacuated only a few moments before. A wave of errant missiles had plowed deep into the bowels of the *Black Talon*, taking out crew quarters and damaging a bay door and two of the DropShip docking collars. Appearing out of nowhere, the enemy fighters had quickly turned his powerful ship into a crippled victim.

Thastus pulled himself up along the bulkhead wall, his sense of balance horribly distorted. Stanley stirred as well, but other than the noise in his ears and the slight hiss of the door, Thastus could not hear anything else. Barry had not made it. Explosive decompression—a human body instantly exploding outward in a vacuum—was a horrific way to die.

It would have been different had his ship been combat-ready, had it had power, had its fighters been on board. Fate had conspired against him. He contemplated his options.

If he fought on, the ship would be lost. Waste was not the way of the Clan. Besides, without the CIC, he had no way to coordinate the activities and fire orders with the weapons bays. And the Inner Sphere fighters were not breaking off, but kept on coming. He slid along the wall toward the intercom, and the lights flickered, damage from another hit.

He reached the intercom and spoke into it. "Jorgass, this is Star Admiral Thastus. Activate the auxiliary comm unit from engineering and signal the Inner Sphere commander. Tell him we concede this battle and to break off his attack."

Martin Thastus could barely hear his own voice as he spoke. It was muffled and lost in the babble of other noises in his head. He heard a mumble from the intercom and realized he would not be able to make out what the officer was saying.

"Jorgass, do as you are ordered. Such is the will of the Jade Falcons."

Having barked out his last order, Martin Thastus, Star Admiral of Clan Jade Falcon, slid down the wall and passed out, giving in to his injuries. A part of him hoped he would die, but as he lost consciousness, he guessed that fate would deny him even that.

On the bridge of the *Colonel Crockett*, Archer stared into the blackness of space.

"You did hear me, didn't you, General?" Fullerton repeated behind him.

"They've surrendered," Archer said, stunned.

"Yes, sir."

"Katya, order our fighters back. Launch rescue craft to recover our injured and the punch-outs," Archer said. Katya moved immediately to the comm system and began to call out orders.

"Lee," Archer said. "Divert us to that ship. Contact Thomas Sherwood and tell him to mount up a team for security and rescue. There's bound to be injured aboard. We're going to help them."

"Yes, sir," Fullerton replied.

Katya returned to where Archer was standing. "Well, General," she said, "you've just taken a Jade Falcon WarShip. What's next?"

"I want you to take a shuttle down to the surface of Butler and get to the HPG station. Send out a priority message to the addresses Gramash set up for himself and for Phelan Kell. I have no idea what to do with a Falcon WarShip, but I'm sure Khan Kell can provide her with a prize crew."

"With pleasure, sir," Katya said, turning toward the door.

"And Katya?"

"Sir?"

"Make sure you say, 'please.'"

=== 17 ===

Asteroid Rothschild III
Malibu System
Jade Falcon Occupation Zone
26 October 3064

"**N**ot exactly the kind of welcome from the locals that I would've expected," Adam Steiner said from the cockpit of his *Thunder Hawk* as the bay door of his DropShip popped open with a hiss, revealing the gray and brown desolation of the Rothschild III asteroid.

"You'd have thought they'd see us as some kind of saviors," Leutnant-General Jeanette Scarlett replied.

"Hard to believe that only ten years ago Malibu was part of the Lyran Alliance," Adam said. "We defeated the only Jade Falcon force in-system, and now Malibu is free from the Clans, even if just for the time being. What do its people do? They order us not to land on their world."

He was still amazed that the civilian population of Malibu had not welcomed his force with open arms. Was it their fear of the Jade Falcons' return? Or was it simply weariness of centuries of warfare in the Inner

Sphere? Either way, he was not welcome in the Malibu system.

Asteroid Rothschild III was only a day and a half's travel from the system nadir jump point, whose recharging station Adam had hoped to capture. Though very few Jade Falcons were in the system, they were not willing to simply surrender the station. Adam had decided not to attack it, as taking it in ruins would defeat the purpose.

Star Colonel Terrence of the Eighth Falcon Regulars, the unit stationed on Malibu, had proposed fighting a formal Clan Trial of Possession on the asteroid, with ownership of the recharging station as the prize. Though Adam wasn't crazy about the idea, he'd given the traditional Clan response of asking with what forces the Falcons would defend the recharging station. Upon receiving word that it would be two trinaries of 'Mechs and Elementals, he had committed two brigades of 'Mechs—one from Colonel Sung's Crucis Lancers and one from Leutnant-General Scarlett's Ninth Lyran Regulars. He would execute the battle on Clan terms, giving them what they considered an honorable fight. From the reaction of Malibu's local population, recapturing the planet itself was not practical.

The surface of the asteroid was typically desolate, consisting mostly of barren rock and dust, and Adam's landing site perpetually faced the red giant star at the center of the Malibu system. Gravity was heavier than he had expected, indicating that most of the rock was impregnated with iron or nickel. It was still only one-seventh of a G, and the lack of atmosphere gave even the slowest of BattleMechs a higher degree of mobility. The asteroid presented a deadly danger, however. A cockpit hit could be fatal.

Adam turned his *Thunder Hawk* so that he could watch the Jade Falcon deployment nearly ten kilometers away. Rather than simply disgorging troops down its ramps, the Broadsword-class DropShips opened up their bay doors at only twenty meters above the ground. The Falcons leaped out, kicking up clouds of dust on landing, and began to bound in short hops toward Adam's force the moment they hit the ground.

"General Steiner," Adam heard Sung say in his earpiece.

"Go, Colonel."

"This is a stretch, sir, but I suggest we hold back a couple of lances of our light 'Mechs from both brigades. Once we engage the Falcon, those lances can skirt the flanks of the fighting and converge on the enemy's rear."

"Lights wouldn't be able to do much, Colonel," Adam replied coldly. He was still uncomfortable with Sung's presence in his task force, knowing that on the civil war field of battle, she would be an enemy commander. Once this operation halted the Jade Falcon incursion—assuming it could—the civil war was still unfinished business. At some point, Victor's people were going to have to be dealt with.

"We can toss in a few mediums, if they've got the speed," Sung returned. "There's not a lot of terrain here to work with, so turning our flanks is about all that's left."

"Your logic is sound," Adam said, as close as he would get to praising the other officer. "Let's deploy the lances to our rear and at the extreme flanks. I've fought the Falcons before, and they'll push to envelop us quickly if they can. If we get those forces in place, we can blunt their attempt to do that."

He stared out at the fog-like cloud of dust kicked up by the Jade Falcons as their DropShips began to settle and their forces approached. It was an almost eerie sight, the BattleMechs and Elementals rushing forward, preceded by a cloud of fine gray dust rolling along the ground in front of them.

The lead Falcon was a *Masakari*—the deadly 'Mech known to the Clans as a *Warhawk*. Bristling with a pair of extended-range PPCs and a matching pair of large pulse lasers, it began firing immediately, not needing to close the distance in the battle. Twin streams of bright, blue-white charged particles from the PPC lashed toward the Inner Sphere line, catching an *Awesome* in mid-torso and one arm. Adam winced as he saw an arc of charged particles leap up from the hit in the chest and seem to dance around the cockpit of the 'Mech, searing the paint job.

As the *Awesome* returned fire, he issued orders for the reserve lances, as Sung had suggested. The rest of his forces moved toward the approaching dust cloud of the Jade Falcons, and in less than two beats of his heart, the air was filled with laser light and missiles streaking back and forth across the space between the two forces.

Out the corner of his eye, Adam saw a flicker along the right flank of the approaching Jade Falcon force. Something fast-moving, almost obscured by the cloud of dust. His sensors picked them up, barely, and he smiled. *Uller*s—quick, light OmniMechs. Star Colonel Terrence was sending a star of them around the far edge of sensor range to his rear. As much as Adam hated to admit it, Anne Sung had been right.

"Colonel Sung, on the right," he said.

"I thought I saw something," Sung answered.

"They're yours. Take them." As Adam spoke, a laser seared his right arm, slashing into an armor plate just above his elbow. One small piece of armored plate spun off slowly in the vacuum and drifted down to the surface of the asteroid, stirring powdery dust. Adam was fixed on it for a moment, reminding himself that there would be no ejections here. To punch out would be certain death.

He twisted his *Thunder Hawk* around toward the advancing Falcons, bringing his targeting reticle onto the *Black Hawk* that had fired at him. As the tone of target-lock rang in his ears and through his brain, he let loose with a pair of his deadly gauss rifles, their hypersonic rounds slamming soundlessly into the

Black Hawk. It was time to make them pay for their boldness.

The battle was surprisingly quick. Star Colonel Terrence was no fool, rushing to a mindless death. He had engaged for several minutes at extreme range, counting on the fact that the extended reach of his superior Clan technology would give him the edge. An edge that was lost quickly. Adam had salvaged enough Falcon weaponry and mounted it on his own 'Mech force that Terrence had no choice but to close range, leveling the odds. Both sides took significant losses, and Adam was on the verge of pulling back when Sung told him that the rear attack had been demolished. This environment would take not only BattleMechs, but warriors as well. Machines could be replaced, but replacing personnel was not so easy.

Adam had just toppled a *Vulture* at almost point-blank range when his comm system came on-line with a transmission from Star Colonel Terrence. He was so close to the *Vulture* when the cockpit exploded that the pilot's water reserves exploded and froze in a clump on his *Thunder Hawk*'s leg. Mingled with blood, the sickly frost told him just how deadly the environment was.

He was sweeping his *Thunder Hawk* around toward another potential victim, when the enemy commander's voice came over the laser commlink.

"General Steiner, this is Star Colonel Terrence."

"Adam Steiner here." Adam half-expected the message to be some kind of taunt.

"This fighting gains for neither of us," Terrence said.

Here it comes, Adam thought. He's going to ask me to surrender.

"As such, I submit to you as the victor. You have won possession of the recharging station. I will disengage my forces if you will yours."

Adam was surprised, but pleased. "Very well. Stand

by." He sent out a quick order for cease-fire and orders to disable the station permanently once his force had recharged their own JumpShips. Let the techs aboard the station take shuttles back to the planet.

There, he thought. That ought to put a subtle crimp in Marthe Pryde's supply pipeline.

"You fought well and with honor," Terrence said, his tone deflated.

"As did you and your people." Adam heard another incoming message on the tactical comm channel and switched to it. The digital prefix told him who it was, and he wondered if this man ever got his timing right.

"Go ahead, Kommandant-General," he said, activating the channel to Seamus Kinnell.

"I have been listening in, sir. Congratulations on yet another victory for the Archon," Kinnell said in his best butt-kissing tone.

"This has nothing to do with my cousin Katrina," Adam retorted.

Kinnell said nothing for a moment, then quickly changed the subject. "I have deployed our recovery teams."

"Good. Send word to our JumpShips to double-charge their drives. We fought hard for that station. We might as well top off the lithium batteries."

"Already done," Kinnell said. "And I have been doing some calculations."

"What kind of calculations?" Adam asked impatiently.

"We are only three jumps from Somerset, General. We're closer now than any other military force has been, sir. We could take the planet, if you wanted."

That got Adam's attention. Somerset had been his home before the Clan invasion, but the Falcons had evacuated much of the civilian population after taking it. He had fought the losing battle to the Falcons, and it had cost him his family, his brother, everything.

He closed his eyes, remembering the last time he

had been on his homeworld, and it seemed more like a dream than a memory. He shook himself free of the longing. "That's not in our mission parameters, Kinnell. My home planet isn't even on the target list. Remember, we're supposed to make the Falcons think they're facing a much larger force before we fall back and rendezvous with Christifori on Blackjack."

"I'm aware of the original plan, General, but as your aide de camp, I'm here to offer alternatives. If we shift and take Somerset, it will still confuse the Jade Falcons. We could secure a logistics chain back into the Melissia Theater, just not the one that Christifori planned."

"What about Christifori and his people?"

There was a pause. "Archer Christifori has proven himself resourceful. He will continue to draw in the Jade Falcons for some time. Chances are he could survive without our cooperation and still make Operation Audacity a success by defeating the Falcons at Twycross. He's really given you a secondary role in this operation anyway."

Adam hesitated. It was seductive. Three short jumps, and he could carve out a place in history, be the man who personally retook his homeworld from the Clans.

Kinnell's voice was like a siren's whisper in his ear. "We may never get this close with this amount for force again."

Adam Steiner sat for a full two minutes in his cockpit, not moving, not speaking, considering the consequences of his next decision.

Little Washington, Crimond
Pandora Theater
Lyran Alliance

Phelan Kell wheeled his *Wolfhound* in place just in time to avoid a stream of autocannon fire from an enemy *Stormcrow*. The rounds tore into the building across the street, gutting its first floor in a roar of explosions and thick brown smoke. The entire structure seemed to moan as Phelan got some distance from it, just in time to avoid its collapse into the street. Bricks and wood spewed out in every direction, and a few slapped against the legs of his 'Mech as he rounded the corner in search of the *Stormcrow*. He charged up the street, then took the next two corners. That brought him up behind the Falcon 'Mech as it headed toward the intersection where Phelan had been a minute earlier.

The town of Little Washington had been evacuated by Phelan just before the Jade Falcons' Seventy-fourth Battle Cluster, known as the Raptors, landed on-planet. He had accepted their batchall challenge for possession of Crimond and then chosen the city as the venue for the fighting for two reasons. First, the fast-moving river that forked in the middle of Little Washington imposed some mobility restrictions on both sides. Second, the heavy, old infrastructure of the buildings that composed the city reduced sensor capability, which would inhibit the Falcons' tendency to rush in for a fast and decisive blow. If they wanted Crimond, he would make them work at it very long and very hard.

The fighting was in its third day, and Phelan was surprised at how quickly the Falcons had adapted to the terrain. Their initial assaults had inflicted more damage than he'd anticipated, but he had turned the tables earlier that morning when he surprised Star Colonel Amado Roshak. After positioning a star of assault-class OmniMechs under the rubble of some of the earlier fighting, Phelan lured the Star Colonel straight into the trap.

Roshak's *Blood Asp*, surely a prize from some battle on the homeworlds, was surrounded and made the mistake of engaging multiple targets in the heat of battle. That action negated the standard Clan rules of one-on-one engagement, and within four minutes had cost him his 'Mech. However, the Falcons did not break at the loss of their commanding officer. If anything, they seemed to fight with even greater savagery.

Phelan brought the *Stormcrow* into his sights and fired everything his *Wolfhound* had into its thin rear armor. The whine of the lasers' discharge was especially comforting. He had been playing tag with the 'Mech for some time, slowly whittling away at it, and now he hit it in its already damaged leg and back. His lasers sliced the armor plating off the *Stormcrow*'s rear torso, and Phelan knew from the way the Falcon 'Mech quaked and staggered forward as well as from his sensors that he had melted away at least part of the gyro housing. His cooling vest did what it could to bleed off the ripple of heat in his cockpit, and he crossed the street as soon as he fired.

The *Stormcrow* turned clumsily as its warrior fought to keep his footing. For a millisecond, Phelan toyed with the idea of racing around the block again, hoping for another rear shot, but decided it was time to end this fight. The Falcon warrior unleashed his ultra autocannon and lasers all at once, a mark, in Phelan's mind, of battlefield desperation. The powerful autocannon went off just to his left, rocking his *Wolfhound* and spraying it with pieces of brick and ferrocrete.

The lasers found their mark, gouging his right torso and arm. The *Wolfhound* twisted slightly at the waist as the lasers mangled and melted armor plating. Phelan juked his gait to the right to throw off his foe's targeting, then threw a quick glance down at his weapons readout to see that his lasers were recharged and ready. With calculated precision, he brought his targeting reticle down on the *Stormcrow*'s legs and tied all his weapons to the thumb trigger of the same target interlock circuit. He heard the tone of weapons-lock at the same instant he fired.

Again, the heat seemed to wash over his body as his *Wolfhound*'s weapons did their work. Three of his lasers lanced into the already damaged leg of the *Stormcrow* while one sliced into the arm on the same side. The tattered and blackened remains of leg armor melted away almost instantly, and the lasers continued to burrow deeper into the leg. One slashed downward and melted the knee joint actuator into a solid blob of worthless scrap.

The *Stormcrow*'s arm burned off at the shoulder joint, dangling from a bundle of half-seared myomer muscle. Sparks danced from the open wound, and Phelan saw globs of green coolant splatter out and down the side of the Falcon OmniMech. The sudden fall of the arm and its jerking stop at the waist threw the already battered 'Mech off balance. It stepped forward drunkenly, then fell face-first onto the road. There was a flash as the CASE system automatically engaged, diverting the blast of the autocannon ammunition out of the crippled 'Mech.

"Excellent work, Khan Kell," a voice said calmly in his ears. It took him a moment to identify the speaker.

"You're following me like a surat in heat, Captain Gramash," Phelan said, moving forward and past the *Stormcrow*, his sensors sweeping out to find other threats in the vicinity. He was disappointed when his sensors gave him nothing else to fight.

"The rest of those I serve have taken off on Audacity and are much harder to contact," Gramash said. "The occupation zone is a tricky place to play."

"You would not be here if you did not have information for me. What is it?"

"Rasalgethi," Gramash said. "The Jade Falcons have just arrived in-system. In two days, they'll be on the planet itself."

"Brion's Legion and the Pandora Theater Militia are there, if I recall," Phelan replied. "That's a serious target for them to have chosen. If the Falcons can take the planet, it widens their front facing Terra." For each of the Clans, the ultimate goal of existence was to push forward and seize control of Terra, to become the ilClan over the whole Inner Sphere.

"That's right," Gramash said. "I have also received word that Precentor Martial Dow is ordering the Com Guard Thirty-ninth Division to Crimond to work in conjunction with your forces."

That surprised Phelan. "I find that remarkable after Precentor Shillery essentially defected with the 388th Division to join us."

"I'm sure it's political. By sending in some token aid, Dow is avoiding having to commit all of the Com Guards in this region. Given the civil war, he doesn't want to have his forces drawn into the middle of Victor's and Katherine's dispute."

"Well, I've sent some of my naval forces into the Falcon occupation zone, per a request from General Christifori."

"I took the liberty of monitoring your communications. I'm sure General Christifori will appreciate getting an operational WarShip."

"You are monitoring *my* communications, quiaff? We are on the same side, spymaster."

Gramash chuckled slightly. "Yes, er, aff, Khan Kell. I am monitoring you. And if the tables were turned, you'd be doing the same to me. We are on the same side, but my role is to ensure coordination and communication of information."

Phelan allowed himself a small laugh in return. "Indeed, Gramash. You keep doing your job, and I will do mine—stopping the Jade Falcons. Please thank the Precentor Martial and have the Thirty-ninth Division coordinate with me as soon as they are in-system. The Falcon incursion is still far from over."

18

DropShip **Colonel Crockett**
Approach Vector, Twycross
Jade Falcon Occupation Zone
28 October 3064

Twycross.

Archer sat alone in his cramped quarters aboard the *Colonel Crockett* and stared at the holographic display. He had not been in this star system since 3050, and back then he'd been a member of the Tenth Lyran Guards, Prince Victor's illustrious Revenants. The Clans had been an unknown terror at the time, high-tech hordes sweeping in from beyond the Periphery, rolling over everything in their path. In memory, it seemed like a time of gallant actions and gallant MechWarriors. But he had been young and idealistic then. Now, he was what they called "seasoned."

Thanks to a single warrior, Kai Allard, the Lyran Guards had lured the Falcon Guards into a narrow pass, where the Clanners had triggered a string of explosions that all but buried them. It had been a turning point for Archer as a young officer, as this was the first time the Inner Sphere had successfully struck at the mysterious Clans and handed them a defeat. The Falcon Guards were seriously dishonored on Twycross, though they eventually redeemed themselves on Tukayyid. Ironically, they had become an elite and almost revered Jade Falcon unit.

The Falcon Guards returned to Twycross a few years later, this time during their war with Clan Wolf. Natasha Kerensky, Khan of the Wolves and known throughout the Inner Sphere as the infamous Black Widow, was killed in a duel in the Great Gash.

Now, Archer had also returned to the planet, again facing the Falcon Guards. The thought stirred him as he sat in the room's one uncomfortable chair, watching the tiny holographic sphere of Twycross spin slowing before him. Despite its dust storms, its widespread desolation, its strategic insignificance, the planet seemed to be a crucible for the Jade Falcons. It was where they had suffered their greatest humiliation, and where they had managed to redeem some of it.

Archer had his doubts about coming back to this swirling dustbowl of a world. He had been lucky to escape from Twycross last time he'd been there, a cocky officer who'd dodged more shots than he'd made in the fight. Now, a great deal hung in the balance. If he lost, he would have done nothing to make the Jade Falcons break off their incursion. If he won, the victory would bring down on his head every Falcon unit in the area to restore their lost honor by wiping him out. A victory on Twycross would come at a high price, but the cost was necessary.

A knock sounded on his cabin door. "Enter," he said, still watching the spinning globe. When he looked up, Archer saw Katya Chaffee in the doorway, looking lithe even in her dull green jumpsuit. He straightened up as she closed the door.

"Please tell me you're not here with some problem," he said half-jokingly.

She smiled as she walked over. "That depends how you define 'problem.' "

Archer gestured for Katya to have a seat on the edge of the fold-down bed next to the desk he was using.

"All right, Katya. Let's have it."

"We just got a message from Captain Gramash. It came hidden in a falsified Jade Falcon transfer manifest, dumped and stored in a relay satellite-signal and encrypted so only we would even spot it. He says he hasn't been in direct contact with Adam Steiner yet, but his agents say it took over two and a half weeks for Steiner to secure Black Earth from the Falcons. No one has heard from him since. In fact, we don't even know if he's still on Black Earth."

"And no word on how Prince Victor's doing?"

"None. We're almost completely cut off from the civil war."

"Blind, alone, behind enemy lines," Archer muttered. "In other words, nothing has changed for us, eh?"

Katya shrugged as if to say what else is new.

Archer rubbed his brow for a moment. "What's different is working with Adam Steiner. You won't say it. You can't. I can, but this stays between us." That went without saying, of course. He trusted Katya perhaps more than any other person alive.

"Adam Steiner may be one hell of a military commander, but he's got a lot to learn about working as part of a larger unit on a coordinated mission," Archer said. "So, now we don't know if he continued on to Malibu, if he's stuck somewhere carrying out repairs, or if he simply diverted directly to Blackjack."

"Frustrating," Katya said.

"To say the least. Did Gramash give any indication that the Falcons might have stopped their incursion?"

Katya shook her head. "They attacked Crimond, where Phelan Kell engaged them. They've also moved into the Rasalgethi system. So far, we haven't been able to attract their notice."

Archer leaned back in the uncomfortable chair,

stretching out his legs as best he could. "That all changes here. Twycross gets their attention. The Falcon Guards will get their attention."

"You're worried?"

Archer gave a small grin. "I'm always worried. Adam's an arrogant little pissant, but he's also supposed to be some sort of tactical genius. If he got tied up on Black Earth, there has to be a good reason. My real fear is that he'll hang us out to dry . . . let us slug it out alone on Twycross, hoping the Jade Falcons will finish us off to save him the trouble when this is all over."

"You don't really think he's going to turn his forces against us if we manage to stop the Falcon invasion?"

"I don't know." Archer gave another long glance at the spinning globe of the world they were approaching. "I've been thinking about it, so I'm sure he's been thinking about it."

"Well, what does your gut tell you?" Katya asked.

Archer looked at her, grateful as ever to have her as a confidante. "My gut tells me that I should proceed as planned and stop worrying about this crap. If Adam wants a piece of us when this is all over with, he's welcome to try."

Katya leaned forward, resting her elbows on her knees. "You started fighting against the Lyran Alliance to honor the memory of your sister. You agreed to this mission because you know that our very homes are at risk if the Falcons aren't stopped. There hasn't been a playbook or set of rules for you to follow up to this point. You've done everything based on your instincts. Why change now?"

Archer looked into her eyes, so full of concern for him. "I think it's facing the Jade Falcons that's doing it to me, Katya. I was younger when I first fought them. I had my whole life ahead of me. Funny, at the time, I even thought I wanted to be a great general, leading BattleMechs into glorious combat. I never thought it would come this way, at this price. Fighting the Falcons has somehow made me feel old, I guess. And the lives of thousands of troops and millions of people hang in the balance of this operation. Before all this, the decisions I had to make involved a raid or an attack against a Lyran world for supplies and munitions. I never had to consider the big picture. Now I do."

"And you're worried that you've made the wrong call?"

Archer nodded. "Maybe I'm not a major general. Maybe I'm just a good old major who should be leading troops into battle rather than planning the entire war."

She patted his hand. "You don't believe that, Archer. Not for a minute. I've known you too long, and we've been too close. I've seen you go from a local businessman to a rebel to a military leader. What's bothering you isn't that maybe you aren't right about Audacity, but that there are parts of the plan you can't control. Up to now, you've enjoyed independent command over a tight, cohesive unit. Now, you're fighting with an exiled Wolf Khan in your rear, a powder keg as an ally, and a deadly enemy who's invaded the homeworlds of the nation you've been fighting to liberate from the Archon's iron fist. You know you're right, but now you have to trust not just your instincts, but other people who you don't know."

Archer said nothing for a long time, turning over her words in his mind. "And here all of this time, I just thought I was getting old."

Her answering smile was like a battery giving him strength. "You're in your mid-forties. I hate to break it to you, General, but that's not that old."

"It is according to the Clans," Archer retorted.

"Well, there's only one Clan we have to worry about, and frankly, I don't give a damn what they think—and as I recall, neither do you."

Archer nodded and reached over to the comm-system control. "Bridge, this is General Christifori.

Patch me in to the Jade Falcon commander on Twycross."

There was a pause, but Archer knew his words had launched a flurry of activity on the bridge. He waited a full minute and a half before he heard the comm tech speak again. "Sir, I have you on laser-relay with a satellite orbiting Twycross. The Falcons can put their Star Colonel on, voice-only at this time."

"Whenever you're ready," Archer said.

"Good to go, sir. You're on."

Archer drew a long breath and sat up tall in his seat, even though he knew the enemy commander could not see him. "Jade Falcon commander, this is Major General Archer Christifori of the Federated Suns; former officer of the Tenth Lyran Guard; officer in the Star League Defense Force; destroyer of Clan Smoke Jaguar; and commanding officer of the task force that is burning in to this system. In keeping with your traditions, I ask you with what forces will you defend Twycross?"

The voice that came back after a pause was almost light and only slightly arrogant, which caught Archer off guard. "This is Star Colonel Ravill Pryde; commanding officer of Gamma Galaxy's Falcon Guards; heir to the legacy of Aidan Pryde; decorated warrior of Clan Jade Falcon. We detected your arrival and respect that you are honoring our traditions. As a former member of the Tenth Lyran Guard, perhaps you doubt our prowess. But to demonstrate to you our skill, I will defend this world with one Trinary of force. Once I have determined which Trinary, I will send you the details of our codexes."

"Very well. I will determine our attacking force and send you the details of their experience as well," Archer said. "I trust that you will grant us safe conduct and landing."

Ravill Pryde's voice sounded almost cocky. "I grant you safcon and salute your knowledge of our ways and traditions. The venue for the battle will be the

Plain of Curtains. I will meet you and your force personally."

"I look forward to meeting you—and to defeating you, Star Colonel," Archer said carefully.

"Indeed. Rest assured that your knowledge of the Clans will not change a thing on the field of honor. Well bargained and done, Archer Christifori." Then the transmission ended.

Archer glanced over at Katya. "Here we go. In a mere two days, Ravill Pryde will learn just why I named this Operation Audacity."

She laughed in response. "Aff, General," she said, mocking Clanspeak. "Aff, he will."

Tech Christopher of the Falcon Guards was on his knees, leaning over the field myomer-monitoring and adjustment system. In front of him stood Star Colonel Ravill Pryde. Seeing the fierce scowl on the Star Colonel's face and the intimidating way he stood with legs wide and hands on his hips, Christopher tried to avert his eyes.

He noticed a film of dust from the constant storms on Twycross on Ravill Pryde's gray uniform tunic, and took some small satisfaction that the warriors also had to deal with the world's infernal dust.

"I just took my *Timber Wolf* on maneuvers for three days," the Star Colonel said. "And are you aware of how it performed?"

"Neg, Star Colonel Pryde," Christopher said, rising slowly to his feet, trying not to shake with fear.

"You rebuilt my cockpit after the last trial. The firing controls are still a disaster. My medium lasers discharged as soon as I switched them over to the target interlock circuit."

"I do not understand, Star Colonel. I replaced that circuit myself." Christopher remembered that the job took nearly a day and a half to complete, though it would have been less without the Star Colonel constantly interrupting his work with pointless queries.

"You do not understand. That is an understatement. Do you know who I am? I am the genetic legacy of Aidan Pryde. I am the commanding officer on this planet. Your understanding is pathetic, you freebirth cur. You are as incompetent as you are filthy." Fire seemed to build in Ravill Pryde's eyes as he spoke. He didn't even give Christopher a chance to explain.

"Fix it. Fix it now. I want my fire-control system to perform above specifications by this time tomorrow. I am about to go into battle. You will fix it, or you and your superior will regret the day you were spawned. I assure you, ignorant Tech, that you do not want to face the full force of my wrath." With those words, Ravill Pryde turned and stormed away.

Tech Felix, who had been watching the little scene, walked over. "The Star Colonel seems slightly irritated with your work, Christopher," he said softly.

"Aye," Christopher said. His face flushed with shame.

"And the problem he speaks of?"

"Minor at best. I will get to it when I can," Christopher said bitterly. "Or perhaps not."

"Don't you fear his wrath?" Felix said, mocking Ravill Pryde's last outburst.

Christopher smiled. "No matter what he says, the most he will do is transfer me. Well, this planet is little more than a hellhole—one giant sand dune of constant storms, unbearable heat, and dust over everything. I've been here for four years, and that's long enough. I would prefer not to repair his little problem and be transferred somewhere else than do what he wants and stay here even five minutes longer."

Felix slapped his shoulder in respect. "You are one wise Tech, Christopher," he said.

19

DropShip Colonel Crockett
Twycross
Jade Falcon Occupation Zone
30 October 3064

Listening to Captain Lee Fullerton's voice from the cockpit of his *Penetrator* filled Archer with a tingle of excitement. "We're going to be down in three. Landing procedures initiated. We have enemy 'Mechs in the LZ—they are not firing." The DropShip door unsealed with a hissing sound that Archer could hear even bundled up inside his 'Mech.

His field of vision, however, was limited. The Diabolis, a massive storm of wind and sand, turned the air outside into little more than a reddish-dull brown blur. With the DropShip's sensors tied into his 'Mech's, he was getting a pretty fair image of the terrain where they were landing—the Plain of Curtains on Twycross. It wasn't just the three-hundred-kph winds of the Diabolis raging over the plains that blurred his vision; it was the memory of returning to this place.

To the east, not far from the Plain of Curtains, was

the Great Gash, a narrow, rock-filled valley where the Falcon Guard had been defeated the last time Archer had been on Twycross. To the west rose the Windbreak Mountains, blocking movement in that direction. The *Crockett* rocked and swayed as it plunged downward, breaking through his reveries of a younger Archer Christifori serving under a much younger Prince Victor Steiner-Davion. As he peered through the raging and twisting vortex of the Diabolis, Archer could see that his troops were not alone.

Star Colonel Ravill Pryde was below, waiting. With a full Trinary in tow, he had formed up as a kind of a greeting party, and Archer assumed this was the unit the Star Colonel had bid to defend the planet. Seeing them standing in a half-circle below the descending DropShip, he activated his gun camera to record the landing and the battle. He wanted evidence to show to the Jade Falcons after he eventually defeated Star Colonel Pryde.

He was landing all three of his own regiments and the Twentieth Arcturan Guards, but their LZ was several kilometers away. The force that would actually fight here was arriving on the Plains with only two DropShips, the massive Overlord-class *Colonel Crockett* and the smaller Union-class *Avatar*. His force was mixed, the best MechWarriors from each of the regiments in his task force. Where possible, he had kept units together that had proven themselves as an excellent fighting force, such as the command lance of the Twentieth Guards under Colonel Gray.

Gray had questioned whether it was wise for Archer, as the commanding general of the whole force, to personally lead the attack units into battle. Archer had taken no offense. Rather, he admired her for challenging his decision, knowing her motives were sincere. He assured her that all would be well, and that he had decided to take command because he thought the mission needed his greater experience in combat with the Clans. Silently, staring at the red soil below on final approach, he wondered for just a millisecond whether she was right . . .

The Falcon Guards would engage with a single Trinary of BattleMechs, a total of fifteen 'Mechs, three of what the Clans called stars. Archer knew that the fight had to be honorable if it was going to succeed, so he would field sixteen 'Mechs, giving himself the extra 'Mech to balance the Clan edge in technology. By keeping the odds so tight, he intended to guarantee not just a chance at victory, but one that would cost the Falcon Guards some of their prestige.

That didn't mean he was going to play dumb, however. Clan warriors were genetically bred for combat, trained for war from the time they could walk. They had a technological edge as well, with weapons that were more efficient and enjoyed better ranges. For that reason, Archer had used the time traveling in-system to make sure that his force had the best of the Clan technology they had salvaged so far. Like his own *Penetrator*, which mounted the lighter and farther-reaching Clan lasers, he made sure that almost every 'Mech in his force had some sort of little surprise aimed at evening the odds.

He had also taken the time to mentally prepare all of the warriors who would take part in the fight, making sure they understood the importance of defeating the Jade Falcons on Twycross on their own terms. "Do this," he'd said, "and the invasion of the Lyran Alliance should stop. Win this victory, and the Falcon Khans will be forced to turn in their tracks to defend a loss of honor in their own backyard."

As the *Crockett* continued its descent, rocking in the winds of the Diabolis, Archer tied his comm channel in to every 'Mech in his fighting force. "Remember, we fight this one on Falcons terms, but we have to beat them. Don't gang up and concentrate fire unless I order it," he said.

"Lance leaders, be sure to run your gun cameras. Ravill Pryde picked this area because it borders on the Diabolis, so don't let yourself get tricked into chasing his forces in there if he heads that way. The particulate matter of that sandstorm is enough to kill communications even at distances of only a hundred meters away.

"So, run your final checks, preheat your weapons. Assume that the fur will begin to fly the moment we land, but wait for my word to engage the enemy." The Diabolis moved around on Twycross, and was receding, but Archer was in no mood to take any risks.

He leaned his *Penetrator* forward slightly and could, for the first time, see the terrain. It was a study in flattened, dull brown hills with hints of red from the stones jutting up from underneath. He saw the Falcon Guard OmniMechs, their green paint scheme clashing with the red of the dirt swirling in the windstorm. They were at least two hundred meters off, forming a ring around the landing DropShips. Most were tipped back at the waist, looking upward at him as he was looking down on them.

He saw a flicker off to his right and felt as much as heard a dull, booming sound from the DropShip. He squinted. Was that a laser burst?

"General!" came a sudden call from Captain Fullerton. "The Jade Falcons fired on us!"

"Confirmed?" Archer replied.

"Damnation, they shot at us," Fullerton said. "Damage confirmed on strut number three."

Archer didn't wait. He had no idea why the Falcons had violated their code of honor by firing on his DropShips. It did not matter. "All units, deploy immediately. *Crockett* and *Avatar*, you are authorized to fire at will. All units, engage immediately. Keep tight to the DropShips for cover and support. I don't know what the Falcons are doing, but they're going to pay. All rules of engagement are off. Attack! Fire at will!"

Just before the *Colonel Crockett* hit the ground, Archer saw its turrets come into play. Long-range missiles twisted and snaked from the turret over his position, while pulse-laser bursts sprayed a number of Jade Falcons in the distance. For a few moments, the Clan 'Mechs did not seem to engage, but then, as if orchestrated, they charged forward, blazing away at the DropShips and their deadly cargo.

Archer didn't wait to see who hit what. He charged his *Penetrator* out of the deployment bay and onto the gritty, reddish-brown surface of Twycross. A *Mad Cat*, the 'Mech the Clans called a *Timber Wolf*, rushed forward at either him or the ship. Archer guided his targeting reticle over the Falcon 'Mech and immediately saw the color change, indicating a lock. He fired his large lasers, followed almost a heartbeat later by two blasts from his medium pulse lasers.

The warrior piloting the *Mad Cat* was good. Caught in the fury of a barrage, he still managed to let loose two racks of long-range missiles. Many of them missed Archer, but they didn't miss the huge DropShip directly behind him.

The *Mad Cat* seemed to twist at first under the fury of the attack. One of Archer's large lasers missed, but another slammed directly into the front of the cockpit, tearing a black scar up through the canopy glass and around to the rear, where it ate away at the armor plates. Green bursts from his medium pulse lasers peppered the upper-torso armor and both weapons-pod arms of the massive Clan OmniMech.

The Falcon 'Mech appeared to stumble, its Mech-Warrior probably shaken up by the cockpit hit. Archer felt the temperature of his own cockpit rise sharply as he broke into a run, crossing the field of fire to put some distance between himself and the DropShip. Images of the battle flashed all around him, lasers and PPC discharges filling the air like fireworks. He swung forward slightly and slowed, bringing the *Mad Cat* into view again.

It had moved forward to pursue him, blazing away

with its twinned pair of large and medium lasers the moment he saw it come into his field of vision. The scarlet beams all found their mark, a sign of the firing warrior's skill. Armor plating on his *Penetrator*'s legs and torso was sliced and seared at the same time, sending molten armor splattering as Archer brought the *Mad Cat* into his targeting sights.

The *Colonel Crockett*'s turrets beat him to the draw. A brilliant white burst of charged particles from a PPC seemed to envelop the *Mad Cat* while another wave of long-range missiles pockmarked the green OmniMech all over. For a moment, Archer could not maintain a visual lock on his foe, who was obscured by the plumes of the missile warheads going off and the smoke from the PPC damage whipped by the winds of the Diabolis. He was on the verge of switching his targeting and tracking system to a magnetic-signal lock when the *Mad Cat* stepped forward, emerging from the smoke that still churned from it.

Archer's secondary display gave him a number of yellow and red warnings showing how much damage the Clansman had already taken, while Archer simply did what any warrior was trained to do—he fired. First, his large lasers, captured Clan gear. The heat they created in his cockpit was bearable. One hit the right arm of the *Mad Cat*; the other burrowed into the already-battered chest armor.

Archer side-stepped just as the *Mad Cat* unleashed its long-range missiles. Forty warheads spiraled in on him, but he was prepared this time, activating his Yori Flyswatter anti-missile system at the last possible moment. It burped a wall of fire at the approaching missiles, devouring a number of them in mid-air before they reached him. The few that did get through battered his *Penetrator* almost everywhere. Archer glanced at his damage readout, and saw that his armor had taken heavy damage, but still held.

Continuing to sidestep, he swung his medium pulse lasers to bear. Split into two batteries of three so that he could manage the heat, Archer brought them in on the *Mad Cat*.

He fired the first three, two of them missing but one stabbing at the already-damaged right arm. As he prepared to fire the other battery, steeling himself to weather the heat he knew would momentarily bake his cockpit, he watched as one of Colonel Gray's four-legged *Barghests* shuffled into a firing stance, stooped, and fired. Its extended-range large lasers had been replaced with a captured Falcon gauss rifle. The awkward BattleMech disgorged its metallic payload into the right side of the *Mad Cat*, knocking it so hard to the side that the MechWarrior had to fight to keep it upright.

Colonel Gray had a Clan short-range missile pack in place of the usual autocannon and let go with a spread of the deadly missiles. Two missed totally, but the others homed in on the legs and arms, forcing the warrior to fight even harder to keep the OmniMech standing, let alone fighting.

She spun, her assist done, and charged away, but she had given Archer's large lasers enough time to recharge. As the *Mad Cat* turned to face him again, he raised his targeting reticle up on the display slightly, and fired. One of the laser beams dug into the remaining armor on the *Mad Cat*'s center torso, plowing deep into the myomer bundling that he could see, sending up white smoke as it ate the muscle material that powered the 'Mech. The smoke lasted only a moment before a buffeting blast of dust-filled wind seemed to evaporate it.

The other laser shot went higher, digging into the center cockpit of the *Mad Cat*. For a moment, Archer thought the crimson beam would deflect off the armor. But it took only a second to burn through and punch straight into the cockpit itself. The interior seemed to flash for an instant. Something inside had exploded, perhaps the warrior himself, then blackness filled the canopy glass as fire raged inside.

The *Mad Cat* looked like a marionette with cut strings as it dropped limply to the ground. Archer charged at it to throw off any shots that might be bearing in on him. Turning wide to the right, away from the DropShips, he saw an Arcturan Guard *Cobra* madly clubbing a *Vulture* with the remains of its left arm, now more scrap metal than weaponry. The *Vulture*'s side was mangled, and slick green coolant oozed from a damaged heat sink like blood from an open wound. The 'Mech attempted to back up, to put some distance between it and the *Cobra*, when suddenly Archer saw it quake and then, in the midst of tremors, fall forward at the feet of the badly battered Guards. Off in the distance, he spotted the final assailant, Colonel Gray in her *Barghest*, standing on a dull-brown clay outcropping of rock. The *Vulture* pilot never saw the gauss rifle slug coming.

Suddenly, a blasting wind from the nearby Diabolis seared across the battlefield. Archer spun slowly, heart pounding, taking in the scene. Six 'Mechs were still standing, including himself. All were damaged, some severely, but they were still alive. In some areas, smoke rose from piles of shattered and burned metal, fallen Jade Falcons. He could see flames, whipped by the wind, coming from a blackened pile that had been a Falcon *Cougar*. Other than the roar of the winds, there was silence, an eerie silence.

"Did any Jade Falcons flee?" he asked over the open commline to his troops.

"None, General," replied Colonel Gray. "I haven't seen anything like it in a long time. They fought to the end, to the very last man and woman. They just kept on coming, but thanks to the DropShips providing some cover fire, we beat them."

"Why in the name of hell did they fire?" Archer asked. "We were meeting them on their terms in a place they chose."

"Unknown, sir," Gray returned.

"Did any Falcon warriors survive?" Archer asked. He hoped that Ravill Pryde might have. He knew Pryde had been piloting a *Mad Cat*, but he hoped it had been another one at the other end of the battlefield. If he was alive, perhaps Archer could get some answers about why the Falcon forces had fired at his ships in violation of their own code of honor.

"A few of the warriors punched out successfully. I suggest we deploy some infantry to round them up," Gray said. There was an uncomfortable pause as she anticipated what Archer was really asking. "That *Mad Cat* you toasted, sir. It appears to have been Ravill Pryde's."

Another voice came on the line. "Isn't that the 'Mech that fired at our DropShip?" Colonel Hogan asked.

"I think so," Archer said. "So we'll never know what happened for sure."

"It all happened so fast," Hogan said.

"Yes, and we caught most of it on holocamera." Then, Archer called to the *Colonel Crockett*. "Katya, this is Christifori. I want you to burn copies of a couple of our battleroms and get the gun-camera footage pulled together. Also, get the repair and salvage teams out here."

"Yes, sir," came Katya's voice from the bridge of the DropShip.

"Then send all the data out to all Jade Falcon commands. We'll tell them that the Falcon Guards violated the Clan terms of honor and that we defeated them here, on Twycross. The wording is important; we're going to soil their honor and reputation. Khan Marthe Pryde and the rest of the Jade Falcons will know that we are here and what her people did. She'll know we beat them using their own code of combat. We need to get a message out to Phelan Kell or Gramash as well. Let them know our status."

"Yes, sir," Katya said. "Anything else?"

"Let's get the repairs going, too. I hope to leave here soon. We've just shaken up a hive of bees, and we don't want to get stung by hanging around too long."

20

DropShip Kearsarge
Approach Trajectory to Hot Springs
Hot Springs
Jade Falcon Occupation Zone
1 November 3064

Adam Steiner looked up from his noteputer at a
knock on his cabin door, then quickly replicated the
data back to the DropShip's main computer for
backup. "Come," he said, sitting up straight and opening his eyes wider to adjust his focus after spending
so much time staring at the data screen.

Colonel Anne Sung entered the cramped quarters,
decked out in her formal dress uniform, right down
to the spurs worn by the officers of the Federated
Suns. The jingle of the spurs was irritating, reminding
Adam that there was still a civil war being fought
elsewhere, while he was here, being forced to work
with people he thought of as enemies. It also reminded
him that they, the forces of Operation Audacity, were
cut off from communications regarding the war between his cousins, Victor and Katrina. He hated that.

Sung stepped in stiffly and saluted, remaining at attention in front of the tiny desk Adam was using. "Colonel Sung, what a surprise to see you." Sung and her battered Second Crucis Lancers RCT were using the DropShip *Ajax.* To get here, she must have taken a shuttle over to the *Kearsarge,* the ship from which Adam commanded the task force.

"General Steiner, sir," Sung said, obviously tense, "I have a matter of some importance to discuss with you."

Adam rather enjoyed seeing Sung's discomfort. It wasn't that he disliked her, just her politics. "Please," he said, gesturing with his open palm, "what's on your mind?"

"Permission to speak freely, General?"

Adam hesitated, more for drama than anything, then nodded once slowly. "If you feel that's necessary."

Sung slipped into a parade rest stance, hands clasped behind her back. "Sir, it's about this strike against Hot Springs. I'm not comfortable with it."

Adam waited, but when she didn't continue, he nodded. "Go ahead."

"Sir, this was a tertiary target on our list. General Christifori and his task force have surely hit Twycross by now. They're planning to meet up with us on Blackjack."

"You're not comfortable with my choice of targets?"

Sung shook her head rapidly. It was obvious that she was still struggling for the right words. "It's not the choice of targets, General Steiner. My people are concerned that we've come here at all. We were already running behind on our timetable. Shouldn't we just bypass this system and move directly to Blackjack, where we're to link up with the rest of General Christifori's force."

Adam drummed his fingers on the tiny desk as he looked up at her. "According to intelligence information, including the information I received from Christifori's own intel officer, Hot Springs may very well be a staging world for the strikes into the Alliance. Doesn't it make sense that we should take it out?"

"I didn't say it's not a worthy target, General," Sung said.

"Then what is it?" Adam smiled as though he hadn't a clue why she was so upset.

"Sir, a lot of people could get killed if we're not on Blackjack when we're supposed to be. If Christifori was successful on Twycross, the Jade Falcons are going to throw everything they've got at him to regain their honor. We're his exit strategy. We hold the back door into the Alliance."

Adam drew a long, audible breath through his nose. "You and your officers believe that I'm going to strand Christifori. That's what this is about, isn't it, Colonel?" He dropped the smile and narrowed his eyes in fury. Sung's face reddened.

"I don't want to think that of you, sir," Sung said, holding up her hands as if to say whoa. "But we've spent the better part of two years trying to kill each other in the civil war. Your striking at Hot Springs, well, it looks like you're not concerned at all about the general or his force."

"And you think that I'm capable of sending those men and women to their death, just because I don't agree with Christifori or my cousin Victor?" Adam demanded, letting his voice get louder.

"To be honest, sir . . . yes." Sung seemed almost relieved to have said it out loud.

"And the rest of your command, they feel this way as well?" Sung's confession did nothing to cool Adam's anger.

"Many do, sir. They've seen the way you've treated the general, and even myself."

"You don't like how I treat you?"

"No. I don't."

"I am a general," Adam said. "I chose to come to Hot Springs because, along with the other worlds we've seized, taking it out might be just enough to get the attention of the Jade Falcon high command. You and your staff may have picked up on the fact that I don't think much of your Archer Christifori. But you had better know this. I'm not in the damn Jade Falcon Occupation Zone to settle personal scores with my cousin. I'm here to do a job, and that job is to stop the Falcon incursion into the Lyran Alliance."

"Sir, I have to know," Sung insisted. "I have to be able to reassure my troops. We *are* going to rendezvous on Blackjack as planned, are we not?"

"I will use whatever means are at my disposal to stop the Falcons. And Colonel, don't forget that you were put under my command by your beloved Christifori. I don't really care what you do or don't think of me, but while you serve under my command, you'll follow my orders without spending a lot of time brooding about some underhanded motives you suspect I might have."

Sung held her ground. "You still haven't answered my question, sir."

Adam opened his mouth to speak just as the comm system in his quarters beeped, two tones, a signal of an incoming message from the bridge. He held up his hand to cut off further discussion and rose slowly to his feet. Propping his hands against the tiny gray table, he leaned on it and said, "This is General Steiner."

A disembodied voice came over the intercom speaker near the ceiling of his cabin. "General, sir. We received a transmission from Hot Springs and the Jade Falcon commander there."

"I'll be right up, and you can tie me in then," Adam said, giving the still angry Sung a quick glance.

"Not possible, General. The Falcon commander sent a transmission to us, voice only, then cut off communication."

Adam paused for three seconds, unsure of what to say next. "Very well, then, pipe it down here."

"Yes, sir," the comm tech said. There was the pop and snap of static, then a deadly silence, and finally the sound of a stern voice. "This is Star Colonel Diane Anu of the Fifth Battle Cluster, the Golden Talons of the Epsilon Galaxy of Clan Jade Falcon. To the commanding officer of the Inner Sphere task force approaching Hot Springs. You have erred in your arrogance in attacking this holding of the Jade Falcons, and it is my duty to teach you the depth of that error. Land on this planet, and know that I shall defend it with anything I can lay my hands on. If you retreat, I will follow and hunt you down.

"Your government's treacherous victory on Twycross shall be avenged. And in the end, it is the grip of the Golden Talon around your throat that will be the last image your brain will process. Prepare to pay the price for your brazenness." There was a final pop of static, then utter silence.

Adam glanced over at Anne Sung. "Well, I guess we know one thing now, Colonel. It looks like Christifori made it to Twycross and that he succeeded in taking it away from the Falcons."

Sung smiled for the first time since she'd come in. "He's got their attention, that's for sure."

Adam didn't smile back. "Well, in the meantime, Colonel, listen up and listen good. I have every intention of getting to Blackjack in time for Christifori to hook up with us. I'm telling this to you, and you can pass it on to your warriors in good faith. I'm in this to drive the Falcons out of the Alliance and I know that means the forces of Operation Audacity must be united, no matter what our political views on the civil war. We must all stay focused on the Jade Falcons, not on what we think a former enemy might be doing."

Sung nodded once. "Yes, sir. And thank you, General, for allowing me to air my concerns."

Adam was curiously relieved all of a sudden, too. No matter how unpleasant, his conversation with Sung had cleared the air. And he believed what he'd told her. Right now, any enemy of the Jade Falcons was a friend of his.

"You might as well stay for dinner, Colonel," he said. "I can use all the help I can get in figuring out how to deal with this Star Colonel Anu."

21

The Great Gash
Twycross
Jade Falcon Occupation Zone
3 November 3064

Archer had assigned a patrol to the area of the Great Gash, which cut through the Windbreak Mountains at the edge of the Plain of Curtains, as a way to secure the landing zone where his regiments had deployed. It was where the Falcon Guards had been utterly defeated in 3050 when he'd first come to Twycross. Explosives set off in the canyon walls had gone off, burying all but one of the Falcon Guard who fought that day in the rubble. For the Falcons, the defeat had been beyond humiliating.

Now, the patrol had found a BattleMech on the canyon floor, and he had come out to see it for himself. Repairs were taking much longer than he'd anticipated, and he'd used the time to interrogate prisoners about why Ravill Pryde had fired at the DropShips before they even touched down. No one knew anything, and all Archer got out of them was that the Star Colonel had been experiencing problems with his weapons systems. Was it possible that he had fired on

Archer's force by accident and that his Falcon arrogance kept him from sending a message to Archer to explain? Had Ravill Pryde led his forces to utter defeat all because he was too proud to admit a mistake? If so, the Clan commander had lost his own life in the process, a fact Archer did not confirm till later.

As he stood in front of the fallen war machine surrounded by a circle of painted white rocks, he was surprised. The Clans, especially the Jade Falcons, abhorred waste. It had apparently been bred into them by the difficulty of surviving in their inhospitable homeworlds. Yet, here was an OmniMech, destroyed in battle, left as a monument. At first, it made no sense to him. He walked around the badly mauled 'Mech. It was a *Daishi*, and Archer couldn't help a shiver of dread at the raw power the machine represented.

As he slowly paced around it, he saw that the paint scheme was chipped and worn, both from battle and from the swirling winds of the nearby Diabolis. The *Daishi*'s cockpit was caved in, burned and gutted by flame, melted to worthless slag, but the insignia of Clan Wolf was still there on the left torso. Archer walked over to a small plaque mounted on a post and wiped off the dust to read it.

It said: "On this spot, 7 December 3057, Wolf Khan Natasha Kerensky was defeated in single combat by a lone warrior of the Jade Falcon Guards. That warrior was the sole survivor of the destruction of the Falcon Guards on this same soil seven years before. The Falcon honor previously lost in this place was restored by this victory."

Reading the words, Archer shuddered slightly. This was the fallen 'Mech of Natasha Kerensky, the notorious Black Widow. The Jade Falcons had left it here despite their hatred of waste because proof of its destruction was worth even more to them. If the Clans recognized the concept of sacredness, then surely this was such a spot to the Falcon Guard, and probably to any warrior of the Falcon Clan.

Looking at the battered 'Mech in awe, Archer

walked closer and touched the ferro-fibrous armor. Almost at the exact moment, his wrist comm beeped, demanding his attention.

"Go," he said, still gazing up raptly at the mighty metal warrior.

"Sir, we just picked up a signal from a pirate jump point in the system," came the voice of Katya Chaffee, her tone sounding almost ominous. "A Jade Falcon task force just emerged from jump and is on a fast burn in-system. They are demanding to know with what forces will defend this planet. They asked for you specifically."

"Unit ID?" Archer asked, turning away from the monument and walking back to the hoverjeep he'd driven out here.

"It is apparently the rest of the Falcon Guard, along with the Ninth Talon Cluster and at least some elements of the First Falcon Hussars. It looks like most of their Gamma Galaxy. I am showing a total of at least twelve trinaries' worth of troops incoming. They'll make planetfall late tomorrow."

Archer shook his head. "You'd almost think we've worn out our welcome."

Katya gave a soft laugh. "Yes, sir," she said.

"Well, I guess our HPG message to the Jade Falcons went out. Assemble our command staff, Katya. We've got plans to make."

He shut off his comm unit, and glanced over his shoulder for a last look at the 'Mech the Black Widow had piloted to her death. "I don't know if I believe in ghosts," Archer said, speaking out loud but to no one in particular, "but if you're here, Natasha Kerensky, I could sure as hell use even your help at this point."

Then he climbed into the hoverjeep and sped back to the LZ.

Bucking and churning, the nine Jade Falcon DropShips blasted through the swirling winds of the Diabolis. Archer and almost every member of his task force stared upward as the DropShips roared less than a hundred meters over their heads before turning and disappearing into the distance. Until now, he'd had no idea where they would deploy, but from the movement of the DropShips, he could see that they were heading off to the west. They were damn gutsy flying through that storm, he thought.

"All right, Colonel Gray. Looks like you and your Twentieth Arcturan Guards will have the first shot at the bogies. The only place they can land is at the far end of the Gash on the Grissom Plateau. I'll move up the Second Thorin Regiment to reinforce you. First Thorin will stay in reserve. Third Thorin, I'm putting you on the edge of the Plain of Curtains in case they send some forces around to our rear."

"They're going to tangle with us in the Great Gash?" Katya said in disbelief.

"Looks like it," Archer replied.

"You must have really put a dent in their honor for them to want to take us on in there," John Kraff said. "Don't worry, sir. We'll teach them a lesson or two."

Archer angled his *Penetrator* toward the Great Gash and pushed the 'Mech forward. Like the Falcon Guards, these Falcon warriors were all part of Gamma Galaxy. They had obviously arrived with one purpose in mind—retribution for the stunning defeat he had handed the trinary of Falcon Guards under Ravill Pryde. The Grissom Plateau was the only place in the direction the DropShips had headed where it was possible to deploy a force of that size.

Archer increased his pace to join up with Colonel Gray, who was already in the depths of the Great Gash in her *Barghest*. Both commanders slowed to a walking speed, and Archer glanced up out of the deep chasm. "We're only a few kilometers from their LZ. They should be on top of us by now."

"General, I have a lance of *Stiletto*s in the lead as scouts. My infantry and light armor are positioned in the narrow passes along the top of the Gash. I've got my artillery as well as that of the Second Thorin Regiment poised for immediate fire support. Putting fighters up didn't seem prudent with that storm kicking up. I don't know what could be holding up the Falcons, but we couldn't be more ready." Her voice in his earpiece was crisp and confident.

"This isn't at all like the Jade Falcons I've fought," Archer said, squirming slightly in his command chair. A nagging feeling tugged at him. The Falcons were famous for their fierce aggressiveness, even among the war-loving Clans. He had impugned their honor with the defeat of Star Colonel Pryde. They should be at his throat, even more so because he was the one who had killed Pryde and because he was the enemy commander.

I'm here, in the front line unit, he felt like shouting. You can come out any time.

He and Gray rounded one of the many bends, and she stopped her *Barghest*. "General, I just got word from our scouts. They have a visual sighting on the Jade Falcon DropShips. They have not debarked their forces."

"What in the hell are they waiting for?" Archer asked. Suddenly it hit him. Either they were deliberately not unloading their 'Mechs . . . or they had already done so.

"My God. Colonel Hogan!" he barked into his helmet mic.

The Odessa Guards company stood looking with awe out over the Plains and at the sheer wall of whirling winds. Assigned rear-guard duty, they were the unit closest to where the Diabolis raged at the edge of the plains. In command was Captain Chip O'Neal. He'd been a member of the Third Thorin Regiment for only a year, and his unit was relatively green. All of the action was at the front door, while his unit was guarding the back door, and that was fine with him.

His short-range sensors had found the Diabolis impossible to penetrate, thanks to the metallic and radioactive dust particles whipped furiously in the winds. For a moment, his display flickered on, having picked up a target, but then the image disappeared. He moved his *JagerMech* III forward slightly, tapping the display controls for resolution. It had to be a ghost image, a sensor reflection off something loose and blowing in the storm.

O'Neal glanced down and saw the image flicker briefly again. That was odd. He reached over to activate his comm system to see if anyone else in his company had picked it up, but all he got was static. Static? His unit wasn't in the Diabolis. He should be able to communicate with them on the tactical channel . . . Then, his mouth hung limp and open. *Unless he was being jammed.*

The realization came too late. His *JagerMech* III reeled backward, nearly tipping over under a devastating blast from two gauss slugs. His brain screamed out in panic, and his arms and legs ached as he struggled to keep his 'Mech upright. Red warning lights flickered on his neurohelmet's visor screen, telling him how bad the damage was. His head throbbed as he used his own sense of balance to get the 'Mech upright.

What he saw was a vision of hell.

Out of the swirling dust of the storm, like a ferrofibrous wall of death and destruction, the Jade Falcon assault force was charging—straight at him and his tiny company. He leveled his PPCs at the wall of enemies and fired, the brilliant azure bursts slamming outward and sending up a shower of sparks downrange as they found targets. His *JagerMech* III teetered under multiple hits, seeming to throb around him. Numbness enveloped his brain. He knew he was yelling warnings, knew that he was ordering his company to fall back, but the words were lost. The Jade Falcons fired back. Not just one 'Mech this time, but many of them. He

saw a bright light, and a warmth like that of a wool
blanket on a cool winter night seemed to wrap around
him. Chip O'Neal was screaming, but as the flames
devoured him, he knew that no one heard.

As Archer Christifori emerged from the Great Gash,
what he saw was like something out of a nightmare.
Where the Plain of Curtains opened outward from the
canyon was a scene of carnage and destruction that
stunned him. Streaks of smoke marked where 'Mechs
had fallen, and the fight was still on, not far from his
position. Explosions rocked him even at this distance
as missile warheads went off and autocannons deliv-
ered their deadly savaging. A light show of crimson
laser beams and pulses of emerald-green laser bursts
raged in the middle of what had been the First Thorin's position. The Third Thorin Regiment, the Minutemen, had been totally overrun and routed.
Somewhere, out there, Katya Chaffee was in the middle of all of the chaos, directing the fight like a traffic
cop trying to clean up a hovercar accident.

He charged out of the Gash seeking any and all
targets. A spray of missiles raced at him from the
Falcons' wavy battle-line, but he managed to turn on
his anti-missile system in time to take out all but four
of the warheads. Those that did get through slammed
into the chest of his *Penetrator* and marred the armor
there. He didn't flinch. He didn't have time to. He
and his commanders had been fooled by the Jade Falcons, who were plowing through the midst of his regiments even though they were outnumbered.

Archer spotted a green-splotched *Cougar* rush along
one flank of the fighting, seeking a target of opportunity. Twisting the *Penetrator*'s torso, he brought his
targeting reticle onto the smaller 'Mech. Anger guided
his fingers as he fired his large lasers. One shot missed,
but the other bore in on the *Cougar*'s leg, which must
have been already damaged. The Jade Falcon hopped
two steps and fell. The 'Mech was not destroyed, but
at least it was out of the fight for a few minutes.

"Artillery, concentrate your fire on the Falcons' rear ranks," Archer said. "Coordinates zero, zero, two, five, and six. Drop your rounds in there and shake them up."

He watched in horror as one of his *Salamander*s came into his field of vision. It was blackened and battered from fire, its metal hide swarming with a star of five Elemental warriors. The genetically altered troops in their power armor were literally ripping the *Salamander* apart, savagely gutting the machine. Archer knew the markings as those of Captain Fitzhugh Cooper of Third Regiment's Ironclad Company.

His fingers danced over the tactical channel. "Captain Cooper, this is General Christifori. I've got your problem in my sights. Stop moving, and I can help."

The voice of Cooper was filled with terror. "My god, sir, they're tearing me apart."

"Hold still, Cooper. That's an order," Archer said, zooming his targeting reticle on the Elementals and bringing his pulse lasers on-line.

The *Salamander* stopped its contorting and attempts to shake off the green Elementals from its limbs and torso. It stopped only forty meters from Archer, and he took careful aim and fired one of his pulse lasers. The burst of green energy slammed into an Elemental, sending him flying. Then he calmly and quickly brought another to bear and fired, missing. While half of his shots missed, half didn't, which let him pick off most of the Elementals. The last one attempted to reach the cockpit of Cooper's 'Mech, a last-ditch attempt at victory. Archer didn't have time to bring another of his medium pulse lasers on line. Instead, he fired his left large laser, and the Elemental seemed to explode under the crimson beam.

"I've never seen anything like that, sir. Thanks!" Cooper called.

"Old trick from my Clan-fighting days," Archer said. "Now, then, let's lock onto that *Mad Cat* at 216 and take him out." Moving up alongside Cooper, he fired at the Falcon, as did what was left of Cooper's *Salamander*.

*   *   *

The battle lasted nearly four hours—or as Leftenant Colonel Kraff put it, "four hours strolling through hell itself." The Falcons had dropped on the far side of the Diabolis and had somehow marched through the storm while their DropShips distracted Archer and his regiments with a diversion. He felt the weight of command but endured it. He'd been tricked, but had managed to win, thanks to numbers and fast thinking on the part of his subordinates. He'd earned that Major General stripe today, he told himself.

The losses had been staggering, though. The Third Thorin Regiment, his greenest unit, had borne the brunt of the fighting, and only a company and a half of their 'Mechs were still operational. Almost half the First Thorin had taken casualties, including its ground armor, and Major Alice Getts herself was in a field hospital. Second Thorin had lost less troops, mostly infantry. Kraff's command company had rushed with Archer into the thick of the battle and emerged with only three operational BattleMechs. The only unit to fare well was the Twentieth Arcturan Guards, which had been suckered deepest into the Gash on their snipe hunt for the Falcons.

If there was any satisfaction to be gained, it was that the Jade Falcon losses were even more devastating. Only five of the Falcon Guard 'Mechs remained standing. The Ninth Talon Cluster was mauled almost as bad. As for the First Falcon Hussars, Archer did not see a single 'Mech bearing the golden falcon with a spear still on its feet.

He had seen ferocity in Clan combat before, during the invasion and on Huntress against the Smoke Jaguars. But nothing like this. The Falcons never stopped. They came with a fury he had ignited, a fire he had stoked into a roaring blaze.

When it was over, the ranking officer, a Star Captain, had ordered a halt and climbed out of what was left of her charred and mangled *Black Hawk* to meet with him. Archer, joined by Katya Chaffee and John Kraff, walked toward her. They met on a rock that seemed to be the only clear space in the vicinity. Archer swept the area with his gaze, seeing rescue and repair crews working furiously trying to recover the injured and to repair the 'Mechs that had been felled.

The officer was a woman with a Roman nose, high cheekbones, and a black smear down one side of her face. Archer couldn't help thinking she was beautiful, an odd thought when it came to Clan warriors. Her cooling vest had been torn and was leaking down her iron-strong thigh, but she seemed not to notice.

This was one tough warrior, he decided, and knew this was probably one of the toughest meetings she would ever have to face. He took off his cooling vest and dropped it onto the rock. Dressed in cut-off shorts and a tee-shirt caked with dirt and drenched in sweat, the only thing that marked him as an officer was his field cap.

The woman stood mutely before him, so Archer spoke first. "Star Captain?"

"Diana Pryde," she said angrily. "Of the Falcon Guard."

"I am Major General Archer Christifori," he said, extending his hand. She did not give it so much as a glance, let alone reach out with her own. He withdrew his hand slowly.

"You have defeated us in battle," she said, obviously hating every word. "I and what is left of my people stand either as your bondsmen, or less." Archer knew that, in her eyes, "or less" might mean outcasts, becoming despised members of the bandit caste. He didn't plan to humiliate her that way. He'd won the battle he'd come to fight.

"It would have never come to this if your people had not invaded the Alliance," he said.

"That is not our concern," Diana Pryde replied.

Archer gave his subordinate staff a quick glance, but they all looked equally blank about how he should deal with this defeated enemy warrior. He turned back to her. "I'm a little familiar with your traditions," he said. "If I don't take you as bondsmen, you become outcasts from your society."

When she said nothing, he went on, "Frankly, given the nature of our mission, I can't afford to take you with us."

He looked down at her torn cooling vest for a moment, then drew a knife from his boot sheath. Reaching out, he pulled her access hose and cut it with a deft swipe of his blade. Diana Pryde didn't flinch at either the knife or his movements. She stood like a statue.

Archer grabbed her wrist and wrapped the coolant hose around it once. Then, with the knife, he cut it loose again. "You and your unit were my bondsmen, now you're free. Your equipment belongs to me, but you are free to return to your Clan with your honor intact."

She scowled at him. "Our honor has been bled dry by your actions and those of Ravill Pryde. The Falcon Guards are no more, thanks to you. I do not know if my Clan will ever accept me after this."

Archer almost saw a piece of himself in her, if only for an instant. She was harder on herself than even he knew how to be. She was kicking herself for failing, but yet the truth was she had managed to salvage something of her command. "We will give you your battleroms to take with you. They should validate your skills. Your people pride themselves on their fighting prowess. I'm sure they'll take you back."

Diana shrugged almost bitterly. "This is a dark day for our Clan."

Archer ignored the comment. "Tell your troops they may leave," he said. "And one more thing . . ."

"Yes, Major General?"

"I want you to give a message to Marthe Pryde for me. Let her know what happened here, and tell her I'm not done with the Jade Falcons just yet."

22

Khan Marthe Pryde stared at the image embedded into the message stream for the tenth time since its arrival but did nothing to betray her profound rage. The screen showed a man with salt-and-pepper hair wearing jumpsuit fatigues and a look of determination. ComStar had gone to great expense and trouble to make the message arrive priority, but Marthe couldn't help thinking that the Primus did so only because it pleased her. Sitting in her Spartan quarters, she pondered the implications of what the man in the message was *really* saying.

His voice was firm and resolute. "Khan Marthe Pryde of the Jade Falcons, I bid you greetings from Twycross. I am Major General Archer Christifori and am here under orders from Prince Victor Steiner-Davion. I have defeated the Falcon Guard forces under Star Colonel Ravill Pryde on Twycross. He violated his code of honor and forced me to destroy his unit. I have taken the liberty of sending you the gun-camera footage and battlerom readouts so that you will know I am speaking the truth.

"Plainly put, Khan Pryde, I am on Twycross for one reason, to persuade you to end your incursion into the Lyran Alliance. My units and their attached task forces have mangled your supply lines. If you continue your assault against the Alliance, I will cut your occupation zone in half. I will do so because you leave me no choice.

"Know this. I have beaten your most elite unit on a world where that unit's honor was scattered over the sands more than a decade ago. I abided by your Clan's rules, only to have your best warriors disregard them. The only way for you to stop me is to stop your invasion. Cease your incursion, and I believe we can find a resolution."

Samantha Clees came up behind Marthe. "I have had our techs review the data," she said. "They detect no tampering with the material he sent."

A wave of bitterness swept over Marthe. "What do you think, Samantha? You've seen the message and the data. Our Clan's honor has been called into question. This general has cost me a heavy cruiser on Butler, and he has seized several of our border worlds. Not to mention the existence of at least one more task force attacking our Occupation Zone."

"He believes himself Scipio Africannis," Samantha said. "He strikes at our holdings to lure us away from his worlds. It is hardly an innovative strategy. We should ignore it and continue our thrust."

Marthe rose from her tiny gray worktable and began to pace the room, arms crossed over her chest. "Phelan Kell and his people have disappeared. I can only assume they will strike across our border as well."

Samantha gave a slight shrug. "The action of renegade Wolves does not worry me."

"Perhaps it should. Phelan Kell has defeated our

forces each time he has fought them. A wolf on the prowl can be a dangerous element, on top of what this general has done."

"Are you saying we should turn around and give up what we have taken?" Samantha seemed shocked by the thought.

Marthe, as leader of the Jade Falcons, did not let her emotions control her actions. "We know this Archer is on Twycross, but he cannot stay there. By now, the rest of Gamma Galaxy will be coming for him. But if they do not defeat him, then, yes, I believe the best course of action is to return to our own worlds."

"Why?"

"Because, Samantha, our honor is at stake. I look down the road to the future. And while it is a long and winding path, you and I know that we invaded the Lyran Alliance to test our warriors' mettle as well as the resolve of the Alliance. Except for Rasalgethi, which we still do not control, none of these holdings is important to us. Continuing to thrust deeper into the Lyran Alliance will gain us nothing."

"It may force this general to come after us, quiaff?" Samantha said.

"Neg. He will not fight us here. He knows that attacking our invasion-corridor holdings could make us appear weak in the eyes of the other Clans. There is more. He is one of Victor Steiner-Davion's people, which means he is no fool. He knows our ways, both on and off the battlefield. How long do you think Vlad of the Wolves will wait when he sees that he can strike toward Twycross from his border and cut our holdings in half?"

Samantha looked angry. "You would have us give up what we have won with honorable blood?"

"Neg, Samantha. We will hold this long string of victories in the Melissia Theater. We will leave behind several galaxies' worth of troops to secure them. The rest will accompany us back to our invasion corridor to rid ourselves of this General Archer and his minions." Marthe refused to use the man's surname, denying him the rank of warrior or peer in her eyes.

"We came so far," Samantha said softly.

"Aff," Marthe said, unable to resist a wistful smile. "But these are not the same Inner Sphere warriors we faced when we first arrived on our crusade to liberate the Inner Sphere. They have learned our ways and constantly find new means to turn our traditions against us. This incursion has gained us much in the way of new resources and skills. Stopping now to consolidate our holdings and to eliminate this new threat is not just logical . . . it is Clanlike, quiaff?"

"It is not the victory I dreamed of," Samantha said.

"Perhaps not. But I would like to face this General Archer in battle. Beating him, a man who crushed the Falcon Guard, would restore some of our honor. And there is more. It would provide a degree of satisfaction." She gave the final word a special emphasis, almost as if she were speaking of some lust of the body.

"Where will you face him?"

"We head for the border," Marthe said. "He will come back, if only for his own supplies. When he does, we will find him and settle this—one way or another."

Samantha's eyes flared wide in pleasure. "It shall be done, my Khan."

"In Flanders, fields of poppies grow,
Between the crosses row by row . . ."

23

Broad Run Delta, Melissia
Jade Falcon Occupation Zone
24 November 3064

The Wolf Clan DropShips fanned out at the last minute, forming a perfect pentagram landing pattern. They landed in the thick sands of the Broad Run Delta, and their landing struts depressed slightly as Khan Kell ordered his forces deployed. Seeing the terrain dotted with copses of trees and other dense brush, he understood why the Jade Falcons had selected it as the venue for the Trial of Possession for the planet Melissia. The deep, wide river would block flanking movements, while the trees offered good cover—for both sides. Phelan appreciated the fact that the Falcon commander had not chosen to fight on the same terrain that General Bryan had chosen as her grave. They were smarter than that.

The Jade Falcon invaders had been using Melissia as a base of operations ever since wrestling it away from Sharon Bryan. Phelan had chosen it for another reason—its position on the map. Christifori and Steiner had managed to pincer the Jade Falcon supply line at Roadside and Black Earth. They hadn't managed to block it, but they had slowed it down. Taking Melissia back would potentially cut off even more the Falcon-captured worlds of Chapultepec and Medellin. If Phelan could take Melissia, it would be much trickier for the Falcons to hold those worlds.

And then he knew he could take them.

"Ranna," Phelan said. "Deploy some of your forces to the east and west to the forks in the river. Have them determine the depth of the water and the flow."

"You have plans for the river?" Ranna asked.

"I am merely assessing the field of this battle," he said, teasing her.

"You *do* have a plan."

"Aye," Phelan said. "The Falcons must have chosen this place for a reason, so I want to learn all I can about it before they arrive."

"The Falcons' Sigma Galaxy suffered some losses on Kikuyu," Ranna said.

"They have had ample time to repair their physical damage. Now, let us see if we can shatter their emotional strength." He tapped on the open comm channel so that the Jade Falcons could hear him. "Galaxy Commander Malthus, I have landed at the designated location. I await the beginning of this trial."

"Phelan Kell," Timur Malthus replied, not using either Phelan's title or the name of his Clan. "Your boldness in coming to Melissia serves your reputation. But you will find that I am not like those other commanders you have faced. My ego will not get the best of me."

"A pity," Phelan replied. "I so looked forward to defeating you as quickly as I have all of the others in this campaign so far."

"Indeed, Kell. This time you have overreached. Khan Marthe Pryde has granted me the chance to end your so-called Clan's threat once and for all."

"I have heard this bravado before, Timur Malthus. I heard it from Star Colonel Daniel Kyle of your Seventh Talon Cluster. He is my bondsman now. If you fight well, you may hope to work beside him scrubbing the mud of this delta off the feet of my 'Mechs.''

Malthus laughed. "We shall see, freebirth scum. We shall see in the morning when my forces arrive. But know this, you will not be my bondsman, Kell. Your genes will be lost forever." Then the comm channel went dead.

Phelan drew a long breath. "Ranna, I want you and your troops to scour every millimeter of this delta. Let's figure out a way to make sure this surat-bait is wrong."

Silver Springs Lava Flows
Hot Springs
Jade Falcon Occupation Zone

Adam wondered why the area known as Silver Springs was so named, as it was far from silvery or spring-like. The ground was black, crusty rock-ash, broken by the occasional outcropping of trees, a smattering of dense jungle, small lakes of brackish water, and jagged rocks. The volcanoes of the nearby Lucas Mountain Range to the west of his position had formed the expanse of Silver Springs. The region was hot, muggy, and from what he had seen, infested with Jade Falcons.

The Fifth Battle Cluster of the Falcons' Epsilon Galaxy did not delay in launching their first attack on his force, striking only thirty minutes after his DropShips had touched down on this blackened hell. They hit hard and fast, taking a toll on the ground armor Felix Blucher had brought with him. Many of his tanks were destroyed within sight of the DropShips while fighting a pitched battle. Then Colonel Anu pulled her forces back as suddenly as she had launched them into battle.

Last night, they hit again. Again, the Jade Falcons

fought furiously for a half an hour, then pulled back. The losses had been significant, but just when Adam would have expected Anu to send in her reserves and press the fight, she had drawn back. Now it was midday, and there was no sign of the Falcons, but Adam knew they were out there . . . biding their time.

Colonel Blucher walked over to him, taking long strides to avoid the deep cracks in the blackened lava flow. Watching his footing, he walked up to the granite rock where Adam stood and saluted.

"Colonel, I take it your troops are positioned on the perimeter?" Adam said.

"Per your orders, General," Blucher replied. "I've also taken the precaution of forming an ad hoc company of fast-moving 'Mechs as a mobile reserve. If the Falcons probe too deep, I can shuffle them to any point on my line in a matter of two minutes."

Adam dusted some gray-black soot off the chest of his jumpsuit. "Everything down here is wet. Leave it to the Falcons to decide to deploy here in the middle of the rainy season."

"I'm not so concerned about the terrain or the weather as I am the tactics they're employing," Blucher said. "They hit us, but pull back just when they should go in for the kill."

"I've been noticing that, too," Adam said. "As a matter of fact, I've been considering changing our deployment so that the next time they attack, we're set to chase them down and finish this contest once and for all." He didn't mention that it was a stand Kinnell had been pushing for.

Colonel Blucher crossed his arms and cradled his chin in thought with one hand. "I can see where that is tempting, General. Only one thing would hold me back from doing it."

"What's that, Colonel?"

"It might be just what the Falcons want us to do."

Adam nodded. "Go on, Colonel . . ."

"There are two reasons you execute a strategy like

the one they've been using. One, you're hoping to tie down the enemy force for a prolonged period. Two, you're trying get their dander up and lure them into a trap.

"If this was a civil war sniper fight or a thrust by the Draconis Combine, the stalling strategy would make sense. It gives a commander time to bring in additional troops. But these are the Jade Falcons we're talking about. They fight honorably as long as we do the same. They don't have a reason to gang up on us. It's not the way they do things."

"I'm listening," Adam said when Blucher seemed to pause.

"That leaves the second reason—to try and get us angry so we do pursue them. Now they're up in those mountains," Blucher said, gesturing to the western range of the Lucas Mountains. "They're probably hoping we'll get frustrated enough to start chasing them. They'll cave in quick, make it look tempting as all hell. We'd follow them into a canyon, a pass, or something like that, then bam!" He slammed his right fist into his left palm. "They drop the hammer on us and take us all out." His Germanic accent became thicker the longer he spoke.

Adam said nothing for a moment. He'd been pondering the enemy's motives for the last day, but Blucher had gone beyond what even he had come up with. "I can see you've been giving this some thought, Colonel."

"Yes, sir," Blucher replied. "I am just doing my job, *ja*?"

"Hell, it sounds like you're doing mine," Adam replied. "I thought they might have figured out that we're linking up with Christifori. Maybe Marthe Pryde wanted to tie us down here to prevent that hook-up."

Blucher nodded. "That's possible, General. I hadn't considered that. Given how limited the Clan intelligence apparatus is, I didn't think that was a viable option."

"Well, if you're right, we're going to have to change our deployment to wear down Star Colonel Anu's forces more with each strike. It will drag out our time on Hot Springs when I had hoped to get in and out of here quickly. But it looks like this will have to become a campaign of defensive fighting for us."

Adam looked off to the mountains in the distance, just visible above a cluster of tall, palm-like trees covered with thick green moss. "If that's their plan, it may have been a mistake to come here in the first place. They may unwittingly prevent us from hooking up with Christifori on Blackjack, as scheduled."

Blucher seemed unshaken. "I've worked alongside Archer Christifori in the past. He's good enough that he could hold out on Blackjack even if we're not there in time."

"Why do you say that? You don't even know his unit's current condition," Adam said.

Blucher smiled broadly. "He would succeed because the price of failure is too great. The Lyran commanders have been misjudging him throughout the civil war. I count myself in that number. Some people have claimed he's a brilliant strategist, but his moves only *appeared* brilliant because of his sheer daring. What people didn't know, and what I did, was that he had no choice but to make do what he did."

"I don't follow," Adam said.

"Have you ever read about the battle of Chancellorsville?"

Adam nodded. "Robert E. Lee. Required reading in every academy, I believe."

"*Ja*, General. Lee was outnumbered by Hooker three to one. In the face of a superior enemy, on terrain of his choosing, he did what most historians have deemed his most brilliant move."

Adam smiled. "I remember studying it. He split his army—twice, if I recall."

"Yes. Violating every military doctrine of the time, Lee divided his forces. It was insane to do so, but he did it. For years, he was considered a genius, but one school of thought says it wasn't so much genius as desperation. Perhaps it wasn't Lee's astuteness, but the fact that he had no other option that made him do what he did."

"You're not comparing Archer Christifori to Robert E. Lee, are you, Colonel?"

Blucher laughed. "No, General Steiner. But what I do know is that since the outbreak of the civil war, the odds have been against Christifori. And no matter what, he always manages to turn the tables. It would be ignorant of us to underestimate his skills. Look at Operation Audacity on paper. In the middle of a civil war, he proposed not to defend, but to go on the offense, into the midst of the Jade Falcons' holdings. If someone had made you such a proposal a year ago, you would have rejected it outright as insane. Now look at us. We're carrying out that plan."

Adam said nothing for a moment. Until this moment, he hadn't really taken the time to understand the military man in Archer Christifori. He couldn't help thinking of him as a media creation, a man deluded by his own press releases. Perhaps that wasn't the case. Maybe there was more to Christifori the general.

Adam looked into the dark eyes of Colonel Blucher. "I appreciate your insights, Colonel," he said quietly.

"Thank you, General."

"Now then, let's you and I draw up a plan for dealing with the Fifth Battle Cluster. And then, let's plan to link up with Archer Christifori. A man that glorious deserves a rescue."

"It's only fair," Blucher said half-jokingly. "He did come to save us once, *ja*?"

"Don't remind me," Adam said.

24

Archer always felt queasy coming out of a hyperspace jump, if only for a moment. It was like riding roller coasters as a boy, when his stomach felt like it was going to fly out of his mouth. And that was exactly how it felt as his task force emerged at the zenith jump point of the Blackjack system, like his guts had been taken for a wild ride. He wasn't complaining, however. It was a small price to pay to travel almost instantaneously across the vast light years of space separating one star system from another.

He didn't feel so philosophical about the high price his task force had paid so far for Operation Audacity. The Third Thorin Regiment had been devastated in the battle with the Falcon Guards. He'd been able to cobble together a battalion's worth of captured Clan hardware and MechWarriors, but their morale was almost shattered. The First Thorin, his core regiment, had suffered losses to its ground armor, infantry, and 'Mech forces, and the injuries filled the hospital bays of the DropShips to capacity. The Muphrid Rangers Regiment had lost several whole companies. The Twentieth Arcturan Guards were down some twenty-five percent of their full force, not including the handful of armor and infantry Archer had left behind on Roadside as additional garrison.

It had taken a week to complete the salvage operations on Twycross. The local population had turned over some supplies, but the Falcons had already gobbled up a lot of what there was to help fuel their assault on the Lyran Alliance. The task force was short of gauss rifle rounds, autocannon ammo, and actuators, but other than that, Archer's units were actually better supplied than when they'd first entered the Falcon OZ. The Avenger techs had managed to repair many of the captured Clan OmniMechs while others were stripped for their high-tech parts and weapons systems. John Kraff described his Muphrid Rangers as, "bastardized-beyond-belief-but-serious-nut-kicking-sons-of-bitches."

Archer had led his regiments back the same way they'd arrived at Twycross, through the Butler system. He had not left a garrison force in-system other than the captured heavy cruiser *Black Talon*. Upon their return, the *Talon* was gone and, almost eerily, the Falcons had not sent in another force to retake the world. Had Phelan sent a naval crew to recover the *Talon*, or had the Jade Falcons retaken the vessel? Or was it simply hidden somewhere in the system? Archer took note of its disappearance, but did not question it aloud. Butler and, for that matter, the *Black Talon*, didn't matter. What mattered was getting to Blackjack for the rendezvous with Adam Steiner.

Afloat on the bridge of the JumpShip *Little Sorrel*, he spun in midair toward Captain Fullerton. "Lee, I need to know what's in the system with us."

Fullerton nodded and quickly gave a string of orders to his officers. The *Little Sorrel* moved out of the immediate area, which was standard procedure when arriving at a jump point. Though the space occupied by system jump points was incredibly large, there was no way of knowing what else, if anything, might suddenly arrive in that same area from another system. And while the odds were against it, no one wanted another JumpShip to materialize in the middle of his or her vessel.

"General," said the comm tech, a young woman whose nameplate read simply Pender, "I'm bouncing a signal off a satellite to get a reading from the nadir jump point. I show no JumpShips or other vessels present, sir."

"What about known pirate jump points?" Archer asked.

"Running through them now, sir," Pender replied. She leaned over the display, her face and body illuminated by its blue and green glow as her fingers danced over the keyboard. "General, the results are negative. I've checked all known pirate coordinates."

Christifori used a bulkhead to give himself enough momentum to swing down to where Katya was standing. His magnetic boots held him in place when his feet touched the deck. He stood there and crossed his arms.

"Adam Steiner isn't here," she said, stating what everyone on the bridge had already guessed.

"It changes nothing," Archer said, looking around at his people. "We're here. Begin detachment procedures. Have the JumpShips move to deploy solar sails and commence recharging."

"Sir!" Pender cried from her station. "General, I am picking up JumpShips materializing at the nadir jump point. Count still coming. Sir, it's three ships and what appears to be a WarShip."

"Good," Archer said, smiling as he threw Katya a look just a hair short of I told you so. "Stand by to send a transmission to General Steiner."

"Sir," Pender said, "I've just confirmed their IFF transponders. The ships are Jade Falcon."

Archer stopped breathing for a moment. "What?"

"Confirmed, General Christifori. It's a Falcon task force, and it looks like they are beginning to deploy to the system."

Field Hospital, Silver Springs Lava Flows
Hot Springs
Jade Falcon Occupation Zone

The fighting for Hot Springs had been brutal, prolonged, and unproductive thus far. Just as Colonel Blucher had predicted, the Falcons had tried to lure Adam into fighting on their terms, but he had refused to do so. As a result, his forces had been hammered at odd intervals, pounded by attempts to goad him into a fast and furious pursuit. It had taken all of his restraint to hold off from such an action.

Walking into the Silver Springs field hospital, Adam approached one of the beds. It was surrounded by field curtains, concealing the occupant from view. A nurse came by, and Adam pointed to the bed. "Is that where the Colonel is?" he asked.

She nodded. "Only a few minutes, General," she said softly, tipping her gaze downward.

Adam pulled open the curtains and saw the battered body of Colonel Anne Sung lying there. The Second Crucis Lancers had been pummeled hard in the last assault by the Falcons. If initial battle damage reports were correct, Colonel Sung in her *Caesar* had tangled directly with Star Colonel Diane Anu, commanding officer of the Golden Talons. As Adam stared down at her burned and broken body, he thought back to the report he'd received.

Colonel Sung had risked her life to buy time for Adam's command company to fall back while under fire. According to one witness, she had almost defeated Anu, but was horribly flash-burned while trying to punch out in the middle of a furious PPC blast of charged particles. Even through the bandages, Adam could see that Sung's right hand was now a stump, wrapped from where her fingers had been up to her neck. Her face was also swathed in gauze except for her mouth and one eye. Her once gray hair was now gone. She was barely alive, and even if she survived, Anne Sung would never pilot a BattleMech in combat again.

"Colonel," Adam said softly to the officer who had been a thorn in his side since the start of the operation. He wasn't even sure she was awake.

"My boys, General," Sung strained to say. "My boys all right?"

"Yes, thanks to you, Colonel. You bought them the time they needed." A sense of awe and profound respect swept over Adam. Here was an officer more dead than alive, and yet all she thought about was her troops. "You almost took out Star Colonel Anu, from what I heard."

Sung's single eye closed in pain and weariness. "Not close. Tough bitch," she said, her words halting. "What day is it?"

"December twelfth."

"General Christifori," Sung said, taking a gulp of air. "Either on Blackjack or on his way now."

Adam nodded, further amazed at Sung's intense devotion to duty, despite her condition and the fact that her mind must certainly be fogged with painkillers. "The Falcons will crumble any time now," he assured her. "As soon as they do, we'll link up with Christifori."

Sung tried to stir, but either didn't have the strength or the will. "Doesn't matter."

"What?" Adam asked softly. "Hooking up with Christifori doesn't matter?"

"No. Hot Springs," she muttered. "None of this matters. Stop the invasion. Nothing else matters." Her last words drifted off to a mutter as she succumbed to sleep.

Adam bowed his head in thought. Here was a woman who had nearly died for him and his command, and her only concerns were her people and her general. Six months ago, Anne Sung had been an enemy. Now, Adam saw a hero to the Lyran Alliance in front of him, and a part of him wished it was him and not her in the bed. He thought he should hate Sung as a traitor, but he simply admired her too much.

"Doesn't matter . . ." came the echo of her words in his mind.

In that moment, Adam realized something. Until now, all he'd wanted was to destroy the Falcons. For years, it had burned in his soul that they had taken Somerset from him, that they'd humiliated the then-Federated Commonwealth so many times on the field of battle. Now, they'd invaded again, and he had believed there was value in defeating Star Colonel Anu's force on Hot Springs. He'd been wrong.

Turning, he slipped through the opening in the curtains, only to find Kommandant-General Seamus Kinnell waiting for him. Adam drew the curtain shut and turned back to his aide.

"How is she?" Kinnell asked.

"Not out of the woods yet," Adam said. "What's the word on the Golden Talons?"

"They've pulled back again. Chances are, they'll hit us again by noon tomorrow. I suggest we rotate in Colonel Blucher's command company into—"

"That won't be necessary," Adam said, waving his hand dismissively.

"Sir?"

"We're leaving Hot Springs. We'll depart under cover of nightfall. If I remember right, a storm front's rolling in, and that'll help conceal our departure." His tone was matter-of-fact.

"Leaving?" Kinnell asked. "Where are we going?"

"Blackjack," Adam replied. "Technically, we'll be a little late, but better late than never."

"Sir, if I may be so bold, perhaps you have not

fully thought through your decision. You don't have to worry about Christifori and his troops. They're rebels who've fought against us. People you know have lost their lives because of traitors like him. Leave him alone on Blackjack. Let the Falcons deal with him. Step away now, and you're already a hero in the eyes of the Archon."

Adam's eyes narrowed. "Politics," he said.

"Sir?"

"The difference between a person like you and one like Sung. Politics. She wants me to go to Blackjack because of honor. I gave Christifori my word. You want me to stay here because of politics. Seeing Sung on the bed reminded me that she's not the enemy. Her injuries were sustained in my name and that of the Alliance. No, it's men like you who are the enemy."

"General!" Kinnell sputtered, his expression one of pure outrage.

"Don't bother yourself, Kinnell. You stand relieved of duty effective immediately."

"Sir, what are you doing?"

"What I should have done months ago. Did you hear me, Kommandant-General? I said you stand relieved of command and duty."

Kinnell just stared at him. Without another word, Adam Steiner turned and left his former aide standing there with his mouth hanging open.

Broad Run Delta, Melissia
Jade Falcon Occupation Zone

Phelan Kell's force huddled in the last clump of trees in the narrow stretch of peninsula that made up the Broad Run Delta. Long days of battling back and forth with the Jade Falcons had slowly and methodically pushed his forces back. They had run out of land.

Forced into a narrow, finger-shaped strip of ground, there was nowhere else to fall back to.

Galaxy Commander Timur Malthus and his command trinary were positioned across a kilometer-long clearing, gathering for the final attack. Phelan knew he'd run out of terrain. Ranna and her people had given better than they'd taken, but the Falcons had bid higher than normal. Apparently, Malthus was willing to sacrifice some of his honor in order to destroy Phelan Kell. That knowledge didn't scare him at all.

In fact, Phelan reveled in it.

As if he had given the order himself, he watched as the Jade Falcons poured out of the woods and into the clearing. On the right and left were the deep waters of the Broad Run River, shimmering in the midday sun. Phelan waited until all of the Falcons emerged, just as his people's long-range weapons went into play. Then he opened the comm channel.

"Galaxy Commander Timur Malthus, this is Khan Phelan Kell."

An arrogant voice came back. "You are beaten, Kell. I have been waiting for this call for three days. Concede the battle. End this senseless waste."

Phelan laughed. "Neg. Check your sensors. How many 'Mechs do you detect?"

Shots continued across the flat open expanse. "Eight. You are grossly outnumbered and outclassed."

Phelan sent a signal on another channel. "Neg, bird-brain. Now, how many 'Mechs do you detect?"

From either side of the open clearing, out of the waters of the Broad Run River, Wolf Clan Omni-Mechs emerged. Phelan smiled. He knew that at least a star's worth of Elementals had worked their way underwater to the rear of the Falcon lines as well, and by now Malthus was detecting them. The Jade Falcons were boxed in, surrounded, and facing more enemies than they could handle.

"You tricked us!" Malthus screamed.

"Aff, I beat you with superior tactics and the fact

that you did not keep count of how many 'Mechs you destroyed over the past few days' fighting. Power down your weapons and concede this fight, Galaxy Commander, and you may yet live. Press on, and the Sigma Galaxy can hold a new Trial of Position to fill your post."

It took a full minute for Timur Malthus to make up his mind. To Phelan Kell, it did not matter. Regardless of the man's decision, the result was the same to him. The world of Melissia once again belonged to the Lyran Alliance.

25

Blackjack Military Academy Ruins
Blackjack
Jade Falcon Occupation Zone
16 December 3064

It was early autumn on the continent of Gray Dusk, where Archer and his force had landed on Blackjack. The trees were just beginning to change color, splashed with bright oranges, dull purples, and pale yellows. From his field tent, a flexiplastic collapsible dome situated near the ruins of a barracks, Archer surveyed the morning and remembered the last time he'd seen these trees and their strange colors. It had been years ago, all the way back to 3048, when he had attended the Blackjack Military Academy.

Any other time, he might have felt some nostalgia, but the fighting on Twycross had purged Archer of his feelings for the past. He had spent several hours shuttling to and from the DropShips visiting the injured after they left the planet. At one point, he'd joined with a tech crew repairing a battered *Atlas*, hoping the physical exertion would clear his mind. His troops probably thought this made him one of them, a hands-on general. The truth was that Archer had to find a way to push down the pain and sadness he felt for the losses they'd sustained. He knew he must stay firmly grounded in the present, where the Jade Falcons were. He would revisit the past later. His losses were bad, but his force had won. That should be enough . . . but was it?

Much had changed in the area of the old Blackjack Military Academy since the days when Archer had been a cadet here. He'd heard the reports of how the Jade Falcons had seized the planet during the initial Clan invasion, crushing the defending students. Then Clan Steel Viper had briefly taken the world from the Falcons, brutally razing the site of the old academy. Soon after, the Falcons had retaken the planet, with no intention of ever letting it go, given its proximity to the border with the Lyran Alliance.

Now that he'd seen the ruins, Archer regretted ordering his regiments to deploy on the site. The academy had been almost leveled, and the few buildings still recognizable as structures were little more than a wall or two and mounds of rubble. The Blackjack Academy HQ building, once large and modern, was now a mere heap of broken, charred bricks and rusted metal, overgrown with dense, thorny vines.

The grounds were the only flat terrain for hundreds of kilometers, which was covered with steep hills sparsely dotted with trees. Ringing the area were low mountains easily traversed in a BattleMech. North of the academy was a semi-cleared area that had previously been the academy training ground. Beyond that was the thick blue ribbon of the Monocacy River. The region was uninhabited, having become almost a wildlife refuge.

If Katya's information was correct, the Jade Falcon task force had gone to ground nearly fifty kilometers north of the Monocacy. Archer had patrols out checking the perimeter, but was in no hurry to engage the enemy, not without some reinforcements. Meanwhile, the Falcons kept the Avenger fighters at bay with combat air patrols. Archer's regiments had not fought a battle since Twycross, and he was worried about them, not so much physically, but mentally. The savaging they'd suffered against the Falcon Gamma Galaxy, and especially the Falcon Guards, had shaken many of the green troops. Even some of the veterans were stunned by the bitter and brutal combat.

Still standing in the doorway of his field tent, Archer was surprised to see Captain Thomas Sherwood, his special operations commander, approaching with another man who appeared to be a beggar. The second man's clothes were tattered and stained with splotches of dark brown and black mud. He was unshaven, and Archer could smell a combination of sweat and urine coming from him even from a distance. Walking behind the pair was Katya Chaffee, her expression dubious as she stared at the beggar from behind.

"What have we got here, Tom?" Archer asked as the trio reached his tent.

"A vagrant, or so we first thought, who was caught by our infantry pickets a little while ago. I figured him to be a camp moocher, looking for a handout. I found him to be much more."

Archer was surprised. The man smiled broadly, shamelessly displaying his yellow teeth. "General Christifori?" he asked in a voice like loose gravel.

"Yes?"

"Only one bird stalks its prey in the night," the man said slowly.

Archer started slightly. He knew the phrase as one he and Anton Gramash had arranged. If this man knew the code, then he was one of the operatives Gramash had scattered throughout the Alliance and the Falcon occupation zone.

"But green is a color that turns men's souls," he replied, giving the counter-phrase.

The man grinned, his dirty face seeming to light up. "Leftenant Joel Jakes," he said, extending his hand.

Archer shook it. "We have a mutual friend, it appears."

"Captain Gramash was worried that a satellite dump might be intercepted by the Falcons. He sent me a series of encrypted messages with orders to personally deliver the information as soon as you got here."

"You're a few days late."

The hobo-spy turned back to Captain Sherwood. "I had to do a little survey work around the Jade Falcons before showing up here. And your pickets are very effective, General."

Archer smiled. "Can I get you something?"

"Coffee, a map, and a table to work on. You've opened quite the can of worms with that victory on Twycross, General Christifori. The Falcons see you as the big prize, and my job is to make sure you have the data you need so you don't end up dead."

"Or as one of their bondsmen," Archer said.

Jakes shook his head. "They aren't here to fight a traditional combat trial with you, General. They want you dead. This is a Trial of Annihilation. I doubt that the Jade Falcon command structure has sanctioned it, however. More likely, they're looking the other way or just plain don't know. That's why you haven't received a batchall from them."

Archer gave Jakes leave to go clean up, and thirty minutes later, the leftenant was back, shaved and showered and wearing a spare jumpsuit. He was a little field-worn, but otherwise every bit an officer of the Federated Suns military.

Waiting for him were Archer and his key staff, consisting of Katya Chaffee, Colonel Gray, Leftenant-Colonel John Kraff, and an injured but functional Colonel Hogan, still heavily bandaged. They stood around the portable holodisplay as Hogan fed in the first chip. A three-dimensional model/map flickered into existence above the projector, showing the area around the ruins of the Blackjack Military Academy.

"First things first," Archer said. "Disposition and composition of the Falcons on Blackjack."

Jakes nodded. "The unit that landed just after you was the Fourth Falcon Striker Cluster, under Star Colonel Jagit Buhallin. Five trinaries. They just linked up yesterday with the Eighth Provisional Garrison Cluster, which was already on Blackjack, but on the Wadswirth Continent and had to be transported here. They're deployed in some hills about fifty-five kilometers north of here, using the village of Orange as their base of operations."

"And separating us," Archer said, pointing at a blue ribbon on the holographic map, "is the Monocacy River. It's about a hundred and fifty meters wide in some spots, with a fast current and a muddy bottom. The banks are rocky, and the river runs deep. One bridge, ninety kilometers upstream. Other than that, the only other crossing in the area is Hinson's Ford. On paper, she's impassible."

"If I were this Star Colonel, I'd want our flank on this side of the river," Gray said. "I'd push across at those points or build my own bridge."

"I agree," Archer said, staring at the map. "So, we need to limit that commander's options. We blow the bridge. That limits them to Hinson's Ford."

"Can you blast it with them on it?" Kraff said to a chorus of chuckles and nods.

Archer joined in, but only briefly. "We can send the Sherwood Foresters across to establish a beachhead and to keep an eye on any Falcon movement. Set up right, they can stay hidden until we need them, then pull off some of their special tricks."

"Combat engineering isn't a Falcon strength," Katya said. "I don't think they'll try and build a bridge."

"We'll keep our eyes peeled anyway, just in case."

"Leftenant Jakes, why haven't they moved on us?" Katya asked.

"The word I get is that Buhallin is waiting for additional forces to arrive in-system in the next few days as part of her bid. Until then, she's content to play the waiting game."

"*More* troops," Colonel Gray half-moaned.

"Yes, but your other task force, under General Steiner, has disappeared," Jakes said. "The Falcons aren't sure if they're headed this way. On top of that, they're apparently missing one of their WarShips." He gave Archer a quick wink. "I'm willing to bet they're bringing in naval support, just in case the *Black Talon* shows up."

"Fat damn chance of that," Kraff said bitterly. "I guess you haven't heard, Leftenant, but we have apparently misplaced our bleeding WarShip."

Jakes smiled. "No, you haven't, sir. The *Black Talon* has been renamed the *Black Paw*. She's in the Blackjack system, hidden in the asteroid belt and running in low-power mode. The Falcons don't know it, so it's something of a trump card. I have the communications protocols for you, General, if you want to contact her."

Archer allowed himself a broad smile. Finally, something was going right. "You mentioned General Steiner. Where is he?"

Jakes punched two buttons on the holographic projector and brought up a map of the Falcon/Alliance border. "He landed on Hot Springs and tangled with the Falcons there for weeks. From what I gather, he was pretty close to victory. Then they just up and took off. So far, we have no sign of them. Hot Springs is still a Falcon holding."

"And we have no idea of Adam's location?"

"No, sir," Jakes said.

"How about Phelan Kell?"

"He managed to take back Melissia from the Falcons a week or so back. I don't know the last bit of data you received, sir, but the Falcons struck at Rasalgethi. The fighting is still bitter there, but our forces seem to be holding on. It's dragging out because Snord's Irregulars, apparently of their own accord, joined in the fight on our side . . . tipping the scales."

Archer smiled. The Irregulars had agreed to stay out of the civil war, but a chance to engage the Jade Falcons must have been too good for them to pass up.

Jakes continued. "The Com Guard 388th Division under Precentor Shillery hit Blair Athol and are fighting with the Provisional Garrison Cluster there."

"So, where are Kell and his Wolves now?" Colonel Hogan asked. "Maybe they're headed this way?"

"Unknown, sir . . . the same as General Steiner."

"Has the Falcon incursion stalled or halted at all?" Archer asked, hopeful.

Leftenant Jakes shrugged. "It's possible, General. Three weeks ago, they struck at Adelaide. The local militia put up a good fight, but they lost. Since then, the Falcons have stopped, but there's no way to confirm if it's because of Operation Audacity or if they're simply catching their breath for the next move."

"What about the civil war?" Archer asked. "We've been cut off from any news for a long time."

"Not so good, sir. Prince Victor's forces are being driven back on Tikonov. It's not looking good."

Archer heard the sadness in the younger man's voice, and he shared it. Still more were dying in this endless circle of fighting.

"Oh, and the Star League has elected a new First Lord," Jakes said.

Kraff laughed out loud. "As long as it's not Katherine, who cares?" A few nervous chuckles seconded that.

Archer held up his hands for silence. "We can't assume that the Falcons are stupid or are just going to sit back and wait for us to die. We need to get the academy airfield serviceable for our fighters. We need to get our people back into fighting trim. If Leftenant

Jakes is right, we've got some time while the Falcon commander waits for additional reinforcements to bid. So, I want everyone to prepare a readiness report and get it to Jakes to pass back to his superiors."

His gaze swept the command tent interior, catching the eyes of each officer present. "We came to Blackjack because it's on the border and a good place to inflict some pain on the Falcons. With us squatting here, on their ground, they have to be close to stopping their push into the Alliance. All we have to do is get their attention—and win."

26

Archer stared at the bridge over the Monocacy River from the cockpit of his *Penetrator*, using the magnification system to bring it into tighter, clearer focus. The river itself was visible just below the steep rock embankments on either side. The highway bridge was the only way to cross the water for kilometers, and he wanted it blown up . . . when the time was right.

To that end, he'd deployed his infantry and supporting forces several days ago. He couldn't say why he was sure the Jade Falcons would try to turn his flank using the bridge, but it was a hunch that had tried his patience over the last five days.

And if Captain Sherwood was right, that hunch was about to pay off. The Sherwood Foresters were the Avengers' special-forces company for unusual missions or operations requiring unorthodox tactics. Thanks to the spywork of Gramash's network, Archer knew every trail, road, creek, hill, valley, and rock in the area, and he'd posted the Foresters across the

Monocacy River with the dangerous task of keeping tabs on the Falcons. Sherwood had found ample nooks and crannies in which to hide.

When they began their flanking move across the river, the Falcons were far from subtle. Archer had received a coded message from Sherwood that a large, cluster-size force was moving down the highway to the bridge. They were traveling in twos through the tree line along the highway on the far bank. Archer watched as at least four of the deadly, long-range *Kraken* BattleMechs deployed on either side of the bridge. A star of lightweight *Vixen*s moved out first, jogging across the bridge toward his position. They looked like second-line hardware, most likely from the provisional garrison cluster.

A full binary of 'Mechs moved onto the bridge, with a line of other 'Mechs holding in column formation on the side. The Falcon commander was cautious, sending one binary at a time across the bridge, just in case a trap was waiting for him.

One binary, ten 'Mechs, was worth the cost. "Icepick One, this is General Christifori," Archer said, signaling Sergeant Major Adrian Glyndon, who commanded the infantry at the base of the bridge. "I was hoping to get more than just a couple of lances' worth on the bridge, but we'll have to take what we can get."

"Understood, sir," she replied. The lead pair of *Vixen*s was near their side of the river. "Permission to give them a bath?"

"Granted," Archer replied.

When the explosion came, it wasn't a single, massive blast, which was more the stuff of holovid dramas. Beginning at either end of the bridge and racing toward the center, it arrived as a wave of tiny little blasts at each of the pylons that supported the bridge. The ferrocrete buckled like a rolling wave from either side, slamming into the middle as the span simply disintegrated under the Falcon 'Mechs. The two lead *Vixen*s seemed to hop over the crumbling bridge just in time, landing on the far embankment. The others weren't as lucky, dropping unceremoniously into the river, along with tons of debris from the bridge itself.

The two warriors piloting the *Vixen*s that made it across must have felt lucky, but only for an instant or two. Icepick Company's infantry were not intimidated by BattleMechs; they were trained to take them out. Before the *Vixen*s could get their bearings, three platoons of infantry opened fire at them with man-pack PPCs and short-range missiles tipped with Inferno warheads. The missiles splattered their cargo all over the light green BattleMechs, igniting them in a millisecond and turning the *Vixen*s into fiery statues.

The war machines reeled, flames lapping up their torsos as if they were scarecrows on fire. The *Kraken*s on the far shore opened fire to provide some assistance, pouring autocannon rounds along the rocky embankments all around the Avenger infantry company, but it was no real help for the now-isolated *Vixen*s. Archer locked on to one of the *Kraken*s and fired his extended-range lasers, stabbing the larger 'Mech with two deep crimson beams.

One of the trapped Jade Falcons pounced on an SRM carrier that had drifted too close to the fighting. Its lasers mauled the missile racks on the top, and Archer watched in agony as the ammo inside the carrier cooked off, sending infantry and vehicle parts flying into the air.

He aimed again at the *Kraken* he had hit previously and fired, again hitting with both of his lasers. Again, it seemed to provoke the enemy. When Archer glanced down, he saw that the *Vixen* that had taken out the SRM carrier was already down, a raging inferno of orange flames and billowing black smoke on the ramp to the bridge.

The remaining *Vixen* was attempting to move along the edge of the river as tanks and infantry poured fire into it. Its machine guns raked one infantry foxhole, quelling all motion and fire from there. Archer didn't have to be there to know that the platoon was dead or dying. The *Vixen*'s large pulse laser tore through the top of one of the heavy APCs on the embankment, half-hidden in a cluster of rocks along the road. It attempted to get away, but the *Vixen* followed up with a set of quick kicks that left the vehicle belching white-gray smoke into the air.

For a moment, it looked as if the *Vixen* might just make it. The fire from the Inferno's napalm seemed to be slowing it, but the flames went out on its arms and legs as they consumed their fuel. As it moved, however, the 'Mech put enough distance between the infantry and itself to diminish their damage, if not their zeal.

The *Vixen*'s MechWarrior next turned to face a Chevalier light tank. Firing its medium extended-range lasers and its large pulse laser into the tank at close range was more than enough to overwhelm the small wheeled vehicle. Archer watched as it tried to back up along the curve in the road, putting it out of his line of sight. What the *Vixen* didn't know was that the previously captured *Goshawk* waited around the bend. He didn't see the results of the fighting, but he saw the light show of crimson beams and emerald bursts from lasers. In a matter of minutes, the firing stopped. Even the *Kraken*s pulled back. Silence filled the air as he mentally tallied the losses.

He switched his comm channel and spoke into his neurohelmet mic. "Katya, we've blown the bridge over the Monocacy and have taken out ten enemy 'Mechs." He paused for a moment, regretting what he had to say next. "Losses were acceptable and less than the Falcons took."

"They probed the ford at the same time," Katya reported back. "Colonel Gray's people took the brunt of it. I don't have word yet on the Falcon losses, but we're down at least a company of 'Mechs."

"What about our fighters?"

"Our combat air patrol has confirmed the arrival of

another cluster in system. They're five days from landing, General. Our recon flights were engaged by a star of Falcon *Visigoth*s and forced to retire, with the loss of two fighters."

Archer bit his lip. He wanted to ask Katya why she hadn't contacted him regarding the probe attempt or the fighter battle, but he knew the answer to the question. His people had things under control. He wasn't needed there, and his knowledge of the probing action wouldn't have changed a thing. It bothered him, but he knew that this was part of the burden of the rank he wore. He couldn't be in every fight at the same time.

For a long moment, he wished he were a major again, leading MechWarriors into battle rather than directing planet-wide operations. Then he purged that thought. The past was gone. This fight would be fought and won based on him being a good general, not a major.

The odds were fair, even in his favor, at this point, but another cluster was burning in system. Their arrival would alter the balance of power. And the Jade Falcons were not playing the way he'd expected. They had not rushed into battle against him, but were taking their time. Jakes had it right. They intended to avenge their loss on Twycross, to pay him back with the destruction of his force.

Archer glanced upward at the sky. *Adam Steiner. Wherever you are, you'd better get here soon.*

27

Blackjack Military Academy Ruins
Blackjack
Jade Falcon Occupation Zone
21 December 3064

"This is Stonewall One," barked company commander Captain "Wild Willy" Hunt, his voice filled with excitement. "They're falling back!"

Archer understood the feeling. At least once a day, the Falcons had tried to cross the river at Hinson's Ford. Each day, he had mounted his *Penetrator* at the command post in the ruins of the old military academy, and prepared to go and face them himself. Each time, the Falcons had pulled back.

He was about to power down and dismount when another voice, that of Katya Chaffee, came over the comm channel. "Like hell, Stonewall One. I'm showing a large number of magnetic and heat signatures across the river. I think they're coming en masse."

Archer's comm channel suddenly sparked with activity, and every muscle in his body seemed to tense up.

"Elementals! The right flank is turned," howled the

voice of John Kraff. "Jumpin' Jesus-H.-Christ-Almighty! Odessa Guards, turn to the right and fall back by numbers! Colonel, get me some air cover on the right and have the infantry start marking artillery targets."

Katya's voice was firm, unwavering. "Sledgehammer Company, switch to Thunder LRMs for the launchers. Icepick One, get your people painting targets. White Tigers, get your TAG folks in position and assume fire control of the area."

Archer wasn't about to leave his cockpit now. He throttled up his *Penetrator* and charged off for Hinson's Ford. Moving at a near gallop for the bird-like 'Mech, he took the worn trail toward the ford. Things had been going all right for a day or two. The Falcons had tried the ford a few times, but never in any real force. Archer was sure they were stalling, waiting for the arrival of the DropShips bringing the additional cluster. Now that they had, the real fun was going to begin.

Plowing through a thin grove of saplings that barely reached the low-slung head of his BattleMech, he saw his first hint of the fighting up ahead. A scarlet laser blast stabbed upward into the sky from the other side of the next line of hills. A missed shot, but a shot nevertheless.

His heart pounded as he started up from the base of the hill-line. His thoughts turned to Adam Steiner, and he forced himself to believe that he had *not* been betrayed. Left on Blackjack with no reinforcements, his units might be crushed by the Falcons. He had to trust that not even Adam Steiner's hatred of Prince Victor would allow him to do that.

He crested the hill and saw the battle raging below. One of the *Behemoth*s that he had captured on Graceland was covered with at least a star's worth of Elementals, each ripping the massive machine apart while the battle raged around them. A *Hauptmann* from the Twentieth Arcturan Guards was pouring fire into a Falcon *Night Gyr*, the air between them filled with raw, brilliant laser fire and splashes of melted armor plating. A flash of white PPC fire lashed into a Myrmidon medium tank, devouring almost half of the armor on its right side. Archer lined up a shot at a *Kraken* that was attempting to seize the high ground on the far ridge line to pour its fire down on the battle. He caught the 'Mech in the rear as it was ascending the hill. One of his shots burrowed deep into the armor and knocked the 'Mech nearly flat on its face.

"Katya," Archer said on the comm channel, "how bad is it?"

"I owe Colonel Gray a beer or two," Katya said. "She tossed in enough for us to stem the tide. The Falcons seem to be pulling back to a beachhead on our side of the river."

Archer fired at the *Kraken* at long range with his pulse lasers, in three separate, paired salvos. A third of his shots missed, but the others tore into the side of the already damaged 'Mech, ripping away what armor remained on its left side and arm. The air in the cockpit was suddenly almost too hot to breathe, and he felt the gurgle of his cooling vest as it began to pump, bleeding away some of the heat from his body. He watched as the *Behemoth* shook off the last Elemental, then fell on its side, crushing the genetically engineered warrior under its massive bulk.

"They've lost their momentum," Archer said to Katya.

"But they're across the river."

He paused as his large lasers came on line. Then he jostled his targeting reticle onto the *Kraken* and fired each of his large lasers, one at a time; just as the Kraken attempted to fire down at the grounded *Behemoth*. The ruby beams found their mark. One took off the left arm of the *Kraken*, sending it rolling down the hill, throwing up sod and smoke on the way. The other stabbed into the 'Mech's left side, passing through the fragmented remains of armor and burrowing deep into the 'Mech's chest. Archer's sensors painted a massive heat spike, and then he watched as the warrior lost whatever control he had left. The *Kraken* tottered, then plunged head-first down the hillside, leaving a trail of coolant and pieces of armor in the gully it dug as it went.

"Katya, do you and Gray think you can hold the Falcons in a pocket along the river for six hours or so?"

"I have no idea, General. I think they might just be holding on their own, waiting for their reinforcements to move into position. If that's the case, yes. If not, well, it's hard to say. What have you got in mind?"

He drew a long breath. "Two ideas actually." He switched to a different channel that tied him in with the Sherwood Foresters. "Tom, this is General Christifori on discreet."

"Yes, sir."

"You've got the green light. You know what to do."

"Yes, sir," Sherwood said calmly.

Archer switched to another channel and popped the visor on his neurohelmet so that he could rub his temple. With the other hand, he reached into a pocket of his shorts and pulled out a tiny card with the communications protocol that Leftenant Jakes had provided him. He punched in the code manually, slowly, methodically. There was a momentary hiss in his ears, then a voice from space spoke to him. "This is Star Captain Rudolph Mehta of the Wolf Heavy Cruiser *Black Paw* on secured channel 211."

"This is General Christifori," Archer said slowly.

"General, you have my thanks for this fine vessel that you provided Khan Kell," Rudolph Mehta said.

"Thank you for being in the neighborhood. I am in need of a favor."

"I assumed as much, or you would not have called. What can I do for you, General?"

"I need you to move in-system and conduct an orbital bombardment. My people on the scene will relay you the coordinates."

"That is not customary for formal Trials, General," Mehta said.

"I understand, but the Falcons are waging a Trial of Annihilation against me and my people."

"Those commanders are acting without the sanction of the High Council of the Clans. This Trial is invalid. It lacks honor becoming Clansmen. For that, we can assist you in making them pay."

"As the target of that trial, I am forced to agree with you, Captain."

"Very well, sir. The Jade Falcons have deployed this vessel's former sister ship, the *White Talon,* in this system. They will detect us as soon as we move. I should be able to get off a few shots for you before I am forced to deal with them."

"Understood," Archer replied. "I appreciate your help."

"Aye, General. And I appreciate this fine ship. Mehta out."

Captain Thomas Sherwood surveyed the tiny village of Orange from his cockpit, able to make out the field gantries of a repair facility at the edge of the cluster of buildings that comprised the community. Nearby were several field ammo-storage containers, large hexagonal-shaped tubes filled with missile and auto-cannon ammunition. There was a lot of activity in the area, damaged 'Mechs being brought back either under their own power or being carried on massive, truck-like Prime Haulers. Techs bustled everywhere, slapping on replacement armor plates. Wisps of smoke from the repair torches rose up in a dozen places.

Though Sherwood had checked out the site three times, he had yet to devise a good way to approach it. His company consisted of three platoons of infantry, a lance of vehicles, and a lance of BattleMechs, all of them behind enemy lines right now, in the heart of the enemy base camp. He had gotten this far inside the perimeter of their defenses using a pair of captured Falcon 'Mechs and Inner Sphere 'Mechs fitted with captured Falcon IFF transponders. Getting in, he knew, was only half the problem. Getting out would be another story.

He had come in with only his lance of 'Mechs and two squads of infantry. The ground-pounders would plant explosives throughout the area with the intent of crippling the base. Some had already been planted alongside the ammo-storage containers. Other bombs, with timers set to go off hours later, had also been concealed to sow confusion in the Falcon ranks for some time to come.

The 'Mechs would take on the repair gantries, wreaking havoc before escaping back into the forest. There, the supporting armor and infantry lay in wait, ready to ambush any Falcon pursuit.

Sherwood edged up the throttle on the *Vulture* replacing the *Nightsky* he usually piloted, and stepped out of the clump of trees that had hidden him. To a casual observer, the *Vulture* would look like any other Falcon 'Mech. He moved to the right, into the open, followed by his lancemates. Slowly, quietly, and carefully, he used his joystick to bring the first repair gantry into his sights. In the gantry was a *Stooping Hawk*, covered with techs. It was the first time he had seen one of these 'Mechs, and he marveled at its sleek outline. Destroying it almost seemed a shame.

"Forester One to Robin's Merry Men," he said. "On my mark . . . engage!" Almost methodically, he fired his long- and short-range missiles at the gantry and the 'Mech it serviced. The explosions and fire were so stunning and bright that he almost didn't notice the approach of the Elementals bearing down on him and his lancemates.

Star Captain Rudolph Mehta sat in the raised center seat of his ship's Combat Information Center and studied the display. He ignored the replacement hardware, the black scars on the walls, the wiring literally taped to the replacement bulkheads. It had taken a lot to get the CIC on the former Jade Falcon vessel operational again, and much of the work was still being done by the prize crew.

"We're only going to get one chance at this," he said to the fire control officer. "Any change from the *White Talon*?"

"Aff, Captain. Missile bay doors are now opening," the tactical officer said.

"Good." Mehta turned to the man next to him, an older man who stood regally, but wore a uniform lacking any insignia. His only mark of rank was a small white chord tied around his wrist.

"Bondsman," Mehta barked. "The captain of the *White Talon*—how will she react when we fire on the surface?"

Former Star Admiral Martin Thastus, now a mere bondsman to Rudolph Mehta, stood at parade rest. "Captain Boyington Von Jankmon is known for over-reacting and for pushing her vessel past its capabilities. It is in her bloodline. I believe she will come straight at you as fast as possible. For her, speed to engagement will be more important than her positioning upon entering the battle."

"Excellent. Bring us into a low orbit—at least she won't be able to get under us. Stand by for bombardment at the coordinates we are getting from ground control. As soon as we fire, execute a lateral starboard battle roll, and swing us to two-five-three mark-four and cut our speed. Missile batteries, you may fire at the *Talon* as soon as she's in range. Have the port batteries stand by to engage the *Talon* as soon as they come into the line of targeting."

"Aye, Captain," the weapons control officer said. "Starboard batteries are prepared for orbital bombardment in five . . . four . . . three . . . two . . . one . . ." The air in the CIC was electric with tension. "Fire!"

The ship's massive lasers and naval autocannon

barked and whined as they disgorged their deadly energy downward at the planet's surface. The crew in the CIC held onto their workstations as the ship began its intricate roll.

"General," Colonel Gray said in an almost pleading voice, "a company of my tanks and a company of 'Mechs just slammed into that beachhead and were slaughtered. The Falcons are in too tight for us to push them out."

Archer turned his *Penetrator* to look to the north. "I understand, Colonel, but we have to hold them there."

"General, those troops have been wiped out. Only two of my BattleMechs got out of there intact." Gray's own *Barghest* was riddled from long- and short-range missile blasts, and a glancing PPC strike had left a deep scar along its right leg.

Archer didn't have to check the cockpit chronograph to know what time it was. In the distance, the air lit up. It looked at first like the sun bursting through storm clouds, but then the light continued to get brighter. There was a rumble like thunder, and Blackjack itself seemed to moan. A black and brown mushroom cloud boiled up from Hinson's Ford, mixed with steam from the shots that had blasted the river.

"What the hell . . ." Gray said.

"Pour them in, Colonel," Archer said. "That was an orbital bombardment from the *Black Paw*. Your troops held the Falcons in place. Now let's push them into the river if we can."

"Star Captain, I confirm seven salvo hits and damage. She's lost power," the tactical officer said. The smell of ozone was still in the air as Star Captain Mehta looked at the tactical display from his seat. The holo-image flickered occasionally, a result of the battle he had been fighting for the last two hours. The image on the screen was of a battered Aegis Heavy Cruiser, with an enormous clump of ice along its spine, the result of a hit. The body of the vessel was bent, as if it had been melted or simply violently twisted.

The two ships had inflicted a great deal of damage on each other. The *White Talon* had dove in fast, almost skimming the atmosphere of Blackjack in pursuit of the *Paw*. Mehta had brought his ship perpendicular to her path, letting his port and starboard batters maul her quickly. The *Talon*'s anti-ship missiles had wreaked havoc, but in the end, it was his broadsides that had carried the day. The Falcon ship was now apparently adrift.

"A trick?" he asked of his bondsman, the former Falcon star admiral.

Martin Thastus shook his head. "The captain of that ship was never so original. If her power levels are low, they are low because of damage you have inflicted. In two more orbits, she will begin to lose hull integrity and burn up."

"We are not much better off. I have lost everything in the port weapons bays, and starboard reports they can barely spit, let alone fire."

"We are picking up some lifeboat launches, Star Captain," his sensors officer called out.

Before Rudolph Mehta could react, he heard the warning from the long-range sensors station and pivoted his chair toward it. "Report."

"We have detected the arrival of multiple JumpShips at a pirate point bearing one-one-three mark-two," the tech said. "Four JumpShips have emerged from hyperspace."

Star Captain Mehta licked his lips in thought. "Transponders?"

"The vessels are showing as belonging to the Lyran Alliance."

Mehta smiled broadly. "Comm officer, send a coded message to General Christifori. Inform him that we think General Steiner has just arrived in the system."

28

Blackjack Military Academy Ruins
Blackjack
Jade Falcon Occupation Zone
24 December 3064

The *Fire Falcon* OmniMech was an emerald blur as it crossed Archer's field of fire. He triggered three of his medium pulse lasers, but only one managed to do any damage. The others tore up the sod and rocks near the ruins of the old military academy, blasting brickwork that had already been turned to rubble years earlier. The damage he did to the *Fire Falcon* was minimal as it turned just enough to unleash its Streak short-range missile pack. Three of the quad-launch of missiles found their mark in his chest, blasting away some of the dull gray replacement armor. One chunk got twisted back by the blast, and a few strands of myomer hung from the jagged metal.

Archer spotted a small hovercraft, a Savannah Master, making a quick pass at the tiny *Fire Falcon*, its small laser blasting away at the 'Mech's rear armor as it went. The Jade Falcon warrior simply ignored it, lining up on Archer's *Penetrator* and blasting away with his medium and small lasers.

The small lasers sent melted scars up the *Penetrator*'s right leg just above the knee while the two medium lasers and the medium pulse laser worked over the right and center torso of his already battered 'Mech. Glancing down from his cockpit, Archer saw, with some twisted satisfaction, that the jagged piece of armor torn by the missile blast had been melted away cleanly by the laser.

This ends now, he vowed. Bringing his large lasers into play, he heard the seductive tone of weapons lock and unleashed the weapons on the *Fire Falcon*. The capacitors whined as they discharged, and the scarlet lances tore into the left arm and side of the small scout 'Mech. The leg was seared off just below the kneecap, and the hit to the 'Mech's side dug deep. A stream of black and gray smoke billowed from the gash, and the *Fire Falcon* quaked for a moment, then toppled over. Archer wasn't sure if whether it was because of the hit to the leg or internal damage, but he didn't care.

He glanced over at the Savannah Master as it swung just in front of him, doing a fast victory spin. "Thanks for the assistance," he said, wondering where the vehicle had come from. Then he saw the insignia of a green bowman on the side. "You're with the Sherwood Foresters?"

"Corporal Franks, General," a voice replied almost gleefully.

"Any word on Captain Sherwood?"

There was a pause. "Sir, we just re-crossed the river at the ford. Had to fight our way across. What a mess. That bombardment turned the terrain over there into a chunk of hell."

"How many made it?"

"The captain and another 'Mech, myself, and one platoon of infantry."

Archer closed his eyes, the news of even more losses like a blow. "Thanks again, Corporal," he said, glancing over at the fallen *Fire Falcon*. He saw the unit insignia on its side, a golden falcon holding a spear in the air. His mind raced. What unit was that? Then he remembered. He had seen it not so long ago, on Twycross. The mark of the First Falcon Hussars, a sister unit to the Falcon Guards.

"Katya," he said into his mic, "we've driven them out of the command post. They damn near overran us here. I've seen one of the new unit's 'Mechs . . . the First Falcon Hussars."

"You'd think Gamma Galaxy would be tired of us by now," she said, sounding weary.

"How are we holding up?"

"Not so good. We're getting plastered."

"Maybe we should fall back, regroup."

"Trying to do that at this stage would cost us dearly. Any word on General Steiner?"

Archer winced slightly at the question. It had been two days since Steiner had arrived on Blackjack, but there had still been no word from him. Archer continued to suppress the thought that Adam Steiner might betray him, but the other officer's lack of communication didn't make sense. "Nothing yet. Probably planning to make a grand entrance."

"Well, he'd better do it soon," Katya said, "or he can break out the shovels for the mass funeral." She was quiet for a moment, then, "Oh God, here they come."

"Size?"

"This is the big push," she said, a hint of desperation in her tone.

The muscles in Archer's shoulders and neck ached with tension. He was about to order up his command company and whatever reserves he could muster when he heard a roar just above the treetops . . . a wave of aerospace fighters heading north, toward the battle. Some were hard to make out, but a pair of *Sabutais*—Clan-made—were outlined against the sun of midday. Falcon fighters. The situation was about to get more desperate.

Then another 'Mech moved up alongside him almost casually, and Archer glanced at it through one side of his viewscreen. Standing only fifteen meters away was a *Thunder Hawk*, covered with replacement armor, battered but battle-ready. The insignia on the left chest portrayed a running *Zeus* BattleMech against the outline of a rising sun—the symbol of the Fourteenth Donegal Guards RCT. Archer knew that unit. It was Adam Steiner's personal command.

He grinned. "General Steiner, you sure took your time getting here . . . but damn it's good to see you."

"What was that line you used on me back on Chapultepec when I was waiting for your help?" Steiner answered. " 'Hold onto your brass?' "

Archer wanted to laugh, but not right now. "I should've held my tongue. General Steiner, allow me to welcome you to Blackjack on behalf of the Avengers and the Twentieth Arcturan Guards."

"I've got the Ninth Lyran Regulars and Colonel Blucher's Hodge Podges dropping along the river to the west of Orange. The Falcons may be pressing forward, but their base is about to crumble."

"Those fighters yours?" Archer asked.

"Some. Most are from the *Black Paw*. She's badly damaged, but her fighters and pilots are fine. Star Captain Rudolph Mehta sent some, with his compliments."

"I'll inform my commands that you and your forces are on the field. If you'll do the honors and take the right flank, I can handle the center and left."

"Very well, Christifori," Steiner said, still avoiding Archer's title. "Have your exec coordinate with mine—Colonel Blucher."

"I hope nothing happened to Kommandant-General Kinnell?"

"He's been relieved of command," Steiner replied flatly. "We'd better get to the battle zone before there's no Falcons left to fight." Then his *Thunder Hawk* lumbered past Archer, heading north.

Archer shut off his comm channel for a moment and, in the privacy of his cockpit, allowed himself a loud, whooping yell, the kind that had not crossed his lips since his early days in the Tenth Lyran Guards. It was the kind of cry that left the throat raw, that had no words, but stirred the soul. With a heart full of hope, he broke his *Penetrator* into a full run to join the battle.

He reached the fighting on a small, grass-covered knoll overlooking the Monocacy River. From the high ground, he could see Hinson's Ford and the area where the orbital bombardment had turned the light woods into a blackened moonscape. Craters dotted the terrain, and burned, spike-like tree stumps stabbed upward in false defiance of the force that had been unleashed on them from orbit.

In the middle of the now-muddied grounds, the Falcon offense was grinding to a stymied halt. Archer watched as a *Masakari*, its right arm no more than a blasted-off stump, poured what firepower it still had into a Ninth Lyran Regular *Blitzkrieg*. Firing on it, Archer hit the *Masakari* in the rear as the *Blitzkrieg* tore into its front. Spinning madly in place, the *Masakari* dropped. When it hit the ground, an infantryman scampered over it, firing at a nearby *Koshi*.

Archer's sensors blared out a threat warning as a wave of missiles raced up the knoll. He attempted to engage his anti-missile system, which roared out in front of him, but it was too late to prevent most of the damage. The Falcon warrior's aim had been true, and the wave of missiles smashed into Archer's front with black and orange fury.

Damn, Archer thought, angry at himself for not paying closer attention. His head rang, and he felt the *Penetrator* totter. He attempted to compensate, but another blast, a PPC, tore into his right leg, and he lost his balance. For a moment, he tunnel-visioned, then the *Penetrator* fell backward, sprawling atop the grassy knoll.

The sound of rolling thunder was in his ears, some of it in his head, some of it from the battle outside of his cockpit. He forced his eyes open and saw a wave of warning lights, yellow and red, from the damage display. They told him he was still operational but that his armor had been torn apart. Looking upward, he saw a single red laser beam pass over his head by less than a meter.

Using the foot pedals, he rocked his *Penetrator* onto its side, and slowly, deliberately, rose to his feet. His stomach pitched slightly as the BattleMech righted itself, but worse than that, he felt like a fool. Here he was a major general, and he'd gotten knocked on his butt in front of his troops. And it was his own damn fault for leading from the front.

At his side was a *Canis* BattleMech, a Jade Falcon machine, but his targeting and tracking system painted it as friendly. It wasn't firing at him, but across the river. A quick glance showed Archer that the *Canis* wore the tiger-in-the-grass emblem of the Fifteenth Arcturan Guards. He knew the unit well. It was the same one to which he'd been attached on Thorin at the start of his fight against the Archon Princess. It was a top-notch unit, and he had beat them. The 'Mech must have been captured by Adam's people. He tapped at his controls, activating the laser comm system to transmit to the warrior next to him.

"Thanks for the cover fire," he said.

"No problem, General," came a voice that Archer recognized almost instantly.

"Colonel Blucher?"

"Yes, sir."

Archer felt even more foolish now. Blucher's career had plummeted when Archer had defeated him on Thorin. Now, on Blackjack, he had come to save

Archer. "Well, this really is a surprise," he said. "I never expected to find you in a captured Falcon 'Mech."

"General, the Falcons seem to be falling back," Blucher said.

Archer glanced around and saw, half-concealed in the hills and trees, the last glimpse of the Jade Falcons starting to pull away from the scene of the fighting. He was tempted to pursue, but his forces were already doing that. Occasional stray shots burst above the tree line in the distance, telling him that the Falcons were not breaking away cleanly. But they were leaving.

"Colonel. Thank you for coming up here and helping. You didn't have to do that."

"You're wrong, sir. I did. Since we first met on Thorin, I had hoped to fight beside you. I got to do that today. It meant a lot to me."

Archer didn't know what to say, but another incoming message intervened. "General Christifori, this is Star Captain Rudolph Mehta of the *Black Paw* on secured channel two."

"Roger that, Star Captain. This is Christifori."

"General, we detected another JumpShip entering the system about twenty minutes ago. I just received a broadcast tagged for you. I am using our laser relay to beam the connection to you now."

Archer switched over to his secondary display and saw the image of a stern woman dressed in a dark green uniform replete with a formal cape in lighter green. He tied in another channel to the command line, linking in Adam Steiner's *Thunder Hawk*. The woman on the display had a muscular physique, and her presence, even on his cockpit's tiny video screen, seemed imposing, almost threatening. Her face was intelligent, but the fierce look in her eyes was all Jade Falcon. Archer leaned back in his command console and stared intently at the image intently.

"You are General Christifori, quiaff?" she asked in a husky voice.

"Yes," he replied, wondering for a moment if additional Jade Falcon reinforcements had just arrived.

"I am saKhan Samantha Clees of Clan Jade Falcon," she said.

Archer squinted slightly. He had seen her face in previous intelligence reports, but the tiny image on his display was different, harder to make out.

"What can I do for you?" he asked as though there was nothing unusual about this unexpected conversation.

"I have ordered our forces on Blackjack to break off. This Trial of Annihilation did not have the sanction of either Khan Pryde, myself, or the Clan leadership."

So, that was the reason the Falcons had not challenged Archer. They were going to pay him back for Twycross and in his destruction, all evidence would be lost.

"Khan Pryde has asked that I escort you and your command staff to a meeting," she added.

Archer cocked his head slightly, doubting that the tiny camera in his cockpit would convey his look of surprise inside his neurohelmet. "And, if I may, the purpose of this meeting?"

She shifted in place, and her expression clouded briefly. "Khan Pryde received your message. She thinks a parlay may be in order." Archer could see that uttering those words did not come easy for her. Negotiation as part of the Clan bidding process was not unheard of, but negotiating peace had no place in their warrior culture.

"And where is this meeting to take place?"

"Fighting continues on Blair Atholl. Marthe Pryde is en route there now to witness the results of that Trial. She suggested we meet there."

Archer paused to consider the implications. "And what of my regiments while we are making this trip?"

"I have been authorized to not only grant you saf-con to Blair Atholl, but I have issued an order to halt all offensive operations along our front until you have met with the Khan."

Archer couldn't resist a smile of satisfaction. "Very well," he said, "I would consider it an honor to have you escort me to this meeting."

"Well bargained and done," she said, bowing slightly, one warrior to another.

29

Sharpsburg City Spaceport
Blair Atholl
Jade Falcon Occupation Zone
27 Feb 3065

The cool afternoon rain whipped at Archer and his group as they hustled from the *Crockett*'s gangway to the shelter of Sharpsburg City's small spaceport control center a hundred meters away. He hunched over, holding his poncho hood on as he ran. His DropShip had been the last of the group to land. Adam Steiner had arrived a half an hour earlier and, from the looks of the Wolf Clan *Broadsword*-class ship sitting on the tarmac, Phelan Kell had been on the planet for at least a few days.

The trip to Blair Atholl had taken some time, with getting started the hardest part. His task force had been in a shambles, and Steiner's people, despite the victory on Blackjack, had suffered serious losses, especially the Ninth Lyran Regulars. During the jumps and recharges, he and Steiner had met to talk, but only in short little bursts. They'd exchanged tactical data on losses, repairs, and so on, but their exchanges had otherwise been icy.

As Archer entered the tiny ferrocrete building, the officers gathered there suddenly fell silent, as if he was interrupting something. He tossed back the hood of his poncho and glanced at Phelan Kell, the man standing nearest him. The Wolf Khan reached out and gave him a hearty handshake. "Good to see you, General Christifori," he said warmly.

"And you as well, Khan Kell. I looked over the after-action reports of your ops on Melissia. Good work."

"We have won battles, General," Kell said. "The question is, can we win peace?"

Archer then looked toward Adam Steiner, who was watching him with a cold, emotionless expression. He reached out and shook Steiner's hand. "I want to thank you again for showing up on Blackjack when you did, General."

"You sound like you thought I might not come, Christifori."

Archer tried to make light of the comment with a false chuckle. "Truth be told, I did have a few moments when I wasn't sure if we'd still be there when you landed." Not wanting to go down that road any further, he turned to the other man in the room. "Gramash," he said, shaking his hand, "before we meet with Khan Pryde, I just wanted to say, 'good job' on the intel. Even in the middle of the occupation zone, I always had some idea of what was going on."

"My pleasure, General Christifori," the spymaster replied. "I came in with Khan Kell. Keeping pace with the Wolves proved challenging." Gramash smiled over at Phelan, who only nodded in response. "Marthe Pryde has been on Blair Atholl for several days already. She has been meeting with her Galaxy Commander, who's been trying to wrestle this planet from Precentor Shillery. The Falcons have driven the Com Guard off of two continents, but have stalled since then."

"Any word from her?" Archer asked.

Adam Steiner answered that. "She signaled me when we landed. She indicated that she wished to meet with us to discuss the current state of the conflict once you got here."

"Apparently, she is planning to meet with one officer as lead and one designated second. Since you command Audacity, General, I believe she assumes that you will lead our group. You can take other people with you, as advisors."

Steiner bit his lower lip and averted his gaze, but not before Archer saw the flash of anger on his face. "Well, Phelan should be there," Archer said. "He understands the Clans better than anyone else here. Given the history between the Wolves and the Jade Falcons, it might throw her off balance if he led off for us."

Phelan shook his head. "Marthe Pryde is behaving in the tradition of the Clans. She's forcing you to bid away negotiators. It is a deliberate act. She has probably pieced together that you, I, and General Steiner represent different interests in the Lyran Alliance. She knows that if our differences are volatile enough, it could divide our unity. There should be a single negotiator with one advisor."

"We haven't been fighting the Falcons all this time to fight each other now," Archer said. He glanced warily at Adam. "Is there a problem, General Steiner?"

"No," Steiner said, obviously lying. His face had been getting redder ever since Gramash suggested that Archer be the lead spokesperson.

"Well, that's good," Archer said, removing his poncho and tossing it onto a chair, "because you are going to be negotiating with Khan Pryde."

Adam's face contorted in surprise. "What? Are you serious?"

"It makes the most sense on a few levels. For one thing, I don't speak for the Lyran Alliance. My commission has been revoked, and with the civil war still on, the Archon Princess would not feel bound to honor anything I negotiate. Sending in Phelan has some appeal, if only to shake up Marthe Pryde, but he only speaks for the ADRC, which isn't even recognized in some circles. When all is said and done, you're the one with the most legitimacy to negotiate this truce or cease-fire, or however it becomes known. Finally, sending you in might just catch her off guard, and from what I know of the Falcons, that counts for something."

"I assumed that you—" Steiner began, then seemed at a loss for words. He had obviously thought that Archer would want to lead the discussions—that he would seek the glory.

"That I would want to head up these talks?" Archer finished for him. "No, General. There's still a civil war on, so if someone is going to broker a deal here with the Falcons, it needs to be someone that both sides in the civil war will support."

"You think Victor would support any agreement I make with them?" Steiner asked.

Archer nodded. "Regardless of what you think of Prince Victor, he only wants justice in the case of his sister. He is not happy at all that it came down to civil war. He'll follow whatever you finally negotiate. I'll back you up, and I believe that will be enough for the Prince."

Adam Steiner seemed to gather his thoughts. "Very well then. Let's go and meet with Marthe Pryde. And General Christifori?" he asked.

"Yes?"

"I'd like you to attend as my second and advisor."

The meeting with Marthe Pryde took place a few days later at a mansion commandeered by the Falcons on the outskirts of Sharpsburg. It was a most dignified-looking place, an older, two-story building with a white stone façade and pillars in front. A handful of Elementals stood guard as Adam splashed toward the entrance through a mud puddle. He noticed that they bore the crest of the Turkina Keshik, the personal command of the Jade Falcon Khan. Behind him by one pace was Archer Christifori.

The Elemental on the porch motioned for them to enter, and Adam was surprised that the guards did not ask for his or Christifori's weapons. Though his pistol was holstered in clear view on his hip, the Falcons were apparently not afraid that he or Christifori would come out shooting. They removed their rain ponchos and hung them on chairs in the main hall. Several rooms were visible off the foyer, but only one, with a set of glass doors, was open. Adam silently glanced at Archer, and the two of them walked into the room.

Though it was probably intended to be a dining room, right now all it contained was a wooden table and a few chairs. Standing at the far end of the room were two Falcon officers. One of them Adam recognized immediately as Marthe Pryde, with her high cheekbones and stern nose. The other woman was slightly shorter, and she wore her hair close-cropped. Unlike Pryde, who seemed at ease, this woman seemed angry, and stood with her arms crossed defiantly.

Adam stepped forward and extended his hand. "I am General Adam Steiner of the Lyran Alliance. I will be leading our discussions. This is Archer Christifori."

Marthe Pryde gave his hand a firm shake. "Khan Marthe Pryde of the Jade Falcons. This is my aide in these talks, Star Captain Diana Pryde."

From behind Adam, Christifori said, "It is good to see you again, Star Captain."

The angry-looking woman nodded slightly in acknowledgement. "When we met on Twycross, you told me to deliver a message to the Khan. As you can see, I have done so." There was a hint of venom in her voice that Adam didn't fully understand or want to. She'd been on Twycross, where Archer had defeated the Falcons. That was probably what had her coolant hose in a knot.

"Star Captain Pryde will fight a Trial of Position shortly. If she succeeds, she will be tasked with the rebuilding of the Falcon Guards," Marthe Pryde said.

Listening to the exchange, Adam reasoned that the

Khan had this Diana Pryde here to point out that Archer's victory was not total. The Falcon Guards would be back.

Marthe gestured toward the chairs, and the two pairs sat down facing each other across the table. For a moment, there was a pregnant silence in the room, charged, almost eerie. Adam hated it. Diplomacy was not his forte. "I trust, Khan Pryde, that your request for a parlay means that you are open to discussing a cession of hostilities?"

Her face betrayed no emotion. "Our operations have achieved their strategic goals. To push further would be to assume unnecessary risk."

Adam smiled slightly. "So, our counterattack in your occupation zone was not to your liking then?"

She almost seemed casual about his barb. "I anticipated that you would try to take some of our planets and had planned accordingly. Even the Wolf Clan actions along our common border were anticipated. The affair on Twycross with the Falcon Guard was, shall I say, disturbing, quiaff?" She glanced quickly at Diana Pryde, whose eyes narrowed with anger.

This was news worthy of note, Adam thought. Information he did not have till just now. The Wolf Clan had apparently struck at the Falcons somewhere.

Christifori put both hands on the table and leaned forward to speak. "We intended to fight honorably on Twycross, Khan Pryde. Our ships were fired upon even before we had landed." Adam knew the importance of Christifori's words. It was important that the Jade Falcons understand that the Falcon Guards had been destroyed in honorable combat.

The Khan lowered her eyes for a moment, perhaps in shame. But when she looked up again, they were as clear as truth. "We have confirmed that you did not alter the recordings of the incident. And with the death of Star Colonel Ravill Pryde, there is no way to know what sparked this unfortunate incident. What matters is what we do from this point forward."

"You have taken a number of worlds from the Lyran Alliance," Adam said. "Just as we have taken a number of Jade Falcon planets. Perhaps an exchange of territories would be in order?"

"Neg," Marthe said, slashing her hand horizontally in the air between them. "Why would my Clan willingly give up what it has won in battle, General?"

Adam stirred slightly in his seat. "With Melissia back in our control, Khan Pryde, some of your worlds are isolated from your other holdings. Namely, Chapultepec and Medellin. You can reach them, but only by jumps through unoccupied systems."

She shook her head. "We will not give back what we have seized purely because of minor logistics problems."

"Very well, then. Several worlds have changed hands." Adam pulled out a hardcopy map of the Falcon/Alliance border from his briefcase and laid it on the table. "Your forces have taken Rasalgethi, Koniz, Kooken's Pleasure Pit, Ballynure, Chahar, Kikuyu, Chapultepec, Medellin, Barcelona, and Newtown Square."

Marthe nodded. "And you have won Trials of Possession for Black Earth, Roadside, Blackjack, Butler, Twycross, and one of the Malibu system's jump points."

Adam did not need to look down at the map. He had examined it dozens of times on the trip to Blair Atholl, and every time, his experience as a general told him the same thing. "Khan Pryde, it would be impractical for us to maintain a foothold on Twycross at this time. Perhaps we could arrange an exchange. I know the world means a great deal to your Clan."

Diana Pryde said nothing, but Adam noticed that she stirred almost imperceptibly in her seat.

Marthe Pryde was cool as ever. "You won possession of the world. Maintaining it is your problem." Then she paused, leaning forward to give emphasis to her words. "Between warriors, I will tell you this,

General Steiner. My Clan will make no attempt to possess that planet."

Her words caught him off guard. "You won't try and take it back?"

"Neg," she said coldly. "It is a desolate world, with little or no resources of any value to my Clan. For my people, it is tainted with dishonor. Cursed soil, as it were."

Adam nodded. "Then the only planet that remains in dispute is this one, Blair Atholl." Rasalgethi had fallen during the trip to Blair Atholl, despite the efforts of the troops sent there.

"The fate of this planet will be settled on the field of battle," Marthe Pryde said curtly.

Adam looked at her for a moment before replying. "Perhaps that make sense. But from what I have seen of your attacks on us, your main concern was testing the mettle of your troops, correct?"

"Perhaps that it is how it seems to you, General. I doubt you could appreciate the depth of our strategies in full."

"And our strategy was to stop your assault by taking worlds you own. But when the dust settles, what assurance do I have that you won't launch another such attempt a year from now?"

Marthe Pryde smiled coldly. "I will give you no such assurance, General Steiner."

Adam rocked back into his seat. "Well, I have another proposition for you, then. You need a place to temper and test your people while the Lyran Alliance wants to prevent another incursion like this last one. Perhaps I can give you a place to test your skills so you will have no need to invade our territory for that. Here . . . Blair Atholl."

Marthe Pryde templed her fingers in front of her chin. "This world would remain contested, then, with our troops allowed to fight yours for Trials of Possession, quiaff?"

"Yes—aff," Adam said. He knew there were risks.

People were still going to die because of this negotiation, but perhaps far less than if the Lyran Alliance sustained another invasion by the Falcons. That would come again, of course, but having a safety valve might postpone it for years. "And with Clan Wolf taking advantage of every incursion you make against us, you would be able to achieve your goals without placing your holdings at risk from those who style themselves your peers."

He phrased his words to show respect for Marthe, while also trying to hint that he had more knowledge of what Vlad's Wolves had been up to than he actually did.

Marthe's eyes narrowed ever so slightly. "In exchange, you gain a handful of worlds and relative peace."

"Yes."

"Then, we have both achieved victory, General Steiner. Since you place a value on peace, and I on the tempering that only battle can bring, we can both face our people," she said, rising to her feet. "Well bargained and done."

Endplay

Sharpsburg City Spaceport
Blair Atholl
Jade Falcon Occupation Zone
27 Feb 3065

While Archer leaned against one cinderblock wall of the spaceport center, Adam Steiner summed up the talks with the Jade Falcons for the other commanders. With his arms crossed casually, he listened to an accurate recounting of the meeting with Marthe Pryde. Gramash showed the most emotion, while the feral grin of Phelan Kell spoke volumes without the need to utter a single word.

"Audacity worked," Gramash said gleefully.

"More or less," Steiner said. "I wasn't able to get exactly what I wanted from the talks. I'd hoped the Jade Falcons would trade back some of the territories they took," he said. "I've left the border a ragged mess."

"They would never have done that," Phelan said. "The Lyran Alliance lost more worlds than it gained, but the greater victory is that the Jade Falcon attack has been blunted. They have halted their incursion.

And here, on Blair Atholl, you've given them a place to fight without having to seize half the Alliance in the process."

"What about the people?" Adam said. "The border's such a mess that Nondi Steiner's going to want my head on a stick."

Phelan shook his head. "As for the people, nothing has changed much on these worlds in the history of the last three hundred years. Oh, a different flag may go up on the pole every morning, but they still wake up, have coffee, go to work. As for Nondi Steiner, I would not worry. The media coverage you'll get for negotiating this peace will insulate some of her anger. You do not give yourself enough credit."

"There is still one issue that is unresolved," Archer said as all eyes turned toward him. "A state of civil war exists, General Steiner. Victor sent me here to help you defeat the Jade Falcons, and we've done that. But now the issue before us is more serious. Will one peace re-ignite another war?"

Adam looked pensive, saying nothing for a moment, and the humid air in the tiny blockhouse became almost leaden with tension. When he did finally speak, it was almost as if he couldn't believe what he was saying. "I have no desire to fight you, General Christifori."

Archer grinned with pleasure. "I think that's the first time you've ever called me that. Thank you."

Steiner nodded. "I have to admit there was a time when I figured you to be more celebrity than Mech-Warrior. But I had to change my mind. Victor *did* send you. Your plan *did* work. If not for you, I would probably either be dead now or still trying to slug it out with the Falcons—probably on Tharkad by now."

Archer reached out and shook Steiner's hand. "I appreciate that, Adam. I really do. I had my doubts about you, too. I figured you'd gotten your rank because of your Steiner name. You proved me dead wrong."

Phelan frowned. "Once you two are done hugging and kissing, would you mind telling me just how you intend to pull this off, quiaff?"

Steiner gave one of his rare laughs. "The fact that Victor sent some of his best commanders and troops to help fight off the Falcons taught me that he isn't fighting Katherine merely to put himself back on his father's throne. I believe he does have the best interests of the Alliance at heart.

"Katherine, on the other hand, *didn't* send reinforcements that she could have. It took men like Blucher. to break the rules and come to my aid. Victor didn't have to send you two. It's no secret it reduced the number of troops available for his own operations. Maybe I've been as wrong about his intentions and motivations as I was about yours, Archer."

He looked down for a moment, pulling on the hem of his dress uniform tunic to smooth it out. "I'll prepare a message for Victor and for Katherine, informing them of my intentions, but I'm telling you all first. As the commanding officer of the Melissia Theater, I'm pulling my forces out of the civil war. We will stand down and refuse to send troops, supplies, or anything else that may be used by Katherine in her war with her brother. I'm saying the same for Victor, but the reality is that it will hurt her more than him."

Phelan bowed slightly with his head. "Well played, General Steiner. Combined with my father's administration and defense of the ADRC, a significant slice of the Lyran Alliance is denied to Katherine."

Steiner looked over at Archer. "Your forces can use our planets to refit and repair. After that, you'll have to move on."

Archer nodded. "I appreciate that. I wasn't planning to stay around much longer anyway."

"Your Avenger regiments suffered fifty percent losses, General Christifori," Steiner reminded him. "It'll take months to get back up to full strength— probably the better part of a year."

Archer waved one hand as if to say that didn't matter. "I'm not going to wait. We'll go with what we have. The rest of the units can rebuild on Blackjack and join us when they're ready."

"Where will you go?"

Archer paused, drew a long breath, and let it out as a sigh. "I'm not all hell-bent on revenge, but the time has come for me to take my forces to wherever Victor is and join up with him. The only way we can stop the killing is to end this civil war. I promised myself I'd be there when it ends, that I would be on hand to take the fight directly to Katherine Steiner-Davion. I intend to do that. If not for myself, then to make sure that those who died fighting did not die in vain."

"I understand," Steiner said.

"I know you do," Archer said. "I'm counting on you to watch the Falcons along the border while I'm gone."

"You have my word on it." Steiner reached out to give Archer's hand another shake.

Archer smiled. "I don't need it. I trust you," he said.

Davion Palace
Avalon City, New Avalon
Federated Suns
15 March 3065

Katrina Steiner-Davion stared at the tiny holographic image of her distant cousin, her ears roaring with anger. The message was coming to her via a direct and expensive HPG link between New Avalon and Tharkad, sent by her aunt Nondi Steiner only a few hours after she herself received it. Katrina listened to the words for the third time, and for the third time, pounded her fists on the desktop. It hurt, but there was no one present to witness her fit.

"Katherine, as I you know by now, the Jade Falcon incursion has been halted," Adam Steiner said. "I wish I could tell you it was because of my actions, but it wasn't. The aid of General Christifori and Phelan Kell, sent by your brother, is what ensured our victory. I imagine that you have also heard from Loki by now that Clan Wolf struck at the Falcons as well. They didn't achieve any real victory, but combined with this Operation Audacity, it was enough to halt the Falcons. I would love to claim the credit the media is heaping on me, but in reality, if not for Victor's actions, we would be in full retreat."

Adam's tone was grim and angry, almost threatening. "Your handling of this crisis has convinced me that there may be some merit in Victor's claims against you. You did not send aid, but saddled me with Sharon Bryan, whose misguided 'leadership' almost got me killed. Resources that I should have had were not available because you allowed a civil war to fester in our realm. Victor's motives seemed to be the protection of the Lyran Alliance—nothing more, nothing less. From the reports I've read, your intention seemed to be to let the conflict happen while you pursued a vendetta against your own brother.

"That is why, to preserve the integrity of the Lyran Alliance and to defend its borders, I am removing the Melissia Theater from your jurisdictional and operational control until matters are brought to a conclusion. I cannot and will not allow my men and women to fight and die under your orders so that you can hold on to power. At the same time, I will not send them to fight under your brother, either. The Theater will be considered neutral space. I am here to protect the people of the Lyran Alliance from the enemies who might attempt to destroy them."

Katrina's eyes flared at those words. He didn't even mention the Clans. Did he believe that she was such a threat? The gall!

"I gain no pleasure from this," Adam Steiner said,

"but do it in the name of our people." With those words, his image faded and was replaced by the aging face of Nondi Steiner.

"He can't do this!" Katrina bellowed.

"I'm afraid he can," Nondi said.

"I'll send in troops to have him arrested. You will appoint a new commander. Have the forces under his command disregard his orders."

Nondi shook her head. "There are no troops to send in. And thanks to the media coverage, Adam Steiner is seen as a hero of the Lyran people. He saved them from the Jade Falcons. His victories have galvanized the forces under his command. I doubt they'd follow my orders to turn against him. If you try and remove him through other means, it will only work against you."

"Bah!" Katrina said. "He lost more worlds than he gained. Adam's no hero."

"He stopped the Falcon invasion. It could have turned out much worse. Regardless of my feelings about his final actions, he did remarkably well against the Falcons."

"The only good thing is that Archer Christifori didn't manage to gobble up the media spotlight from my dear little cousin," Katrina said bitterly. "And you'd have thought that at least *he* would have had the courtesy to die when facing the Jade Falcons."

"There are other issues around General Christifori that we should be more concerned about, Archon," Nondi said.

"Such as?"

"He and his Avengers have disappeared."

"Disappeared? What do you mean?"

Nondi straightened in her seat. "Our Loki agents believe that he and his forces have gone to link up with Victor. To put it bluntly, Archon, I believe that Archer Christifori is coming for you."

About the Author

Amissville, The Piedmont
Virginia, United States of America
Terra
9 June 2001

Blaine Pardoe was born in Virginia and raised outside Battle Creek, Michigan, and he earned his bachelor's and master's degrees from Central Michigan University. He works for Vcampus as the Senior Director of Products and Services. He resides in Virginia and swears it is the best and most beautiful place to live in the known universe.

Pardoe has published more than forty books, including a number of computer game guides, science fiction sourcebooks for BattleTech® and other series, and the best-selling business book, *Cubicle Warfare*. He has authored material for FASA's game universes for more than fourteen years. His several novels for the BattleTech® and MechWarrior® series include *Highlander Gambit*, *Impetus of War*, *Exodus Road*, *Roar of Honor*, *By Blood Betrayed*, *Measure of a Hero*, and *Call of Duty*.

Blaine is a Civil War buff, and when he can, he hunts for war relics in the old camp and skirmish sites near his home. He also plays the Great Highland Bag-pipes when the mood strikes him. He can be reached at **bpardoe870@aol.com.** for those fans who might want to track him down.

(0451)

See what's coming in July...

THE DISAPPEARED
by Kristine Kathryn Rusch   45888-5
In a world where humans and aliens co-exist, where
murder is sanctioned, and where no one can find safe
haven, one police detective is willing to risk everything
to help those who must Disappear...

"One of the most sure-footed authors in science fiction."
                              —*Science Fiction Weekly*

ONCE UPON A WINTER'S NIGHT
by Dennis L. McKiernan   45854-0
From the bestselling author of the Mithgar novels
comes a new version of a classic French fairy tale. A
young woman marries a mysterious Prince, only to
have magic steal him away—and, once upon a winter's
night, her quest begins...

"McKiernan brews magic with an insightful blend of
laughter, tears, and high courage."   —**Janny Wurts**

To order call: 1-800-788-6262

R402

BATTLETECH®

Loren L. Coleman

THREADS OF AMBITION

Sun-Tzu Liao is the First Lord of the resurrected Star League. In the last year of his reign, he decides to milk his power for every ounce of benefit to himself. His dream to rebuild his Capellan Confederation at any cost is about to become a reality. His first victim: his own aunt, Candace Liao, who deserted the Confederation in the Fourth Succession War, taking the St. Ives Compact with her. And as Capellan fights Capellan, the high price of glory will be paid in full....

(0-451-45744-7)

To order call: 1-800-788-6262

(0451)

DEEP-SPACE INTRIGUE AND ACTION FROM
BATTLETECH ®

LETHAL HERITAGE by Michael A. Stackpole.
Who are the Clans? One Inner Sphere warrior, Phelan Kell of the
mercenary group Kell Hounds, finds out the hard way—as their
prisoner and protégé.

(453832)

BLOOD LEGACY by Michael A. Stackpole.
Jaime Wolf brought all the key leaders of the Inner Sphere together at his base
on Outreach in an attempt to put to rest old blood feuds and power struggles. For
only if all the Successor States unite their forces do they have any hope of defeating this invasion by warriors equipped with BattleMechs far superior to their own.

(453840)

LOST DESTINY by Michael A. Stackpole.
As the Clans' BattleMech warriors continue their inward drive, with Terra itself as
their true goal, can Comstar mobilize the Inner Sphere's last defenses—or will
their own internal political warfare provide the final death blow to the empire
they are sworn to protect?

(453859)

To order call: 1-800-788-6262

S452/BattleTech

(0451)

More Deep-Space Action & Intrigue From
BATTLETECH®

PATH OF GLORY *by Randall N. Bills* (458079)
When the Nova Cat Clan is forced to ally with the Inner Sphere it forces two MechWarriors from different worlds into a precarious friendship. For Zane and Yoshio, the line between ally and enemy will be drawn in blood. . . .

ILLUSIONS OF VICTORY *by Loren L. Coleman* (457900)
Solaris VII, home of the ultimate sporting event—war. Now, ancient grudges have reached beyond the arena and given rise to a championship match where the winner is the last man alive.

MEASURE OF A HERO *by Blaine Lee Pardoe* (457943)
As the fires of rebellion burn on Thorin, a local militia leader holds the fate of the world in his hands. . . .

To order call: 1-800-788-6262

Don't miss out on any of the deep-space adventure

of the Bestselling **BATTLETECH**® *Series.*

LETHAL HERITAGE #1 *BLOOD OF KERENSKY* Michael A. Stackpole	453832
BLOOD LEGACY #2 *BLOOD OF KERENSKY* Michael A. Stackpole	453840
LOST DESTINY #3 *BLOOD OF KERENSKY* Michael A. Stackpole	453859
EXODUS ROAD #1 *TWILIGHT OF THE CLANS* Blaine Lee Pardoe	456122
GRAVE COVENANT #2 *TWILIGHT OF THE CLANS* Michael A. Stackpole	456130
THE HUNTERS #3 *TWILIGHT OF THE CLANS* Thomas S. Gressman	456246
FREEBIRTH #4 *TWILIGHT OF THE CLANS* Robert Thurston	456653
SWORD AND FIRE #5 *TWILIGHT OF THE CLANS* Thomas S. Gressman	456769
SHADOWS OF WAR #6 *TWILIGHT OF THE CLANS* Thomas S. Gressman	457072
PRINCE OF HAVOC #7 *TWILIGHT OF THE CLANS* Michael A. Stackpole	457064
FALCON RISING #8 *TWILIGHT OF THE CLANS* Robert Thurston	457382
DAGGER POINT Thomas S. Gressman	457838
ILLUSIONS OF VICTORY Loren L. Coleman	457900
MEASURE OF A HERO Blaine Lee Pardoe	457943
PATH OF GLORY Randall N. Bills	458079
THREADS OF AMBITION Loren L. Coleman	457447

To order call: 1-800-788-6262

PENGUIN PUTNAM INC.
Online

Your Internet gateway to a virtual environment with
hundreds of entertaining and enlightening books
from Penguin Putnam Inc.

*While you're there, get the latest buzz on
the best authors and books around—*

Tom Clancy, Patricia Cornwell, W.E.B. Griffin,
Nora Roberts, William Gibson, Robin Cook,
Brian Jacques, Catherine Coulter, Stephen King,
Ken Follett, Terry McMillan, and many more!

**Penguin Putnam Online is located at
http://www.penguinputnam.com**

PENGUIN PUTNAM NEWS

Every month you'll get an inside look at our upcom-
ing books and new features on our site. This is an
ongoing effort to provide you with the most
up-to-date information about
our books and authors.

Subscribe to Penguin Putnam News at
http://www.penguinputnam.com/newsletters